THE SPACE BETWEEN

THE SPACE BETWEEN

LAUREN KEENAN

PENGUIN BOOKS

PENGUIN

UK | USA | Canada | Ireland | Australia
India | New Zealand | South Africa | China

Penguin is an imprint of the Penguin Random House group of companies, whose addresses can be found at global.penguinrandomhouse.com.

Penguin Random House New Zealand

First published by Penguin Random House New Zealand, 2024

1 3 5 7 9 10 8 6 4 2

Design by Cat Taylor © Penguin Random House New Zealand
Cover photograph by Soldiers Road
Background cover photograph by Westend61, Alamy Ltd
Prepress by Soar Communications Group
Printed and bound in Australia by Griffin Press, an Accredited ISO AS/NZS 14001 Environmental Management Systems Printer

A catalogue record for this book is available from the National Library of New Zealand.

ISBN 978-1-77695-081-2
eISBN 978-1-77695-390-5

The assistance of Creative New Zealand towards the production of this book is gratefully acknowledged by the publisher.

creative nz
Arts Council of New Zealand Toi Aotearoa

penguin.co.nz

MIX
Paper | Supporting responsible forestry
FSC® C018684

This book is dedicated to all people
who sit, or have sat,
in that uncomfortable space between.

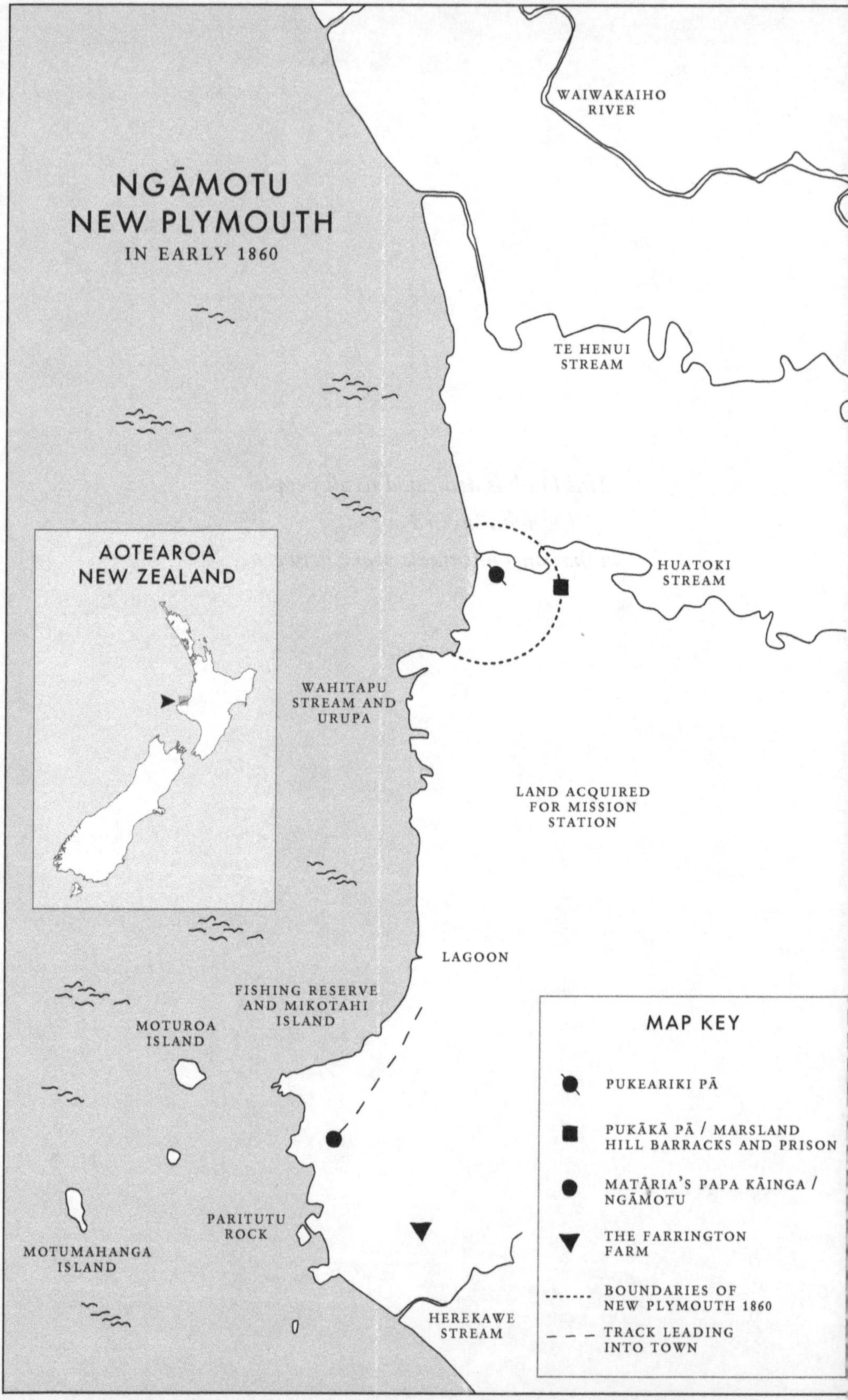
NGĀMOTU
NEW PLYMOUTH
IN EARLY 1860
WAIWAKAIHO
RIVER
TE HENUI
STREAM
HUATOKI
STREAM
AOTEAROA
NEW ZEALAND
WAHITAPU
STREAM AND
URUPA
LAND ACQUIRED
FOR MISSION
STATION
LAGOON
FISHING RESERVE
AND MIKOTAHI
ISLAND
MOTUROA
ISLAND
PARITUTU
ROCK
MOTUMAHANGA
ISLAND
HEREKAWE
STREAM
MAP KEY
PUKEARIKI PĀ
PUKĀKĀ PĀ / MARSLAND
HILL BARRACKS AND PRISON
MATĀRIA'S PAPA KĀINGA /
NGĀMOTU
THE FARRINGTON
FARM
BOUNDARIES OF
NEW PLYMOUTH 1860
TRACK LEADING
INTO TOWN

CONTENTS

CHAPTER ONE

FRANCES

NEW PLYMOUTH, FEBRUARY 1860

Frances heard the commotion before she saw it: a man being arrested by two soldiers of the Crown, right in front of Thorpe's General Store.

'I belong here!' the man shouted. 'Nō Te Ātiawa au. This is our place.' He wore a European shirt over trousers that were far too short. His black hair was unkempt, his eyes bright.

'You need a pass to enter the township,' one of the soldiers said, hands gripping his rifle. The soldier's uniform was crisp and tidy: black trousers and a navy-blue tunic with shiny buttons. 'Natives are not allowed here without swearing allegiance to the Queen. You should all know that by now. And you're disturbing the peace by yelling.'

'Go,' the other soldier said. 'Move.'

The man was led away, head bowed, past the staring customers at the butcher's, the seamstress's workshop and the bakery. Past the pile of cut wood that would soon be another military blockhouse, built to ensure that the likes of this loud, shabby man were kept out of the settlement. *How unpleasant*. Frances preferred not to think about what the newspapers called the 'native troubles' — it was all too frightening. So, she wouldn't. She'd think about something else instead.

Frances turned towards the general store: a low, rectangular building made of roughly cut timber, with a small six-pane window so her view was not clear, which was no doubt why she mistook the man on the other side for Henry. All thoughts of the arrest flew from Frances's mind. *Henry?* She thought. *Is it you?*

Of course it wasn't him. Frances sighed. She couldn't decide if she would rather Henry was dead or alive. She saw him far too often: outside the public house, mounted on a passing horse or strolling down the street. Each time she would turn towards the man, mouth dry. *Oh, Henry*, she'd think. *Is it you?* But then 'Henry' would transform into someone else with broader stature and darker colouring. Frances would be left with a dull ache in her stomach and a single thought swirling around her mind: *What happened to him?*

Moving to this remote backwater was supposed to make her visions of Henry go away — indeed, that hope had sustained her during the long, arduous voyage from England. But it hadn't worked out that way, for she saw him just as often here in New Plymouth as she had in London. Last week he rode a horse through a paddock near her farm. Two days later he marched in formation with a garrison of soldiers, rifle pointed at the sky. Yesterday was worse than usual: Henry was a workman building the blockhouse; he was a drunken wastrel begging outside the hotel; he was yet another soldier — an officer this time, rather than one of the rank and file. He was everywhere. And here he was again, stepping out of Thorpe's General Store, sack of flour in his arms.

He stepped around a muddy puddle, narrowly avoiding a pile of horse manure. This man had Henry's agile footwork; Henry had been a fine dancer. Was it him? Frances knew it couldn't be. Twelve years had passed: it was time to stop looking. And sure enough, this wasn't Henry. This man was older and rather dishevelled, with no hat and tattered moleskin trousers, as well as a cloak of leaves, the sort one usually saw worn by Māori. Her Henry had never even seen a Māori, let alone donned their garments. Henry was a man of London, not the colonies.

The man with the flour stopped in front of the noticeboard, just as Frances herself had done before she'd heard the commotion. There were only two updates today: the mail coach was due on Monday afternoon; and a new public establishment had opened, offering rooms and stables. The man shook his head and turned away — he obviously found the news as dull as Frances had.

Stop staring, Frances! she admonished herself. *It's not Henry.* No amount of unseemly gaping would change that fact. Frances scanned the street. It wasn't long before her brother George would return with the cart, and she had several items on her shopping list: cloves, flour, carrots, lard, treacle. Candles, though George said they needed to make their own, and she had no idea how.

Once finished at the store, Frances would fetch some beef from the butcher, but only if it was fresh off the cow. Milking their own cow had caused her hands — mercifully hidden in her gloves — to grow thick and raw since they'd left London; they were stronger, but so much less ladylike. Nor were they improved by the dirt under her nails from tending the vegetable patch, or the network of scars from a particularly feisty hen that had taken exception to her eggs being collected. If only they had enough servants to do this work.

Henry was hard to forget. He had always been brimming with energy; not overburdened with riches, but a man with prospects. He was a valued assistant to a wealthy merchant who shipped all sorts of expensive goods up the Thames from the far reaches of the world. The merchant was an acquaintance of George's, which was how

Frances had met Henry, and then just when she thought nothing but happiness lay ahead for her, Henry had disappeared.

Mother had the bizarre notion that he must have ended up working on London's docks and had likely perished there, as so many men did — especially, Mother said, those of Henry's ilk. According to Mother, Henry might have been the son of a doctor, but that didn't make him a gentleman. Or perhaps he had been caught in some nefarious dealings, Mother had mused, pointing out that Frances had never actually met Henry's family, so who could attest to either their respectability or their solvency?

'Stop being so self-indulgent,' Mother initially complained. 'Thinking too much is like walking around an object and poking it with sticks. Doing so does not change the object in question. All it does is weaken one's sticks.' She usually followed this with a litany of her own woes: 'Do you think I wallow about all day, crying about my husband passing away? Or my darling Albert, gone too young? Such a charming, clever man he would have grown to be, had the fates not been so cruel.' The litany was to get longer soon after, as the truth about Father emerged. 'Thank the Lord,' Mother then reiterated on a regular basis, 'that George has found a way to restore our fortunes, even if it means we must travel so very far from home.'

Yes, they were lucky to have George, but over the years Frances had been unable to stop herself from constant imaginings of a life with Henry. What would it have been like? What *had* happened to him? She'd already lost Father and her other brother Albert, so the thought of Henry also being dead was too much to bear.

As was the thought of him being alive.

Had Henry died, he'd left this Earth wanting to marry her, which meant she hadn't been abandoned by the only man she'd ever loved. But if he were alive, he'd dropped her, probably for a far superior and more beautiful heiress, not even caring enough to write. That opened too painful a chasm of speculation. If she knew Henry were dead, Frances would feel sad, bereft and melancholy. The idea of him being alive awakened much more uncomfortable feelings, such as anger, infused with regret. Not knowing meant she did not know what to feel.

Frances shook her head: she mustn't wander down the dark and murky path of *wishing* Henry dead. Surely, Henry being alive but elsewhere was better? She was wicked for entertaining thoughts to the contrary. And yet, if Henry were alive, what did that make Frances — she who had mourned his loss for over a decade?

She shivered and pulled her shawl tightly around her shoulders. New Plymouth wasn't cold like England, but there was a dampness that seeped into her skin and sat in her lungs, even in summer. It crept from the undergrowth of the dark forest that surrounded the township, bush that was filled with birds the size of small chickens. The trees stretched all the way from the recently cleared farmland to the large inland mountain. It was thick and impassable — claustrophobically so. And there was little in the drab wooden shops straggling along the muddy street to lift her spirits. What a pity the store didn't stock vibrant fabrics or interesting ornaments to brighten her mood . . . what a pity she'd had to move here at all.

A sound caught Frances's attention: a cry, followed by a sharp inhalation of breath. The man with the flour had dropped the sack, which hit the ground with a thud. Frances turned to see him looking down at the flour and back up at her.

'Frances?' he said. 'Is that you?'

Frances's stomach lurched.

'It *is* you!' Henry went to lift his hat to her, but realised he did not have one. The Henry she once knew would never have ventured out bare headed. 'Frances Farrington. What are *you* doing here?'

CHAPTER TWO

MATĀRIA

Matāria sat beside her sleeping mat and hugged her knees. Henry should be back by now, where *was* he? She hoped he was safe. *Hope*. What a useless word: hope didn't fill the fishing net with kai moana; hope wouldn't keep her husband safe if Tūmatauenga, that unpredictable god of war, was brandishing his taiaha. It was a useless word yet still so fitting because Henry wasn't here, and Matāria couldn't do anything about it. She was as useless as hope, like a fish floundering on the shore: thrashing, gasping, wiggling — but not getting any closer to safety.

She faced most challenges as steadfastly as a carved kāhia on a meeting house, but knew only too well it was best to flee the god of war. Matāria could sense Tūmatauenga all around her. He vibrated in the soldiers' boots as they marched to and from the barracks on the old pā site they'd taken for themselves; he danced in the silences between her cousins' angry words; and when Matāria closed her eyes at night, Tūmatauenga invaded her sleep, lurking in the deep crevices of her mind and threatening her twins. In Matāria's darkest nightmares her children were taken, just as Matāria herself had been at the very same age. But in those nightmares, her children didn't come back.

She pulled herself up and shuffled out of the low doorway. Henry often complained that their hut was far too cramped, with barely enough space for sleeping mats, their clothes, and Henry's meagre belongings. But, as she would argue back, it was no smaller than most wharepuni at the papakāinga. The walls were made of bundles of raupō, so were sturdy enough to withstand strong winds. Better still, the hut was dry — the thatched roof stopped Ranginui's tears from splashing on their sleeping faces.

It wasn't perfect, of course, nowhere was. The hut's location was less than ideal: directly beside the kūmara storehouses. The low dugouts were lined with ponga logs and built into the side of the hill, so every now and again a rat would scuttle into their whare after being unable to reach the sweet-smelling kūmara: an unwelcome, ravenous guest that Henry would chase away with angry English words and a swiftly thrown boot. Their hut also sat near where people gathered around the fire, so loud voices carried in their direction, long after the sun, Tama-nui-te-rā, had returned to his pit.

Loud voices — and smoke. Henry couldn't endure the smoke filling the hut so had insisted they build a chimney, which still drew mockery from others in the papakāinga. Matāria ignored them. Although her clothes and bedding still carried the dusty scent of fire, the twins coughed less often now. What a shame a hole to the skies didn't drive away the rats as well.

Ow. Her leg throbbed worse than usual today — she should never have joined the women to wash blankets in the river. It had been too much for her. To distract herself from the pain, Matāria once again tried to assess the escape routes they might take if war came. Probably not west, in the direction of Paritutu, much as she loved that rock, even though it was so high that only the most able-bodied were able to scramble up it. To the south, Matāria could see down the hill and over the jagged walls of the papakāinga to where her people's boundaries met those of other iwi. That way would be easier to walk, for inland was the mountain that the settlers called Mount Egmont, ignoring his true name of Taranaki. Not Mount Taranaki — just Taranaki, a name for this mountain that was also Matāria's tupuna. Taranaki hid his face today. Grey, cloudy skies sat above the vast expanse of bush and scrub between the coast and the mountain — an area that was almost impassable if you didn't know where the old paths were. Knowledge Matāria did not have.

Alongside the papakāinga was a muddy road that followed the coast northeast towards New Plymouth. Matāria watched as some women returned to their village along it, arms full of flax. Harakeke: both plant and descendant of Tāne-nui-a-Rangi. That was why she was not permitted to weave: the ones chosen to be taught were not unclean like Matāria. Flax had a mauri of its own, so only those women now walking towards the papakāinga could use the leaves. Only they knew how to give the flax the respect it deserved by transforming it into something beautiful and worthy: a kete to carry food, a woven bird, a mat. Today the women would strip the hard harakeke and turn the sinewy strands into bales. Bales of flax fetched a good price nowadays — more than potato or kūmara; more than kai moana, fresh from the sea. More money to buy useful things: blankets, razors, nails.

Rifles.

Matāria didn't know where all these new rifles would be housed. The storage hut was full: there were a few already stacked beside the numerous shorter, heavier muskets and their bayonets. The older people in the papakāinga spoke of a time before muskets — it was hard for them to understand that these muskets were now being replaced by rifles that were more accurate and could cause even more harm. Her cousins reassured Matāria that Te Ātiawa would not start a war, reminding her they had tilled the land to appease

Rongomotāne, so in following the god of peace it was not they who had summoned Tūmatauenga, it was the settlers. Settlers who wanted land that held the bones of Te Ātiawa tūpuna. It was because of this that they needed as many firearms as they could get. Tama tū, tama ora; tama noho, tama mate. They would not sit. They would not die.

Matāria sank onto the sodden earth and rested against the hut's hard walls. Her breathing was ragged, she needed to still her mind. *Tīhei*, Matāria thought as she inhaled deeply, just as her māmā had taught her to do. After holding her breath for a moment, she let it out slowly. *Mauri ora.* Tūmatauenga might be close, but tīhei mauri ora reminded Matāria that she was still here, grounded, and alive.

She looked back towards the road, which was busier now. Some dogs sniffed around in the middle of the path, but a rattling cart hurtled past, sending the strays running for the gutter. The cart threw up a splatter of mud onto the plain trousers, off-white shirts and cloth hats of some settler men. Closer to the papakāinga, a group of children played a game with sticks and a ball. Matāria could hear their laughter on the wind: happy shrieking that almost made her forget Tūmatauenga was sharpening his koikoi nearby.

So many people were on the road this afternoon, but not Henry. The sun had been high when her husband had mounted one of the papakāinga horses and ridden into the township. Now the sky was dark blue, and soon the children would be called inside by their mothers. Kai moana was no doubt already being cooked by the older women — there were no slaves here to do that job anymore; Matāria was adamant on that point.

Were the kuia preparing mangō, kina and mussels from the sea tonight or kōura, inanga and piharau from the river? Both bodies of water sustained the people of Ngāmotu over the warm part of the year, but after the next cycle of the moon, or even the one after that, the kaumātua would decree the ocean and the waters flowing from Taranaki were to be left alone. Henry complained that through the cold months they were only allowed to eat crops, but the rāhui was to ensure the creatures could replenish to feed them all in the future. Why could he not understand that he mustn't go off and fish whenever he wanted?

The smell of cooking meat wafted over to where Matāria sat. *Mmmm.* It seemed the women had decided to smoke the birds that had been stewing in their own fat inside gourds. Not that Matāria and her small family would ever get to eat those — it would be fish for them. In time, darkness would descend and the fire in the marae ātea would be lit. Another day would be done.

Matāria scanned the road again: no change. That husband of hers had better be back soon — at least before the twins. If he wasn't, they wouldn't be able to talk in private and decide what stars to follow when Tūmatauenga came. There was no time to lose.

Two children burst from around the kūmara storehouses. Henry was too late. The twins were back, their smiling faces covered in sand.

'Māmā!' they called as they ran. 'Māmā!'

Edwin and Betsy may carry names from their father's culture, but they looked almost like the other children in the papakāinga, certainly dressing in similar clothing: Betsy in her loose smock; Edwin in his coverall. And, like the other tamariki, they usually wore much less on hot days — a simple maro hanging from the waist now they were older, though nothing at all when they were young. Papakāinga children were often sent home from the mission school for not wearing enough. Some of Matāria's cousins didn't like that: their tūpuna hadn't had to cover their whole bodies, they said, and, as for having to put on strange clothing, it wasn't right to let something touch your skin when you didn't know where it came from or who made it, for how could you know what sort of mauri the material contained? But those old ideas were slowly ebbing away with the passing of the years — so different from what Matāria remembered of her own childhood.

Betsy ran ahead of her brother, light-brown hair streaming behind her. 'Māmā!' she said. 'I got a special stone. Look, Māmā. Look!' Betsy rummaged around inside the front pocket of her smock. She pulled out a stick, followed by a handful of leaves. 'It's in here somewhere.' She waved a pebble in the air. 'Look!'

'Look at Betsy's stone!' Edwin had the same dusty-brown hair as his twin but a narrower face. He was also slightly taller — not that Betsy would ever admit it.

'I see.' Matāria inspected the grey, smooth pebble the size of Betsy's palm. 'It looks very special — a taonga.'

'It is,' Betsy said. 'Isn't it, Edwin?'

'Yes. It's very special.'

Matāria flicked some sand off Betsy's collar. 'You need to return it to the beach tomorrow, though. That's where it belongs.'

'Of course,' Betsy agreed. 'I'll put it back where I found it. Right where the sand gets wet.'

'And guess what, Māmā?' Edwin said. 'Betsy saw a big fish. A really, really, really big one.'

'Is that so?' Betsy's stories often had a shimmer and shine that caused them to stray from reality. 'You saw a big fish?'

Betsy waved her arms. 'Yes! I titiro au te ika nui.'

Matāria felt a warmth creep up her body. The children speaking her language was a gift, especially as they hadn't been among her people their whole lives. And Henry needed to learn more — so the more the twins spoke in his presence, the better.

'Te ika nui?' Matāria asked. 'And what sort of fish was it?'

'The biggest fish in all the sea!' Betsy said. 'But it swam away before Edwin or Whaea Atarangi saw it.'

'As big as Te-Ika-a-Māui?'

Betsy scoffed. 'Of course not, Māmā. Te-Ika-a-Māui is the whole land we're standing on — that's what Whaea Atarangi told me. It's not in the sea like a fish. It's right here.'

'The land is in the sea.' Edwin's voice was soft. 'It is surrounded by ocean— '

Betsy spoke over her brother. 'This fish wasn't as big as Te-Ika-a-Māui. But it was a hundred times better to look at.'

'What a shame no one else saw this large fish,' Matāria said. 'Are you sure it wasn't a trick of the light?'

'I'm telling the truth, Māmā. The fish was huge. And it was pink and blue and all the colours.'

Edwin tilted his head to one side. 'I thought you said it was brown and red like a kākā.'

'Brown and red were the colours I meant when I said all the colours.' Betsy pulled on Matāria's arm. 'I'm not lying, Māmā. I'm not. The big fish was in the ocean. It was a fish-bird. But not like Manaia. This was something else. The kākā of the sea.'

The kākā of the sea? Time to change the subject. Matāria would speak to Betsy again about telling lies — especially stories that might cause offence — but if she did so in front of Edwin the shame would be a heavy cloak on Betsy's shoulders.

'Where's Whaea Atarangi?' Matāria said. 'Did Aunty bring you back from the beach?'

But Betsy and Edwin didn't reply, too intent on joining the children playing by the gate, neither so much as looking back as they ran off.

At least they're happy, Matāria thought. *Long may they stay that way.*

Her thoughts were interrupted by a cough: Atarangi was glaring down at her.

'Oh,' Matāria said. 'Here you are.'

'Āe.'

Matāria and Atarangi had the same black hair, full lips and high foreheads. Even their eyes and nose were similar. But no one would guess they were sisters unless they looked closely. Atarangi had a moko kauae on her chin and lips; the only marks Matāria had on her face were deep lines: it was little wonder some thought she'd been born long before the whalers came to Ngāmotu, not the very same year. Atarangi stood proud in her cape made of kiekie — there was no mistaking the expertise in its weaving. While it would keep Atarangi dry and warm, Matāria knew her sister was wearing it only to display her skill at the craft that Matāria was denied.

Around Atarangi's neck was a large pounamu, and her hair cascaded over her shoulders and down her back, the front swept back and kept in place with a heru. Matāria, in her unadorned off-white cotton dress, had much plainer plumage, and her hair was secured at the nape of her neck with a small wooden comb. The missionary's wife had taught her to set it this way and she preferred it, especially on windy days. In spite of these differences, Matāria was determined not to be cowed by her sister.

Atarangi looked as if she'd eaten a sour berry — the sort even the hungriest of birds knew not to touch. 'Your children need to be taught to behave, Minnie.'

Matāria fixed her eyes on the ground at Atarangi's bare feet. Only Henry was allowed to call her Minnie. It was soft and loving coming from his lips — a name he'd bestowed upon her, before he could say Matāria, back when they'd first met. When Atarangi said Minnie, it sounded like a curse.

'The Boy and The Girl are naughty, Minnie. They need to be disciplined.' *The Boy* and *The Girl*, Te Tama and Te Kōtiro; never Betsy and Edwin.

Atarangi's sharp words snapped Matāria out of her self-pity. She stared up at her sister. 'E noho. You don't need to hover over me like that. Sit down beside me.'

'I can't be idle like you, Matāria. The kai needs to be prepared before the kuia cook it. And The Girl was too slow walking back from the beach. She kept looking for a fish that exists only in her mind — a fish that is also a bird, as if such a thing exists! We already have kōrero about Tangaroa's creatures, and already tell stories about Manaia. It is disrespectful to invent more.' Atarangi sniffed and looked around. 'Kei whea Henare Mā? And did he bring my flour?'

'He's not back yet.'

'Is he at that place where the settler men drink?'

'No.' Though, now that she thought about it, he had mentioned a new establishment that had opened. But Henry wouldn't do that to her, not today.

'Are you sure? I know your husband likes to sit with the other white men, abusing the tapu of his body by filling it with poison.'

'Henry doesn't do that,' Matāria said. 'He'll be back soon.'

'So where is he?'

I don't know, Matāria thought, but she wasn't going to admit that to her sister. Henry wasn't a bad husband, no matter what Atarangi said. *Moe atu ngā ringa raupo*. Matāria had married a man with calloused hands, just as the whakataukī said a woman ought to. He didn't mind Matāria's bad leg, where other men would have left her by the side of the road to die like a wild dog. Nor did Henry pay heed to the other whakataukī about marriage: *aitia te wahine i roto i te pā harakeke*. He didn't need to marry a woman who was good at weaving flax: Henry didn't understand the mauri of the harakeke, or care why Matāria had never been taught. Besides, it was Henry who had helped her find her way back to the papakāinga, after all those years away.

'He'll be back soon,' Matāria said. 'And sit down. You know I can't stand for long, and it hurts my neck to look up at you like a kōtuku.'

'Hmph. A sore neck is the least of your problems, Minnie. And kōtuku have legs that work. Otherwise, they die.'

Matāria flinched. 'It's not my fault. I came back. I tried to come earlier. And now Tūmatauenga is close—'

'No, *Minnie* came back. And she brought Tūmatauenga with her.'

Atarangi turned and strode away, past the kūmara storehouses and around the back of another hut. Right before disappearing out of sight, she spun back around.

'Tell The Boy and The Girl I'll take them back to the beach tomorrow,' she called. 'At first light, before I collect kānga.'

Matāria sat up straight. 'Collecting the maize already? But it's not time. The crops might not be fully grown. It's still the time for eating kai moana—'

'We're doing it early this year and eating both at the same time. Unless you want to go hungry?' Atarangi's voice was sharp. 'Are you going to complain to me about it, just like all those other women are doing?'

Matāria shook her head; it wasn't her place to criticise whoever had decided to bring the harvest forward, though she railed at having to concede to her sister.

'And tell The Boy and The Girl: no more lies about rainbow birds that look like fish. When you're done telling them that, get your husband to bring me that flour.'

Atarangi swept around the side of the hut, hair flying in the wind. Matāria made a face but Atarangi didn't see, as she didn't so much as glance back.

CHAPTER THREE

FRANCES

Frances stared: *Henry*, right in front of her. She studied his face, which was different from how she remembered him: eyes bluer; hair a dustier shade of blond; nose both larger and redder. He had new lines on his face, and more girth around his middle. But it was definitely still him. Henry hadn't perished at the docks or met his end after becoming embroiled in nefarious dealings. Mother was wrong. Frances's corset suddenly felt much too tight. She closed her eyes. An image of Henry stole into her mind, an image from twelve years earlier . . .

'Frances?'

Her eyes opened. Imagined-Henry's face changed into that of the man standing in front of her.

'Frances?' he said again. 'Surely you remember me. It's Henry. Henry White.'

Be pretty and clever, she thought. The rest could wait until later, particularly the knot of rage that sat heavily inside her stomach. It was all too much to think through now, including at whom, specifically, her anger was directed: Henry, herself, or a mix of both.

'Yes, I remember, I . . . yes. Henry, Mr White, I mean. Good afternoon. How do you do?'

Henry bowed. 'Well, thank you. How do *you* do?'

'I am also well, thank you.'

The cool wind tickled the back of Frances's neck; her stockinged legs were cold under her crinoline. She glanced down at her dress. If only she'd worn her blue gown today. It suited her much better than the brown, had larger skirts, and was less frayed around the hems and cuffs. The brown had replaced the mourning black she had worn for two years, and at the time was a welcome change, but was now so out of fashion it was what Frances put on when it didn't matter how she looked. Which was more days than not — there was very little to dress nicely for here. Even the blue dress was tired. George said Frances didn't need another: why did a spinster need expensive clothes, especially when they cannot yet sell pork, and their eggs only fetched two shillings a dozen? But even the blue would have been an improvement on this fabric that had faded to the colour of cow manure.

Frances had felt pretty the last time she'd seen Henry. They'd met in Hyde Park for a stroll. Clementine acted as chaperone, trailing a tactful distance behind. Clementine had earlier decided Frances would wear a gown made of muslin with an open neckline. The dress would be terribly unfashionable now, and wouldn't have lasted a week being worn while tending to the animals. But it was what all the young ladies in London had on that season. Clementine had also insisted Frances curl her hair, so their lady's maid had spent over an hour making Frances's locks fall perfectly. *Imagine that*: Frances could barely remember how it felt to have a lady's maid attend to her. Their current maid-of-all-work, Kitty, was far too busy with washing, polishing and cooking to see to Frances's needs. Kitty and the stable boy were their only servants now — Frances had to do a great number of chores herself just to keep the household running. The memory of having a maid to arrange her hair felt as distant as the moon.

Henry looked from Frances to the road.

'Well,' he said. 'So . . .'

Heart speeding up, Frances tightened her fist around her shopping basket. Henry couldn't leave — there was too much to say. She needed to think of something more intriguing than 'how do you do?' to entice him to linger. *Think, Frances, think. Be clever if you can't be pretty.*

'You dropped your sack of flour,' she said. 'Unless you intended to gift it to me, of course?'

Henry moved his gaze from the road and back to Frances. 'Indeed, I did.'

'It's on the ground. Down there.' Frances said. 'It's on the ground.' She exhaled deeply. Repeating *on the ground* ad nauseam was neither clever nor pretty. It didn't matter about being witty anymore. She'd settle for not sounding like an imbecile. 'That's a large sack. Is Mr Thorpe still selling flour for three shillings a stone? It's on my own shopping list.' She waved the crinkled paper in the air.

'I don't know,' Henry said. 'I had pork and potatoes to trade; no money passed hands.'

'I see.'

Henry must be a farmer, like George. Although, if Henry had pork to trade, he was obviously someone who had the stomach to slaughter the beasts and prepare them for sale. Quite unlike George, then.

Henry ignored the flour, his eyes flickering over Frances's face. 'What's it been — nine or ten years?'

'Twelve.' Frances's voice was hoarse. Twelve anniversaries of the day he disappeared, twelve years seeing him in every shadow. How dare he not remember? 'It's been twelve years, Henry.'

Henry winced. She'd spoken too sharply. It wasn't seemly to

lurch from imbecilic to horrid in one conversation. This wouldn't do; Frances needed to better control her emotions.

'Twelve years?' he said. 'I suppose it was, wasn't it? Back in the late forties, when I was twenty. Or was it one and twenty?'

'You were one and twenty. I was eighteen.'

Eighteen. What an age. Old enough to have big dreams about what life could be. Not old enough to know that, in actuality, one's dreams were rarely realised.

'Ha! You have a better memory than I do. Half the time I wouldn't even know which way was up without my wife Minnie to remind me.'

The air stilled.

Minnie. What a glamorous name — short for Minerva, goddess of wisdom, perhaps? No doubt this Minnie has Greek curls, porcelain skin and blue eyes. She wouldn't wear a dung-coloured dress resembling a sack.

'Minnie.' Her voice was strained. 'How lovely.'

'And your husband?' Henry looked around. 'Is he here? And what about your children? I dare say you must have plenty. It *has* been over a decade, after all.'

'No.' Frances bowed her head. 'I have no husband. Or children.'

'You are a widow?'

'No, I am not a widow either. I . . . I remain unmarried.'

Henry didn't respond. He looked past Frances and clenched his jaw. Frances turned to see George striding towards them, his coat tails flapping in the wind. He must have returned with the cart. *A cart*: what would Henry think of that? Her family kept a carriage in London when Henry disappeared. Now, all her family owned was an uncomfortable, rattly, wooden contraption made for transporting firewood and produce. Their carriage in London had been sold the same week the lady's maid was let go. A month later, all of Frances's fine shoes and dresses had been sold as well, including the muslin she had worn to the park.

George stopped and stared at Henry, his newly grown moustache twitching. George was proud of that moustache. Frances had spied her brother admiring its reflection in their windows on more than one occasion.

'Henry White.'

'George Farrington.' Henry's voice was low. 'Fancy seeing you here. I didn't pick you as someone who would venture to the colonies.'

'Oh,' Frances said. 'You two remember each other then.'

The two men glared without speaking. Frances looked from one to the other.

'George?' she said. 'Henry?'

George tugged on his moustache. 'What in God's name are you doing here, wearing that native cloak?'

Yes: the cloak. Frances had forgotten to ask the same. There was a handful of settlers who adopted such items — those who had lived here since New Plymouth was first settled almost twenty years ago, or the whalers who arrived even earlier than that, but they weren't Henry.

Henry tapped his tobacco pouch. 'That's none of your business, Farrington.'

'Why would you wear such a garment?'

'Do you need your ears seen to, Farrington? I said to mind your own business.'

'You look like a heathen.'

Henry shrugged. 'I can't hear you properly, sir. That dead animal on your upper lip obstructs your words. What is it, a rat?'

George reddened. 'I'll teach you to mind your manners, you impertinent—'

Henry turned to Frances, cutting George off. 'Good day, Frances, I must go. Minnie and I have things to discuss.' He spun around and walked briskly towards his horse.

'Good riddance,' George said, though not loudly enough for his words to carry.

Henry can't leave, Frances thought. She still had too many questions to ask him.

'Wait! Henry!' She looked at her feet. 'Your flour! You've forgotten your flour.'

But Henry was gone.

CHAPTER FOUR

MATĀRIA

Henry still wasn't back. Matāria sat by the fire with a group of children, half listening as Betsy talked loudly about colourful fish. It was cloudy tonight; no moonlight lit the papakāinga, just the fire. The dancing flame cast long shadows over the people huddled nearby. It gave little warmth, although no one else seemed to notice that the breeze from the sea blew sharp and cool. Only Matāria.

She never should have let Henry take her cloak. He preferred it to his old, worn jacket; cloaks didn't wear through at the elbows like his English garments. Of course Matāria could have wrapped herself in one of their blankets, but her leg was sore and the hut felt too far away to go there and back. Nor did she want to interrupt her twins to fetch it for her: the other children didn't always include Betsy and Edwin in their kōrero so it would be a pity to pull them away. Matāria wrapped her arms around her body and listened to the children's conversation to distract herself.

Betsy was waving her hands in the air, eyes sparkling. 'It was an orange fish. And it looked like a boat.'

'Was it bigger than those?' Edwin pointed at a row of tuna being smoked over a small fire nearby.

'Yes, much bigger. And not as smelly.'

'You said it was all the colours. Then you said it was the colour of a kākā. But now you say it was orange?'

'Oh.' Betsy giggled. 'I was confused. It *was* all the colours. Not orange.'

'Fishhhhh.' Another boy spoke, trying the word out. Niko was his name. He was the oldest son of Matāria's cousin and close to the twins in age. Niko was also one of the loudest children in the papakāinga, well known for his hair that stuck in all directions like the tuakura fern, his large grin, and the twinkle in his eyes. 'Fishhhh. Ika.'

Betsy shook her head. 'Kāo. Fish. Not fishhhhh.'

Niko told Betsy in rapid Māori that she looked like a stinking dead fish. All the other children except Edwin laughed.

'Fishhhh!' they yelled. 'Fishhhh! The Boy and The Girl smell like *fishhhhhhhhhh!*'

Matāria looked around at the gathered adults. Surely someone would tell Niko to behave? On the other side of the fire were the men of the hapū: crowding together, anger on their faces. In the flickering light it was hard to see where the men stopped and Tūmatauenga began. None of them was going to stop the children from laughing at Betsy.

Near the men, Atarangi and some of the other women crouched and stripped flax with mussel shells. They weren't paying attention to the children either. Matāria watched as they pulled the thick green blades with their fingernails until it was nothing but wiry strands, which they tied into bundles with twine. The women sat most evenings in a tight circle, talking. Matāria could usually hear their conversations from where she sat. She knew all about their lives, thoughts and opinions. She'd heard them lament about when her people had left Ngāmotu after the Waikato troubles, only to later return in a great fleet: a generation of Te Ātiawa in forty-four waka, coming back to their ancestral homeland to join those hardy few who had remained behind. Matāria knew all of the gossip about the women's husbands and how proud they were of their children. Sometimes, a woman in the circle would nod at Matāria, but she was never invited to join them.

Niko leapt to his feet and darted away. He yelled back, right before turning the corner: '*Fishhhhhh!*'

The other children followed, leaving Betsy and Edwin alone with Matāria. Betsy glowered at the boy's retreating form. 'I didn't even want to play with Niko.' Betsy looked so much like Atarangi when she was cross. The likeness would have amused Matāria if Atarangi's constant disapproval didn't cut like māpere.

'No.' Edwin shook his head. 'I didn't want to play with him either. He's too loud.'

'It doesn't matter what they say about us, because we don't like them anyway,' Betsy said. 'They're not important.'

Edwin rested a hand on his sister's arm. 'Let's talk more about the fish, Betsy. They're not important.'

'Yes. And it's fish. Not fishhhh.'

Matāria glanced towards the women huddled around the flax, most draped in cloaks or blankets. Not all of them wore a moko kauae like Atarangi — the younger of the group weren't yet ready, as they were still learning about harakeke. One of the older women told a joke in a quiet voice; Atarangi threw back her head and laughed. Others joined in, stealing glances at Matāria and the twins. Matāria leaned forward to try to catch what was being said but she was too late: Tāwhirimātea had already carried the woman's words away on his wind.

She looked away, determined to show she did not care. Like her, these people were of Ngāmotu: from Te Rau o te Hui Pā in the north to the Herekawe Stream in the south, they all called the same whenua home. These people looked up at Taranaki the same as Matāria, and felt the comforting gaze of their tūpuna upon them. They were all descendants of Te Awanui-a-Rangi the Second, who traced his own lineage all the way back to Ranginui and Papatūānuku. As the whakataukī proclaimed: *Te Ātiawa i runga o te Rangi*. They were all from the skies. And, like the strands of rope used to tie waka, they were joined together.

Betsy was wrong: these people *were* important. But Matāria still didn't actually need the women in that circle, however important they were. Let them have their fun at her expense. Their rope would not help her find the stars. And she wasn't completely alone: she had the twins and her husband.

But where was he? The road was lost in a vast expanse of gloom. There had been so much rain lately that Ranginui's tears had transformed the pathway into mud. Henry would have to watch his footing so he didn't slip in a ditch. Or, even worse, into one of the rivers that travelled from Taranaki and flowed into the sea. A young settler child had drowned in one recently, and, whenever the rains were heavy, the rivers overflowed and seeped into some of the settler houses nearby. Henry said there was talk in the town of taming the rivers: walling them in; building fences; changing their course. Matāria hated that idea. What was wrong with how things were now? The awa didn't need to be altered, just respected, which included not building too close to them, or falling into them after dark.

Something caught her eye: a slow-moving object, close to the ground. Matāria squinted into the darkness. Was it him? *No*. The thing she could see was too large to be a man. She shivered and moved closer to the fire. The flames burned low; it was almost time to retreat to the hut, but she didn't want to lie on her mat until Henry was back. She had trouble sleeping unless he lay beside her. It would be even more difficult if he was out in the night, defenceless against whatever strange being had crept out of the depths of Rarohenga and was crawling right outside the papakāinga walls.

She knew her mind was tricking her. The danger wasn't real. Henry wasn't going to meet any creatures from the underworld out there on the road — he had enough demons of his own. His biggest danger was slipping into the river.

Edwin curled into Matāria and yawned. She couldn't wait any longer.

'It's time for bed.'

'Yes, Māmā,' said Edwin.

Betsy crossed her arms across her chest. 'I'm not tired.' She covered her mouth with her hand to hide her own yawning. 'Besides, Pāpā isn't home yet.'

Matāria struggled to her feet. 'It's time to rest. Pāpā is busy tonight.'

'Even the rainbow fish is asleep. What is Pāpā doing?'

'He's working.' Matāria didn't meet Betsy's eye. 'He's working in the township.'

Thud.

It was the sound of something landing heavily at the gate. The women with the flax stopped talking and turned to stare.

'He aha tēnei?' Atarangi's question carried to where Matāria stood. How was she meant to know what it was?

It must be what I saw on the road, Matāria thought, balling her hands. The beast from Rarohenga. Or worse: a British soldier from the barracks up the hill, ready to fight. Betsy and Edwin wrapped their arms around Matāria's middle like Te Wheke. Edwin whimpered softly.

'There's someone keeping watch,' Matāria whispered. 'We're

safe here behind the papakāinga walls. If something were wrong, we would have heard the pahū being struck by the men at the gates.'

'Then why is your heart beating so fast?' Edwin asked. There was nothing she could say to that.

Thud. Thud.

One of the men leapt to his feet. No one else spoke. Then Matāria could hear the sound of something heavy being pulled across the stones. That, and the waves behind the papakāinga breaking — a sinister contrast of natural and unnatural.

Thud. Scrape. Thud.

A song filled the air: a waiata, sung with vigour. The merry tune ricocheted off the hut walls.

Edwin let go of Matāria. 'It's not a monster, it's Pāpā!'

'I knew that all along,' said Betsy.

The man who'd leapt to his feet shrugged and sat back down. The women stripping the flax turned back to their conversation. Atarangi muttered something; the other women laughed.

Matāria sank back to the ground. That wasn't a Te Ātiawa waiata, or a song from another iwi; nor was it one of the hymns she'd been taught by the missionaries: high, trilling songs about the Holy Book. This was what her husband had once described as a 'sea shanty'.

How could you, Henry?

Hair hanging limply over his forehead, Henry staggered around the corner, dragging a large wooden object behind him. His shirt was untucked, her cloak sat lopsided across his shoulders.

'The king cannot swagger, nor get drunk like a beggar,' he sang. 'Nor be so happy as I . . .' He stretched his arms out wide and looked around. 'And where are my children?'

Edwin and Betsy ran towards him. Betsy reached Henry first. 'Māmā thought you were a monster! But I knew it was you!'

‘I knew too,’ said Edwin.

‘I knew it more,’ Betsy said. ‘Māmā said you were busy working.’

‘Yes, I was,’ Henry said, ‘but I am finished my work now.’

A large chair sat behind Henry; he had dragged it from who knew where. Not just any chair, either. It had a thick round back and an intricate floral design on the soft cushion. Its curved wooden legs had feet shaped like a dog’s paws. The missionaries didn’t own chairs like this — theirs were plain and made simply of wood. So this was what Matāria had seen on the road — Henry and this ridiculous seat. Maybe a beast from Rarohenga would have been better, for Matāria wouldn’t feel so much shame.

‘Look, children!’ Henry pointed at his new acquisition. ‘A chair! I dare say this is the first one ever brought to this papakāinga. And it’s such a good one for sitting on. I should know. Whenever I felt tired walking from the stables, I took a moment to see how it felt. My legs were well pleased. As was my bottom.’

‘How did you carry the chair on the horse, Pāpā?’ Betsy asked.

Henry stroked his chin. ‘With well-honed skills and finesse. Little did you know that your father is an expert at balancing. A great attribute indeed.’

The twins laughed. They took it in turns to sit on the chair. Other children emerged from the shadows to stare. The boy who’d called Betsy a stinking fish ran his hand around and over the rounded back. Niko’s eyes were wide. ‘Te tūru o ngā kurī,’ he said slowly.

Henry grinned. ‘Āe, Niko! A dog chair. Woof! Woof, woof!’

Laughter echoed from the circle of women. Matāria’s skin prickled as their words reached her ears.

‘I knew he’d be polluting his body with drink.’ *Atarangi.* Matāria would recognise her sister’s voice anywhere. The other women laughed even louder.

‘Look at Matāria’s husband. Is he barking like a dog?’

'Not a tame dog, either. He sounds like one of those wild dogs you find in the bushes.'

'What does he need a chair for? Does that man think his nono is more important than ours?'

'That thing will take up half their hut. As if their hut isn't strange enough with that chimney.'

'It belongs on the fire, dog feet and all.'

'At least then his stupidity will keep us warm.'

Henry grinned at the women. His grasp of their language wasn't good enough to keep up. Unlike Niko, the women spoke quickly and Henry seemed to think they were laughing with him. They weren't. The women were laughing *at* him: at Henry and Matāria both.

At least the twins didn't notice, as they played on the chair with the other children. Betsy contorted her body to crawl underneath. Edwin sat on the seat, and Niko sat on Edwin. All of them barked loudly between bursts of laughter. Others stood nearby, pointing with glee.

'My pāpā is so funny,' Betsy yelled from below the seat.

'Fishhhhhhh,' Niko replied, wriggling around on top of Edwin. 'Fishhhhhhhh and . . . Woof!'

One of the men waved at Henry. 'Homai te tupeka, Henare Mā?'

That he had understood, for he reached into his pocket and pulled out a leather pouch. The tobacco he had purchased meant he had been welcomed with his Māori name.

Henry shooed the children away and dragged his chair over to the other side of the fire, humming the shanty quietly. Placing the chair on the edge of the circle he sat down, back as straight as a tōtara.

'How do you do? How do you do?' Henry said in English. Not his normal English, either. This was the sort of accent the wealthy settlers had — those new arrivals with fancy clothes and nice things.

Henry dissolved into giggles. 'How do you do?'

The men smiled, clustering around Henry to reach for the tobacco.

'How do you do, Governor?' one of the men said, also in English. 'How do you do?'

Another man chuckled. 'How do you do, Sir Henare Mā?'

'Yes sir,' Henry said. 'Yesssir!'

The men plucked small burning embers from the fire and rolled them into their pipes, fingers moving quickly to avoid getting burnt. Henry did the same. The smell of tobacco filled the air, mingling with the smoked eel cooking over the smaller fire.

'Ahhh,' one of the men sighed. 'Thank you, Henare Mā.'

'My pleasure,' Henry said, still perched on the chair. Matāria flinched. Henry shouldn't have put himself higher than all of the others like that; if he'd been a man from another iwi, it might have caused offence. Although perhaps it was worse that none of the men seemed bothered by Henry's actions, as if they regarded him as like a child.

Matāria turned to the twins, who stood beside her, gaping at their father. 'Edwin. Betsy. It's time to sleep. We need to go.'

'But look at Pāpā's chair,' Betsy said. 'It's like the ones at the mission school, but softer. And the feet! Do you see the feet, Māmā?

'You'll have plenty more time to sit on that chair when it's squashed in the corner of our whare puni. Come along. Kia tere.'

Matāria brushed down the front of her skirts and limped towards their hut. The sound of laughter burst from the group by the bonfire, Henry's louder than most. A tear ran down Matāria's cheek but she brushed it away. The children must not see her cry.

Today was supposed to be when she and Henry talked about the map to help them out of the darkness. But all she had was a chair with dog feet and shame so heavy it gnawed at her belly. And no idea what to do when Tūmatauenga finally arrived.

CHAPTER FIVE

FRANCES

Frances lay on her bed in the semi-darkness, the smell of mutton fat from her candle hanging heavy in the air. Her bed was in a narrow room at the back of the house — a place more befitting a servant than a member of the household. But Kitty, the maid-of-all-work, had been put in a small lean-to beside the outdoor kitchen, so here Frances stayed. As Mother was so fond of saying, beggars could not be choosers — meaning, of course, a spinster wholly reliant on her family. And this room was homely enough. It had space for the trunk she'd brought on the boat from England, as well as a chest of drawers. She'd hung some needlework on the wall; though it didn't quite cover where the wallpaper had peeled to expose the scrim underneath, it was still better than nothing. Her narrow bed made of split logs was much more comfortable than the straw pallet Kitty slept on. On the bed was a small cushion filled with feathers from a hen that Frances had plucked and baked herself, just how Kitty had taught her. And being squirrelled away at the back of the house had the added benefit of being far from the drawing room, where George and Mother spent most of their time.

Not that Frances paid much attention to her surroundings this evening. When she did, it was only to observe how much the gloom suited her mood. She was too busy thinking about Henry. Was he happy? Mother said happiness was a ridiculous concept designed by folk with too much time on their hands. She claimed being content with one's lot was more than enough, for happiness is merely the absence of melancholy or illness. Mother was wrong. Frances had been happy that day at the park, when Henry had outlined his hopes for the future. The way Frances had felt back then wasn't the absence of bad feelings — it was much more pleasant than that. And Henry was probably happy with his Grecian goddess, Minnie. Happy, when Frances was the opposite. It was quite unfair, considering how he had up and left her. If Frances saw Henry again, she'd have to try her hardest not to throw propriety to the wind and give him a piece of her mind. Or cry. Or both.

Outside, through the window, lay George's two paddocks separated by a ditch, and the fowl yard off to the side. Alongside the fowl yard was what would eventually be the vegetable garden. Frances prayed this season would yield better crops than the last, for she had done everything she could to encourage the harvest. Mrs Archer had been so kind, offering her advice on how and when to plant, lending her a trowel and hoe, even giving her seedlings and cuttings from her own garden. If it didn't work this year she didn't know what else to do. Hearing the other settlers wax lyrical about how good the Taranaki soil was for growing food did not help her own carrots, onions and potatoes flourish.

Behind the paddocks was a bare hill. Māori land, apparently. Not that they used it very often, apart from crossing the hill to access their maize on the other side. George said the hill would be perfect for his own farm — it would be ideal for sheep. He had a vision of a fine estate of many acres, starting his expansion with grazing for sheep, and one day building a proper homestead and installing a farm manager in their current cottage. But the hill wasn't his to use, so it remained wasted.

If Henry had traded pork and potatoes at the store, he must be doing a fine job of taming the land. But where was his farm? The township of New Plymouth wasn't very large: some said there were around 2000 residents, and the same number of soldiers on top. Given that and the size of the surrounds, there weren't many options for where Henry might live. She'd not seen him in the area near the giant rock with the name she could never remember, nor seen him on the road to the south. He wouldn't be further inland, for there was nothing there: impenetrable bush as far as the eye could see. Perhaps he lived to the north. People said the land closer to Waitara had excellent soil, even better than here. They said that so long as you had a stomach for the natives fighting one another on your land, you could make a good living up there. Perhaps that was where Henry was.

Closing her eyes, Frances allowed herself to imagine Henry's farm. It would be the sort of land the new middle classes travelled all this way for, dreaming of social betterment and fresh air. Henry's farm probably afforded him luxuries he would never have experienced in London as a doctor's son, even with Frances's marital settlement. Minnie was likely the mistress of a beautiful, well-appointed home bursting with finely made furniture and other comforts — perhaps even a wardrobe. Minnie would run the household from her very own sitting room, assisted by more than one maid, as Henry would be able to afford the extortionate wages demanded by servants in the colonies. Minnie would not have to feed chickens, mend clothing, starch linens or any of the other things Frances was required to do every single day. At night, Minnie would sleep in a large bed in the finest bedroom of the house, warmed with its very own fireplace. Unlike this cold, narrow room, overlooking nothing but two paddocks, a hill and a failed vegetable garden.

A knock. 'Frances! I know you're in there; I can see the candlelight. Don't pretend you're not. May I come in?'

Mother. Frances opened her eyes and turned towards the wall. What a ridiculous thing for Mother to say. Of course Frances was in here. Where else would she be? Galivanting around in the dark?

'I'm changing into my other dress,' Frances said. 'I'll be out soon.'

'I want to talk.'

'Please, Mother. I'll join you in the drawing room shortly.'

The door swung open and Mother bustled inside. 'You're not dressing yourself at all. You're doing nothing but lying on your bed.' Mother wore a dark-red gown, her perfectly formed grey curls bouncing from her bonnet. Around her shoulders was a black shawl.

Frances rolled over and sat up. 'If I *had* been changing, you might have seen me in my undergarments!'

Mrs Farrington reared backwards. 'I only wanted to ask if you wanted a slice of cake. I know we have already had supper, but cake is such a nice treat, is it not?'

'Sorry, Mother.' Frances needed to keep her temper in check, even when Mother was being especially vexing. 'I'm sorry for being ill-mannered.'

'Apology accepted. And — if you *were* dressing yourself, it's nothing I haven't seen before. Besides which, a lady doesn't speak about such things. I know it's near impossible to know who is a lady in this town and who is not. But we both know that we are in the former category and must continue to conduct ourselves as such.'

Mother straightened her back before continuing: 'It's so hard to know nowadays, isn't it? Just look at Mary Paske's betrothal to that doctor from the 65th Regiment. Her mother carries on as if they are the sort of people who kept a carriage in England, forcing me to bite my tongue every time I see the wretched woman. I am pleased you are a spinster, for I do not understand the etiquette of courting in this town. But, as I was saying to Mrs Archer just the other day, at least I saw one daughter married, even though Clementine remained in England . . .'

Frances noted Mother's shawl — it was well worn from when she had only dressed in black. The tassels shook as Mother spoke, triggering an unwelcome memory: Mother in that very same shawl at Father's funeral, tassels quaking as she wept. It was a recollection Frances preferred not to linger on.

Today had been altogether too much. Frances felt as if she had walked the full gauntlet of emotions. She turned her face away. If she were to cry, Mother mustn't see. She'd find out about Henry eventually, of course, but not right now — Frances couldn't bear to talk about it.

'Is something the matter, Frances?'

'No. I am perfectly fine.' Her voice wobbled. 'There is nothing the matter.'

'You seem very pale, even in the candlelight. And I know you. Your voice is thick with tears.' Mother sat on the small chair beside Frances's writing desk and stared intently at her daughter. 'Have you eaten too many peaches again, my dear?'

'Peaches? Why are you talking about peaches? I don't even like them.'

'Is that so?' Mother shook her head sadly. 'Because all of the peaches are gone from the bowl in the kitchen, and George said it wasn't he who ate them.'

'It wasn't me. They're too furry.'

'They're not furry when you cut off the skins. They are delicious and juicy. The peaches are gone, and now you need to change your dress,' Mother said, squinting at Frances with suspicion. 'Is it because you dribbled peach juice down your front and feel ashamed of your gluttony? Is that why you don't want to join me for cake?'

Frances searched for something to say that wouldn't make her sound like a petulant child, but no words presented themselves.

Mother turned her attention to the tassels on her shawl, stroking the thin threads draped over her shoulders. 'I am sad you couldn't buy any fresh beef,' she said. 'But at least we have flour. How lucky we are that George procured an entire sack, and for such a good price too. We'd be lost without him looking after us so well.'

Silence hung in the air. Mother waited for Frances to embrace the subject change and enlighten her about the good fortune with the flour.

'Yes,' Frances said eventually. 'So very lucky, particularly as we were not able to take in any pork to trade.'

Mother sighed. 'It's not your brother's fault the farm boy left the job so soon. George was paying him a full ten shillings a week, as well. It would be daylight robbery to pay a penny more.'

'The Archers now pay him twelve shillings a week.'

'Well, more fool them. As I was saying to Mrs Archer last week, the servants here are so terribly uppish, are they not? I even spied Kitty making herself a crinoline of reeds — a crinoline! — as if she were a woman of high fashion rather than our help. It's not right. And now the tradesmen and their families presume to attend dances and other such events. I signed the petition to keep them away, but was only the fourth person to do so. The fourth! And here we are.'

'Indeed. Here we are. Without any meat bought and none to trade.'

Mother wrinkled her nose. 'It's so unpleasant, all that blood. The sooner George finds some workmen, the better. And let us talk no more of household finances. I despair how often people in this settlement talk about money; it is all one hears about at times.

It's terribly vulgar, and not something a lady should have to think about.'

'As you wish, Mother.'

'Anyway, brush your hair and come into the drawing room for a slice of cake.'

The door closed behind her. Frances sat on the edge of her bed, head in hands. Then, with a sigh, she slipped out of her bedroom and walked down the dim hallway, candle in hand, past George's room on the left, past Mother's room on the right. Past the daguerreotypes of Father and Albert hanging on the wall. Albert's had been turned. *How odd.* Frances set it right. As she did so, her eldest brother's dark eyes looked down at her. Albert had been fourteen when he cut his leg and succumbed to infection. Had Mother worn the same black shawl after Albert died? Frances couldn't remember; she and Clementine had been young when it happened. Over the years between that time and this she'd heard many stories about Albert from her parents. In time, her own memories had become entwined with their reminiscences. But she was sure of one thing: Albert had been good.

At the end of the hallway, the sitting-room door was ajar. Mother and George's voices wafted out. Frances was nearing the door when a single word reached her ears and froze her to the spot. *Frances.* They were talking about her. She quietly pulled herself back against the wall.

'I know Frances ate the peaches,' Mother said. 'You told me so.'

'Of course she did,' George replied. 'Kitty might be uppity, but she knows not to eat food without permission. The stable boy never comes anywhere near the house. And it wasn't either of us, was it?'

'Yet she denied it so vehemently. But you are quite right, George. Who else could it be? Especially as Frances has looked poorly ever since you both returned from the store this afternoon.'

'Ah,' George said. 'That we cannot blame on peaches. Something occurred in town that you will want to hear about.'

Frances listened closely. At least she wouldn't have to tell Mother herself about seeing Henry. She trusted her mother would be kinder when she knew the real reason Frances was so out of sorts.

'Oh? What happened?' Mother said. Frances could imagine her bending towards George, face lit up with excitement. 'Did you meet a nice young woman of marriageable age?'

'No, not today, alas. The few women in evidence were the usual assortment of silly girls swooning over the soldiers.'

'Did you not remind them you are landed gentry? That is so much finer than a man in a blue coat waving around a weapon.'

'Of course I did.' George coughed. 'No, this was something else. Remember Henry White? That scoundrel who asked me for Frances's hand in marriage, shortly after Father died?'

Mother gasped. 'How could I forget?'

'Well . . .'

George's voice lowered; Frances couldn't hear a word. She tilted her head to one side and concentrated as hard as she could, but to no avail. George barely spoke above a murmur.

Mother was not so quiet. 'Oh, my goodness!' she said. 'What should we do? I thought you'd put an end to the matter.'

George's voice was loud and clear again. 'I didn't know he'd end up here, did I? He was supposed to . . .' His voice dropped again to a whisper, and Mother's response was equally inaudible.

'Mother!' George spoke loudly again. 'Henry White was only making mischief with his allegations.'

Frances shivered. This made no sense. None whatsoever.

CHAPTER SIX

MATĀRIA

The morning light peeked through the cracks of the hut's raupō walls. Matāria could hear the waves crashing against the beach in a steady rhythm. When she was a child she'd lie awake in her parents' hut in this very same papakāinga and listen to the very same sea. She could picture it now: a blue expanse, stretching past where kina were collected, past where the creatures of Tangaroa swam, past the reef where the old people used to place the bones of the dead. Life and death: not two separate things, but linked together as part of the same landscape. The land and ocean around Ngāmotu were a constant reminder of how change and sameness intertwine. Matāria was different, but the sea was the same. Māmā and Pāpā were long gone, yet the giant rock Paritutu looked down on the papakāinga exactly as it always had.

Matāria rolled over and snuggled against Henry. He wrapped his arms around her, pulling her close. She opened her eyes. A large chair with dog paws for feet came into focus. *That's right*. She turned her back on her husband, hunching into a ball.

Behind her, Henry's body stiffened. 'I said I was sorry, Minnie. I really am.'

'And I said that you needed to sleep on that chair,' Matāria said.

'I tried!'

Matāria turned back to see Henry rolling off the mat and standing up in his filthy white shirt and linen drawers.

'Have you ever slept in a chair?' Henry continued. 'My poor back will never recover.'

'What else are we to do with the thing if you won't sleep in it? Give it to the rats to sit on?'

'We can sit on it ourselves; we don't need to waste it on the rats. Besides, they haven't shown their faces in at least a month. Not since I demonstrated my excellent aim when throwing my boot. And this chair is far too elegant for vermin.'

'It's far too elegant for *me*.'

Matāria considered making a scene about how ridiculous it was to buy furniture. How stupid it was for a man who constantly complained about the size of the whare puni to acquire an item that took up more space than anything else they owned. But there was no point. It wouldn't achieve anything except make Matāria feel like a nag, with a voice drip-dripping like the rain. *He manako te kōura i kore ai.* And just as wishing for the crayfish won't bring it, berating Henry wouldn't banish the memory of how she'd felt last night.

She reached towards the pile of clothes in the corner and picked up the dress she'd worn yesterday. Matāria was lucky to own two dresses — both gifts from the missionaries, who'd been given them by a settler whose wife had died of the coughing disease. Matāria preferred to wear the simpler of the two frocks as the other was much less comfortable: the bodice was tighter and it had a larger skirt — the sort the settler women wore with a crinoline to make the skirts appear fulsome and round. Without a crinoline, the dress's fabric fell in limp, heavy folds around Matāria's legs. Of course wearing a crinoline was out of the question: it would get in the way when she did her chores, it would invite mockery in the papakāinga, and it wouldn't fit in the hut, even without the chair.

Pulling the preferred dress over her head, she patted down the skirts. Then she fixed her hair at the back of her head, fastening it with the small wooden comb.

As Matāria dressed, Henry looked around. 'Where are the twins?'

'Atarangi said she would take them to the beach. They must have slipped away while we were sleeping.'

Henry snorted. 'I thought she was too busy hating us to show our children kindness.'

'She doesn't hate us. She just doesn't approve of us. And can you blame her? Look what you did with my cloak — you wore it to a public house, of all places. Such disregard of tapu! My māmā would have had some hard words to say to you. If things go badly today, it will be your fault.'

'Sorry, Minnie. I'm learning your ways — I'm just slow. I forgot, and I was thirsty. I'd had a terrible day, you see. I saw a bad man.'

'A bad man?' Matāria spun to face her husband. 'Who?'

'George Farrington.' Henry sat on the chair and put his hands behind his head. 'I knew him in London, would you believe it? I recognised him right away, even if he is hairier now. And I caught him in the most barefaced lie, the scoundrel.'

Henry spoke rarely about his life in London, and couldn't even describe the land where he grew up. *It's flat*, was all he said, *with a river full of offal.* London was somewhere Henry used to live, a place he wanted to forget — not somewhere he was from.

'George Farrington?' she said. 'Was he a friend?'

'I would sooner drink from a sewer than call that man anything other than what he is — a nasty brute disguised as a gentleman.'

Such angry words, Matāria thought. Henry must have good reason to hate the man. 'Where did you see him? Was it when you went to the store?'

'Yes, outside the store. You know the spot, beside the notices. Seeing him gave me such a start I dropped my sack of flour, right where we were standing.' Henry reached out towards Matāria. 'I'm sorry, Minnie. I was so flustered after seeing that swine, I completely lost my mind and forgot to pick the flour up. I'll make it up to you, I promise.'

'I'll explain about the flour to Atarangi. She might understand.' Probably not, in fact, but Matāria would at least try to redeem her husband's reputation. Matāria might be hōhā with Henry, but that would remain within the walls of this hut. It was not for the women in the harakeke circle to discuss with delight.

'I doubt your sister will understand,' Henry said. 'She'll speak ill of me. Like the time you said you admired my calloused hands and she said I had a calloused brain. Then she'll give you that look. You know the one . . .' He puckered his lips and crossed his eyes in imitation.

Matāria hid a smile. She couldn't indulge Henry, he was still in disgrace. 'You were meant to bring something we could cook with. Not a chair.'

Henry's eyes twinkled. 'We could cook with the chair, Minnie. It would make good firewood!'

'Tell me more about Mr Farrington. Who is he?'

Henry rested his chin in his hands. 'I was so startled to see him after all this time. Last time I saw him wasn't in the most pleasant of circumstances. I want to know what he's doing in New Plymouth.'

'He's probably the same as those other men who have arrived recently: he wants to take from Tāne-nui-a-Rangi to build more blockhouses.'

'Oi. Some of us came for adventure and have no intention to offend your forest god. But Farrington is another breed altogether. I saw his sister first. He has two sisters, Clementine and Frances. I knew both of them fairly well, I suppose, especially Frances. And there Frances was, standing outside the general store. I hardly recognised her. The poor woman used to have some spark but not anymore. She's about as lively as a wet cloth. She and I spoke for a short while, then Farrington appeared.'

Henry broke eye contact with Matāria when he spoke of Frances. How curious.

'Is Frances as bad as her brother?'

Henry shook his head. 'No. She's perfectly tolerable. Probably the only agreeable person in her family, if I'm honest. Her sister Clementine was far too talkative, and the mother a frightful snob. And the less said about George, the better.'

Henry leapt up from the chair and paced up and down inside the small hut: two small steps one direction, two in the other. 'Let's not talk about George Farrington any longer. We have other, more pressing concerns to discuss.'

Matāria's chest tightened. Henry was right — the chair and George Farrington were trivial matters next to Tūmatauenga.

'We need to keep ourselves and the children safe, Minnie,' Henry said. 'I shared a pint of ale with some soldiers from the 65th last night. They told me a thing or two.'

'The Hikete Piwhete,' Matāria said, using the nickname the Māori had given the troops.

Henry threw back his head and laughed. 'I call them the Hickety Pips to their faces, and they have no idea they're being made fun of.'

How familiar, Matāria thought, recalling the previous evening. But she kept the thought to herself.

Henry continued. 'Goodness knows, there are enough of them here now, whatever you want to call them. Seems to me your cousins living in the other papakāinga in town are not going to be able to stay there for much longer, either. There's talk of kicking them out.'

'Why? The people at Pukeariki aren't doing any harm.'

'I don't disagree, Minnie. But the papakāinga is slap-bang in the middle of New Plymouth. It makes the army nervous.'

'What else did the soldiers tell you?' There was no way Matāria could have learned these things for herself. It was good being able to hear it from Henry.

'They talked about those passes Māori have carry to enter the township. Another man was arrested yesterday for not having one.'

Matāria frowned. 'Why do we have to carry passes when the settlers don't? It's so unfair.'

'I know. It makes no sense, but your cousin Wiremu Kīngi is heading for war, whether we understand it or not.'

'Wiremu Kīngi Te Rangitāke. That's his name.'

'Well, his name is being dragged through the mud, regardless of what it is. The men in the public house were also ablaze with anger at those Te Ātiawa factions that had a skirmish on some poor farmer's land — a sheep was shot by accident. And I won't repeat what was said about your cloak.'

Matāria's breath became shallow. Scenes from the last war flashed into her mind: running, screaming, begging, crying. Henry didn't notice, and kept talking: 'I spoke to Kuru last night, after all the tobacco was gone and the women had gone to bed.'

Pulling her mind out of its dark depths, Matāria thought about Kuru: Atarangi's husband, a tall man with thick hair and eyes the colour of the night. Kuru was of a tuakana line, as her sister never tired of saying, a first-born son of a first-born son of a first-born son, going back further than even the most learned tohunga could recite. Atarangi's boasting aside, Matāria had to concede that Kuru was a wise leader, a just decision-maker and a skilled carver. It was said he'd been trained for warfare ever since he was a young boy, when his father would wake him with a slap to teach him to be alert to danger. Matāria hadn't seen Kuru by the fire last night, though she knew not to ask too many questions about his whereabouts — sometimes, true wisdom is found in silence, not words. But she had pieced together enough to know Kuru was close to Wiremu Kīngi Te Rangitāke.

'What did you tell Kuru?'

'Just what the settlers and soldiers told me,' Henry said. 'This problem isn't going away, Minnie.'

The sound of agitated voices came from outside the hut.

Matāria rushed through the door, Henry right behind her. A small cluster of people stood beside the kūmara storehouses, pointing over the wooden fence to the sea. Among the noisy group were Kuru and the young boy Niko. Matāria limped towards them, stopping beside Kuru. Henry stood on the other side, still in his shirt and undergarments. No one noticed his pale legs, they were too distracted by the large vessel gliding across the ocean.

Matāria gasped. It was the largest ship she'd ever seen, sailing past the rocky islands off the Ngāmotu coast. It had more sails than Matāria could count, billowing from masts so tall they must have been made from one of the kauri in the north. Kuru clenched his jaw, while Henry stared into the distance, a serious expression on his face. The ship sailed closer and closer to shore.

Māmā used to teach that Tangaroa said *Tiaki mai i ahau, māku anō koe e tiaki*, so Matāria knew that if they looked after the god of the sea, he would look after them in return. All the people of Ngāmotu thought of Tangaroa whenever they did anything within his domain, respecting his generosity by not cracking sea-eggs or opening shellfish lower than where the high tide brushed against the shore, and acknowledging his power by not straying too far into the ocean's depths. Go past that spot without a waka, and Tangaroa might sweep you away forever.

The people of the papakāinga would never swim further than that point; and neither could the ship come in any closer. A handful of smaller vessels were now being rowed out towards the ship by workers from the waterfront: *lightermen*, Henry had called them. Matāria couldn't think of an equivalent Māori word for the porters who transfer passengers to the smaller boats and take them to the beach. Perhaps there wasn't one. And why would there be? Māori waka could be dragged ashore, for they weren't this large.

'Thank you, Henare Mā.' Kuru turned to Henry and spoke in English. 'You had good information last night. Even if you did have a foolish chair.'

Henry shrugged. 'This fool knows one thing, Kuru. Those junior members of the regiment will say anything when plied with enough liquor.'

'I am sure you were more than willing to help them with that.'

'Anything to assist,' Henry said with a wink.

Matāria touched Henry lightly on the arm. He had done a good deed, but maybe next time he shouldn't drink so much himself. Not that she would trample on Henry's mana by saying that in front of Kuru.

'Who's on this ship?' she asked instead. 'And what's so important that you needed to tell Kuru last night?'

'It's—' Before Henry could finish his sentence he was interrupted by Niko, who jiggled from leg to leg and pointed into the distance.

'Look! Fishhhhhh, Māmā! Down there. Look!'

Matāria followed the boy's gaze. The smaller boats steered by the lightermen had pulled alongside the large ship and begun helping passengers disembark. Incoming ships usually had a range of people onboard: men, women, children. Not this one. All of those climbing down the ropes and into the smaller boats were men. Young men in their prime, recognisable by their tunics.

'Soldiers,' Henry said. 'The Governor has sent reinforcements from Auckland, and more are coming from Australia. That boat is full of soldiers of the Crown.'

Kuru pulled Henry away. 'We need more information, Henare Mā.'

'Shall I go back into the settlement and ask around?'

'Get us some more tobacco as well,' Kuru said. 'Take some kūmara with you to trade, and some kānga. We're preparing it early this year; some of it is ready to sell now.'

Henry nodded. 'I'll go to the store tomorrow afternoon, after I've earned some money doing odd jobs in the township. I'll spend some time talking to the settlers. And I'll buy another sack of flour for Atarangi, I promise.'

Matāria wasn't really listening. She stood watching the soldiers below. One boatload rowed to shore, then another, then another. So many men, in New Plymouth. To fight.

Tūmatauenga had arrived.

CHAPTER SEVEN

FRANCES

It had been two days since Frances had seen Henry. She decided to go to the store that afternoon — she needed to get away from the farm for her own sanity. And if she should encounter Henry again, all the better. Not that she knew what she might ask him. Her pile of questions was large and tangled, and she had no sense of the order in which they ought to be retrieved. But that was a decision for later. Now was for getting ready.

Her hair was smooth, parted in the centre and gathered low at the back of her head. The tendrils that fell around her face were curled — it might not be the height of fashion to curl one's hair, but Frances still liked to do so as it made her feel pretty. The blue dress sat nicely on her shoulders, its full skirts shimmering with every movement. The colour had dulled over the past year, but was still much more handsome than the brown. That morning Frances had also fetched some water from the stream to wash her whole body. It was quite an effort, boiling all the water on the fire, but worth it for how fresh she now felt.

She peered into the mirror atop her chest of drawers. A tired woman looked back: sunken eyes, sallow skin, pale lips. Her only colour was the small red marks from squeezing her cheeks in a misguided attempt to appear more spirited. Her face still betrayed how wretched she felt, and was that any wonder? The past two nights had been spent staring at the darkest corner of her room, wondering what George and Mother knew about Henry that she did not. Without sleep, time had passed in a foggy blur.

Nothing brought her pleasure, not even the needlework she was sewing to accompany the one above her bed. Her waking hours were spent in sluggish misery, the daily chores more of a grind than usual. Frances collected the eggs so slowly the chickens pecked and fussed, and her attempts to rouse the vegetable garden had amounted to little more than prodding the soil and thinking dark thoughts about the lack of sustenance growing within. While mending George's clothes, she'd been so distracted she'd misdirected the needle, drawing blood.

Neither Mother nor George had commented on her mood. Only Kitty had said anything, intercepting Frances as she boiled water for her bath in the scullery.

'I thought you were milking the cow today. Did you forget?' the maid had asked, glaring at Frances and waving a half-scrubbed pot in the air. 'And which of us will wash the clothes? I'm a maid, not a washerwoman. Next time your mother complains, I've a mind to tell her the same.'

Kitty had come out from Devon just before Frances had arrived, and gave every impression of having adapted to this place so much better. If the rumours were true, Kitty had been seen stepping out with an army administration assistant, something that would have been unheard of back in England.

'If you want me to do everything,' Kitty continued, 'as well as live out here in the middle of nowhere in your leaky shack, I want an extra shilling a week — not to mention last week's pay in time for me to spend it on my day off. My mother says there's lots of families around here looking for help. It's not like the old country out here. And you can tell your brother I said so.'

At least you get paid for your labour, Frances thought but didn't say. She was being uncharitable on account of being so tired, and there was far too much work for Kitty alone.

'I'll milk the cow, and I'll pass your message to George,' Frances said. 'Don't mind me, my head is in the clouds — I've not been sleeping well.'

Kitty's face softened. 'Thank you, miss. I don't mean for *you* to catch the sharp end of my tongue. It's not you I take issue with.'

'I understand. Perhaps once I've milked the cow you can help me turn that jug of sour cream into butter? I am unable to do it on my own.'

'Of course, miss. And I haven't forgotten that we'll be making bread as well. Once you're less tired, that is.'

Kitty had turned her back on Frances and continued scrubbing the pot. Frances finished boiling the water in silence. Even though they often worked side by side, the two of them could never talk for long. Mother took exception to anything she considered a breach of class boundaries. Kitty and Frances hadn't spoken again since that morning.

Frances sat back from the mirror, regarding her reflection from a distance — the sort of distance at which a person might stand to speak to her. She looked much better from here, especially now the red marks were fading from her cheeks. She turned her head this way and that, tucked a curl behind her ear and patted down her skirts. That would have to do. Then she tugged on her grey gloves, covering her work-worn hands. Not a blemish to be seen. She was ready.

Picking invisible lint off her sleeve, Frances ran through the afternoon's events in her mind. George would drop her off and take the cart elsewhere. He had important things to do, he'd said, things a woman needn't worry about. 'I'll be back at three sharp. You had better not be late, dilly-dallying by the river or some other nonsense.' In the meantime, Frances would look around New Plymouth. Where, God willing, she would see Henry again. That would be her chance to demand an explanation for why he had left. If she were prettier and wittier than the last time, all the better. Not because she thought she could compete with Henry's Grecian goddess. Frances hoped to present herself in better light so she could feel less embarrassed about the lonely spinster she had become.

She walked down the hallway. Sun streamed through the windows; it was warmer than it had been in some weeks. Perhaps today she would find something to lighten her mood.

Mother sailed out from the drawing room, blocking Frances's path. She wore a different dress, but had on the same black shawl.

'Where are you going?' she said. 'I had thought we would spend the afternoon together. You've been so busy with Kitty and the animals, I've scarcely seen you. Those chickens spend more time with you than I.'

Frances took a step back. Mother mustn't know Frances hoped to see Henry — she'd have to think of another excuse. Something that wasn't a rude retort about how the time Frances spent in the company of chickens was hardly by choice.

'I'm going to the grocer with George,' she said. 'Didn't he tell you at breakfast?'

'Why? We have all the supplies we need. And I would benefit from your company this afternoon. The sun is so pleasant; it would be such a shame to sit by myself. We could read from a serial, or finish our sewing?'

'I thought it might be worth looking for new supplies in the store, given we weren't able to purchase any fresh beef from the butcher last time . . .'

Mother shook her head. 'There won't be any. I have it on good authority from Mrs Archer, who heard from Mrs Leigh who had it from Mrs Bowen, that there will be no fresh beef to be had at the butcher all week, only brawn and ham bones.'

'I didn't mean meat, Mother. There might be a new delivery of dry goods, and Kitty said we are nearly out of sago. I also had a mind to visit Black's to see if there are any wedding cakes on display — remember those we saw not so long ago, during that period of so many weddings? I like studying the handiwork on the cakes; there might be some new ones to admire.'

'There are no wedding cakes on display at Black's — I looked myself not two days ago. Who would get married now? This weather is far too dreary.'

'I thought there had been a boat yesterday?'

'Mrs Archer said the boat was packed full of regimental men and carried no additional supplies for the store whatsoever — not even a grain of sugar. Unless another boat comes in the next week, we won't be eating cake for some time. I said to Mrs Archer, it was a large sloop, so surely it had food stores below? But it didn't, would you believe it? Mrs Archer was quite rude about it in fact. She said it was irrelevant to be talking about cake when those Māori troublemakers were causing such friction. But, as I said to her, one can care about both cake *and* war, can one not? Might not cake ease the pain of battle? She's such a strange woman, that Mrs Archer. I have a mind not to call on her again until she apologises for casting aspersions on my love of baked goods.'

As Mother went on, Frances murmured in all the appropriate places: *ah*; *hmmm*; *oh no*. The longer Mother talked about Mrs Archer the better to distract her from thwarting Frances's outing. Mother always made friends easily — she and other women would become the closest of confidantes within a month of meeting.

Keeping those friends was a different matter entirely. Mother would soon run out of women to befriend in this small town.

The tirade continued: 'Mrs Archer has been here too long. I keep trying to educate her in how backward some of these colonial ways are, but does she hear me? No, and she is terribly ungrateful. I think she's jealous that my George owns all this land — twice as much as her wastrel son. And it's just a matter of time before George finds a way to bring that empty hill behind our house into his possession as well, for the sheep we shall acquire.' Mother clapped her hands. 'Yes, that's it! Mrs Archer is consumed by envy. Envy of George's future landholdings.'

'Indeed,' Frances looked past Mother through the open door, where she could see the stable boy preparing the horse.

'She is alone of course, Mrs Archer,' Mother said. 'She does not have a daughter to stay with her as I do, and her son is always tomcatting around town. George is much less of a cad — he will have a good wife soon, I am sure of it. Albert would have had one too, God rest his soul. My Albert would have been a firm favourite of the young ladies, and might have had even more children than our Clementine.'

'Yes, Mother,' Frances said. 'But I really must be going. George is ready, and I don't want to make him late for his important business.'

'Oh, yes.' Mother looked Frances up and down. 'You're going to the store to look for new supplies that I just clearly established will not be there. Unless you have another reason for rejecting my company?'

Frances tugged at her nicely curled tendrils — a nervous habit from childhood. *Think, Frances. Think.* What were the notices last time she was there? Something about a new public house, and the arrival of the mail. *Yes.* That was it.

'I want to see if anything from Clementine came in the mail.

I read a notice that said the post would arrive today.'

Mother squinted at her. 'What makes you think your sister would write now, when she hasn't done so for at least six months? Clementine is far too busy for her family, and don't we all know it.'

'She might not have had the correct address before. Or she might have written a letter with poor handwriting that went astray. It might have gone to Plymouth, not New Plymouth.'

'You're wearing your finest gown to collect a letter that won't be there. Are you hoping to impress the shopkeeper? I hope not. That man is nice enough, I suppose, but he *does* keep a shop. Or is there someone else you plan to see?'

'Not at all. I'm simply taking your advice. I thought you wanted me to take more care with my appearance?'

'Balderdash! I know you, Frances. You had your first bath in who knows how long in an attempt to tempt that man Henry with your feminine wiles.'

Frances steadied herself against the wall. Of course Mother had guessed her intentions. And Frances was far too tired to think of a plausible response.

Mother put her hands on her hips. 'You are *not* to seek out Henry White, do you hear me? I have waited night and day for you to tell me of your encounter with him, yet you did not say a word. Me, your own Mother! Am I not to be trusted? Do you care so little for me that you would keep such a dark secret? At least George would not lie to me. At least one of my living children is honest.'

'I . . .' Frances could not confess to having overheard the conversation between Mother and George the other evening.

'He is trouble, that Henry White. Nothing but trouble.'

'I need to pass by, Mother. I *want* to go to the store. I've already told George I would. We can talk about this later, after we've read that serial and done our sewing. I promise.'

'Look me in the eye, Frances. Please.'

Frances turned her gaze back to Mother. All the tiredness and confusion of the past two days suddenly overwhelmed her. A tear rolled down her cheek.

'I thought Henry might have been dead.' She dabbed at her cheek with her gloved hand. 'But he's here, in New Plymouth! I want to talk to him and find out why he went away.'

Mother's expression softened. 'You may never find out, Frances. Who knows what goes through the mind of such a man? I wager he left you because he was chasing some other woman, and washed up here when his various crimes caught up with him. And George says he is married, so he will not have you regardless.'

'I . . . I didn't know where he was. The torment I have felt, not knowing . . .'

'My dear, you must move on. Of course you'll never marry now — you're too far old — but George and I want the best for you, you know that. And we agree that you need to forget Henry White once and for all — just as you should have done all those years ago.'

'How can a person forget a thing they do not understand? One cannot close a book before reading the ending.'

'Yes you can.'

Frances pulled her arm away. 'Did *you* know, Mother? Did you know what had happened to Henry?'

'How would I know what caused Henry White to leave London? That's ridiculous. Just ridiculous.' Mother suddenly drew in a breath. 'I know! I have an idea. Perhaps an outing *is* the best thing for you. You seem so melancholy. As I was saying to Mrs Archer, this climate does not suit your disposition at all. So wet, even in summer. I will accompany you today. I haven't been to the store myself for some time. And I wouldn't want to miss out if a letter does arrive from Clementine after all.'

No, no, no, Frances thought. But she said nothing.

Mother continued. 'We can go to together. Won't that be lovely?'

CHAPTER EIGHT

MATĀRIA

Matāria sat on the chair with dog feet. The cushion was very comfortable, and she liked being able to extend her sore leg while leaning into the thick padded back. Not that she'd ever admit it to Henry.

Henry rummaged around the hut, getting dressed for his visit to the store. He pulled on a shirt, followed by his trousers. Last was a black hat, perched on top of his head. He turned to Matāria and waggled his eyebrows. 'Lo! Behold: I dare say I am wearing the most wrinkled shirt of all of the white men in this town.'

Matāria inspected her husband. 'It looks perfectly respectable if you ignore that mark on the right sleeve. What is that?'

Henry grinned, the large gap between his front teeth on full display. 'Treacle. The cook at the public house was generously offering it by the spoonful to the regimental men when I happened to be sitting with them.'

'What do those men need treacle for?'

'They take anything they can get to sweeten their lives. Those tents they live in look like they'd blow over in a gentle breeze. And anything that might hurt their teeth would help your cause, surely? Men with toothache cannot fight at their best.'

Matāria thought about the last tooth Henry had lost. 'They become grouchy and have swollen faces — especially without boiling the right plants to help with the pain.'

Henry spat on his finger and rubbed away the treacle from his shirt. 'Exactly.'

'Anyway, your shirt looks fine, treacle aside. It seems like any other shirt you'd see a white man wearing on Devon Road.'

'Don't ruin my fantasy of looking different to those other men. I laugh to think about what the genteel settlers must say about me in my absence. That fiend George Farrington in particular.'

George Farrington again, Matāria thought. 'You still haven't told me what that man did.'

'Let's just say he is the sort of man who would not approve of a wrinkled shirt,' Henry said, dodging her question with an answer that was slippery like tuna. 'What is the point of ironing a shirt anyway? It will only wrinkle again. I'm not lazy. I am merely efficient.'

Matāria could wait — he would talk when he was ready. She leaned back even deeper into the chair's padded back.

Henry patted her shoulder. 'You look very comfortable sitting on that chair. Isn't it a work of art?'

'No. I hate it.'

'You don't hate it enough to sit on the floor instead.'

'I thought I might as try out the chair before we turn it into firewood,' she said. 'I've not sat on kindling before.'

'Oh? And how do you find sitting on kindling?'

'Uncomfortable,' she lied.

'I don't know how you bear the pain.'

'Neither do I.'

Henry's blue eyes twinkled. He knew she'd forgiven him again — at least, as much as she ever would. 'Come with me to the store,' he said. 'We can take the papakāinga cart — Kuru said I could use it — and we haven't been on an outing together for ages. Maybe we could go for a stroll around the town? And Betsy and Edwin are busy collecting kānga with Atarangi and the other women.'

Matāria shook her head. 'I can't. I don't have a pass, remember?'

Henry's face fell. 'Oh. That's right. You really ought to get one, Minnie. I'll take you to the border fort myself.'

'No. This is our land. I should not need to plead allegiance to a queen I've never met to walk in the steps of my ancestors.'

'You sound like Kuru.'

'Kuru is right.'

Henry looked solemn. 'You're both right. I don't like what's happening any more than you do, and I say as much to the settlers. But I still think you should get one. Then you can come with me to the township every now and again.'

'Maybe.' Matāria stood up and stooped outside. The wind was cool on her face. She turned to look out over the sea and towards the land stretched out in the distance: one of only two ways to leave Ngāmotu without a boat. She knew the journey north: through New Plymouth and past the turnoff to the old pā site of Pukerangiora, where so many Te Ātiawa had thrown themselves off cliffs when the Waikato came. Further on, the road passed the land at Puketapu that Wiremu Kīngi refused to sell, over the northern tip of Te Ātiawa's boundary and, eventually, into the lands of Ngāti Mutunga and Ngāti Tama. All the while, the path passed beaches with sand so black it would burn your feet on a hot day.

The other way out was the road to the south, which wound all the way around Taranaki and, after days of walking, reached the Whanganui River. Not that Matāria had seen that great river. She'd only heard the stories: about the deep grooves of the riverbed made by Taranaki himself after being exiled from the middle of Te-Ika-a-Māui, the water his tears. There were other ways to leave through the thick inland bush — Ngāmotu scouts knew which trails to follow — all the way to the southern tip of the island, but Matāria herself would get lost.

Coming up behind her, Henry wrapped his arms around her waist. Matāria rested against him.

'Remember meeting up there?' she said. 'In the north?'

Henry chuckled. 'Of course. How could I forget? That reminds me. We must write to our missionary friends up in the Waikato. The more I spend time with that German missionary here, the more fondly I think of those other two.'

'Yes, we will, but for now we need to decide what to do if we are attacked. We need to have a plan.'

'I know, you're right. I think the best option is going north. We could stay with the missionaries. You getting a pass would help us move through New Plymouth on the way.'

Sometimes sour berries needed to be swallowed, and Matāria would swallow a thousand to keep her children safe. She agreed this was the best option — to return to stay with the missionary and his wife in the Waikato if danger drew any closer.

Henry pulled her close. 'I'm sorry I promised you a proper conversation and came home drunk with a chair instead. But what I planned to say was that we should start making preparations to take the twins and go.'

Matāria thought of how she had wept after laying eyes on Taranaki for the first time. The tears came again. 'I don't want to leave here. Nō Te Ātiawa au.'

'I don't want to leave either. It's not something we'll do unless we have to.'

Matāria pulled away and looked up at her husband. 'We could visit the border fort to get my pass on the way to the store.'

'Good idea. Let's leave as soon as we can. I don't know how long we'll be at the fort. And I have to get to the store.'

'Yes, we mustn't forget Atarangi's flour.'

'I wouldn't dare forget. Your sister's wrath haunts my dreams.'

Matāria fetched her shawl from the hut and wrapped it around her shoulders. It was a warm afternoon, but it might get cold later. She patted her hair: it was tied sturdily, just as she liked it. She bent over and laced up her leather boots. The heavy shoes made Matāria's feet feel heavy and hot — she was so much less nimble when walking in them, and their hard flatness sometimes made her leg even sorer — but it was better to go into the town with shoes on. It wouldn't pay to stand out too much before getting the pass.

She held out her hand to Henry. 'Let's go.'

CHAPTER NINE

FRANCES

Frances stepped towards the cart.

George held up his hand. 'One moment, Frances. As Mother is joining us, you need to sit in the back.'

'Ah,' Frances said. 'Yes, of course.'

'You don't mind sitting back there, do you, Frances?' Mother asked. 'Of course you don't.'

Most of the planks in the back of the cart were damp, and it was neither pretty nor clever to be seen in a sodden dress. All her hard work and preparation would be for naught. 'It *is* a little wet.'

'Oh, how I miss our old carriage!' Mother said. 'It was never wet inside, was it? Even during the rains of '46, when your father and I agreed we had never seen such a downpour. Do you remember, George?'

'The cart is passable,' Frances said before George could reply. It would be unwise to linger on their family's former fortune — she felt unsettled enough as it was.

Mother reached to pat Frances on the shoulder, then climbed up into the cart. 'You are too kind,' she said. 'Even if you did insist on us travelling into the township instead of remaining in the warm drawing room, as was my preference.'

George snorted. 'I don't know why we're even talking about this. No one will notice Frances, wet or dry. She could wear a sack for all people would care. Half the women here barely pay *me* any attention, and I am a landowner. A real landowner — carriage or no carriage. Just as Father hoped I would be.'

'If I were to wear a sack, people would surely notice,' Frances said. 'Fashions in the colonies are not that uncivilised.'

'You flatter yourself, sister.'

Frances turned to Mother, waiting for her to intervene. She didn't — of course she didn't.

'Climb inside the cart, Frances,' Mother said instead. 'Hurry along now.'

Frances lowered herself onto the damp wood. She shuffled around to position herself on an empty sack and bunched her dress so it was touching as little wood as possible. Perhaps she would stay dry after all.

George flicked the reins and they were on their way.

They travelled over the hill and down towards the sea. Seated facing backwards, Frances watched their house in the distance, solitary in its paddock. The further away they travelled, the more their house became eclipsed by the harsh landscape surrounding it: the hill, the dark forest that undulated all the way to the mountain in the distance. Frances had once visited the Yorkshire Moors, when Father had rented a house for a month to take the waters in Harrogate. But even that wild and strangely forlorn landscape had felt tamer than this place, where the paths were hardly more than a slash of mud in the long grass, and there wasn't a stone wall to be seen.

They passed the Archer homestead. The house was similar to their own — wooden with a shingle roof and small windows — but everything looked that much finer. The path leading to the house was scattered with shells: ideal for seeing where to walk in the dark, and enabling the household to hear whenever someone approached. Mrs Archer's home had trees around the boundary line, and the paddocks were full of cows. A long rectangle of soil stretched out in front of the house, a garden Frances knew to be filled to the brim with carrots and potatoes and all sorts of herbs. Nearby were the chickens: happy, fat creatures that laid much bigger eggs than those Frances collected every morning.

'Oh!' Mother said. 'Look in the field behind the house. Is that a second bullock I spy, or do my eyes deceive me?'

Frances followed her mother's gaze. 'It is.'

'How is it they have two bullocks, when we have only one?' Mother asked. 'And all those cows! Mrs Archer must be surrounded by sweet, clotted, creamy goodness, night and day. What a glutton.'

'What do we want a second bullock for?' George's voice was sharp. 'The one we have is more than enough.'

'Yes,' Mother said. 'You are right, George. I would not want another bullock. I'm not greedy like Mrs Archer.'

'I'm glad you feel that way, Mother, because I will not be buying a second. We have enough demands on my hard-earned money as it is.'

'George,' Mother said, 'that reminds me: Kitty was very curt this morning. She made a comment about how she isn't a slave, whatever we may think.'

George shrugged. 'I wouldn't concern yourself with Kitty. She's a temperamental girl, always in this mood or that.'

'She said something to me also,' Frances added. 'She said she's a maid, not a washerwoman.'

'That girl!' Mother's voice was loud. 'So uppity. Kitty needs reminding that she is a maid-of-all-work. Not a maid-of-whatever-work-tickles-her-fancy.'

'I'll speak to her,' George said. 'I'll remind her to speak with respect.'

Poor Kitty, Frances thought. A lecture from George. No wonder the other two maids had left.

They passed a group of Māori women trailing up the hill towards their crops. Some had tattoos on their chins — what a shock it had been seeing *those* when Frances first arrived. She'd written to Clementine about it in her very first letter, going so far as to attempt to draw the pattern. Frances's rendition was little more than childish scribbles, whereas the tattoos themselves looked almost noble when one became accustomed to black ink so close to a person's mouth.

Frances looked more closely at the passing party. All the women had long black hair, falling loose below their shoulders, and they wore a mix of blankets, cloaks and simple cotton. One woman had a baby saddled to her front, another walked between a boy and a girl of perhaps seven or eight years of age. The boy and girl were very pale for Māori children, their hair a lighter shade of brown, their skin olive. The boy wore tattered coveralls, the girl a dark blue dress that came down to her knees.

'Look at those two,' Mother said. 'They don't look native at all. I hope they were not kidnapped for ransom.'

'Quite a few Englishmen have taken up with these women, Mother,' George said. 'I've even heard stories of a settler woman who married a Māori man, if you can believe it. Quite shocking, really.'

Mother tut-tutted. 'They're not even Christians. I know that some come to church and claim to have converted, but it's not the same, is it?'

'It is not,' George said. 'And they insist on wasting land. Like the hill behind our house.'

'The sooner that is yours, the better. Mrs Archer said there was a reason the natives didn't put their crops there — she had it from her late husband who had it from an old Māori man who used to live nearby. But what does she know, really? She more than likely made up the story to appear more interesting.'

'I know you have your disagreements with Mrs Archer,' George said, 'but please remember I need to remain on good terms with her son. I don't deny they're a family of uncultured imbeciles, but we have to keep borrowing their plough until I can buy one of my own.'

'Hmph,' Mother said. 'I shall remain civil, although I can't promise to be her friend. She flaunted her second bullock in our faces just now, not to mention all that cream she must eat. She's not one of us. Mr Archer was no gentleman, something I have on very good authority. Merely turning a profit on land is not what makes a person landed gentry, like yourself, George.'

'Indeed.'

Frances opened her mouth to comment, but closed it again. Neither of them would welcome her observation that she worked alongside Kitty more days than not, which was hardly the behaviour of landed gentry. Surely, all her chicken-feeding and cow-milking disqualified Frances well and truly from a title that George and Mother felt they retained? Perhaps a compromise could be had: she was landed gentry with only two dresses and raw hands. Who knew? These rules and distinctions had been much clearer in London.

The cart turned the bend and the sea stretched out in front of them. In the distance were the rocky islands called the Sugar Loaves, rising out of the water underneath the giant rock that had a name Frances could never remember. Closer to the shore was a large sloop with tall masts.

Mother shuddered. 'Those ships conjure the most horrid memories. Oh, that journey here was vile. I dare say the soldiers must be pleased to have arrived.'

'There are so many more reinforcements to the regiment now,' George said. 'That's what I've been told. Those Maoris will regret making trouble.'

'Good,' Mother said.

They passed a group of dusty men digging hastily to erect a wooden palisade around the outer rim of New Plymouth. Frances watched as three new logs were tied to those already standing, the defence growing incrementally. Could there actually be conflict? Conversations of war and land and the sneaky, dishonest Mr Kīngi had been swirling around the town ever since the Farringtons had arrived last year. But now — and she remembered the Māori man she had seen arrested, right before Henry had driven all other thoughts from her head — it was all taking a disturbingly concrete form.

Mother gaped at the men. 'For goodness' sake!' she said. 'They ought to be building that fence further out if they want to keep our farm safe. Great lot of good a fence as sharp as sharks' teeth will be if we are to be on the wrong side of it.'

George didn't reply, silently directing the horse and cart into the township. Frances looked at the small houses that lined the streets. Some were made from what the locals called raupō: bundles of reeds tied to a wooden frame under thatched roofs. Homes made of bulrush didn't look like terribly appealing places to live. How did they withstand strong wind?

Most of the houses were sturdier: wooden cottages with small, square windows, many clad with vertical sawn boards, a feature Frances had never seen prior to coming here. It gave them a distinctive look that served to remind her of how far away she was from what she'd always known. The homes were surrounded by low wooden fences to mark the boundary between the property and the road, and to keep the domestic animals from straying, although many failed to do so. On more than one occasion George had yelled at a chicken or pig to leave the road or be squashed by the horse's hoofs.

The cart turned onto Devon Road and trundled past a group of soldiers marching in formation. Their rifles caught the sun; the men's legs moved in unison. Frances felt reassured by the sight of them. How could there be war with such an army on hand to prevent it? George said there were at least a thousand regimental men in New Plymouth now, if not more. Most lived in the barracks up on Marsland Hill, the flat hill that loomed over the city — even from here, Frances could see the military camp surrounded by fences and defended by cannons. It was a formidable sight. Wiremu Kīngi and his band of renegades trying to block the land sales might be troublemakers, but they weren't stupid. Surely they wouldn't take on the might of the British Empire?

George tipped his hat at the soldiers, while Frances and Mother inclined their heads respectfully. A senior officer overseeing the palisade's construction from his horse saluted back. The cart rumbled onwards, dust flying in its wake. They arrived at the first of the shops at the end of the street. Men and women walked up and down on either side of the unpaved road, some stopping to chat. Frances recognised many of them, but not all. And none were Henry.

Henry. He was a much more familiar subject to think about than soldiers and conflict. Frances shifted her position, turning to study George and Mother's backs, sitting up the front of the cart. They had long filled her head with suppositions about where Henry had gone, yet now it seemed they had somehow been involved in his disappearance. Or at least they knew more than they had ever told her.

Frances's hands shook; she bit her lip. A dull pulse charged through her body. Mother always said anger was an emotion for men, so ought to be avoided at all costs. Unlike melancholy or contrariness, which were both acceptable in women in small doses. She shook her head and calmed herself; the feeling dissipated. *Thank goodness.* Anger was so much more frightening than sadness or malaise. Frances understood the contours of her melancholy self — her limits, how it manifested itself — but not so her angry self: that was a complete unknown. And should she ever surrender to that unladylike emotion, it would serve no end other than to expose her as unstable.

She returned to listening to the conversation in the front of the cart. George was talking, though Frances didn't know what about. That was another reason not to be angry — it took one out of oneself, in a way that dulled the mind.

'I wouldn't know, Mother,' George was saying. 'You know Clementine and I weren't close — we never have been. She was always far too hysterical for me, particularly over the past two or three years.'

What an odd conversation. Frances hadn't seen Clementine once in the past three years. Had George? And, if so, why had Frances not been told? And there had been no letters for so long, at least none that she knew about.

'It does vex me that she changed so much,' Mother said. 'And on the rare occasions Clementine did write, she did not pass on her regards to you. Don't think I didn't notice — I did.'

'Clementine's determined to act like a raving lunatic,' George said. 'Frances might be a sad old spinster who ate all the peaches, but Clementine is another kettle of fish entirely.'

Frances turned to George's back. She would ignore the comment about the peaches for now — she had something more pressing to ask. 'You saw Clementine before we left? You said "the past two or three years". We left England a year ago, and Clementine didn't visit the year before that. Or the year before *that*.'

George stiffened. 'No. You must have misheard me. I said these last *ten* years. Why would I see Clementine in secret? You do come out with the most ridiculous things at times.'

Frances didn't reply. She was distracted by an uncomfortable sensation spreading over her legs as the wetness from the damp wood seeped into her skirts. Of course it had.

George pulled on the reins and the horse stopped. Frances climbed out of the cart, followed by Mother. Instructing them to be back in that precise spot in two hours, George drove away.

'Oh!' Mother squinted past Frances. 'The women from the Floral Society look as if they're having an outing together. They must have forgotten to invite me. Wait here, Frances. I'll go bid them good afternoon.'

Rushing off, Mother left Frances alone in the exact place she'd seen Henry the day before yesterday. Frances tried to look at her rear to assess how damp it was, but couldn't twist her body far enough around. She imagined a giant wet blotch so vivid that an onlooker would assume she had been slow to reach the chamber pot. Why hadn't she bunched up her skirts in the cart and sat on her petticoats?

Mother walked briskly towards a group of well-dressed women, their bonnets decorated with brightly coloured ribbons. 'Yoohoo!' Frances could hear her mother's voice above the street sounds. 'Yoohoo! It's me, Mrs Farrington!'

Sinking onto a nearby bench, Frances put her head in her hands. She couldn't bear to watch the round of awkward curtseying. This outing was not what she'd hoped for: Frances had only just arrived and already had skirts that would remain wet until George returned to take her home. It would be a long few hours indeed.

CHAPTER TEN

MATĀRIA

Matāria stood by the cart outside the papakāinga. Beside her, Henry loaded the goods into the back: sacks of kūmara, kānga and potatoes, along with two kete of karaka berries, fresh from the stream, where the waters had washed away their poison. These were what the settlers liked to eat — unlike most of the seafood Māori collected, or the taro plants the newcomers didn't know how to prepare.

Many of the nearby settler farms grew similar crops. Matāria had seen their plots of land, divided into neat parcels, some ready to harvest but others producing little. The farmers hadn't yet come to understand how best to work the black earth of Taranaki. They also knew nothing about rāhui, or the local climate, and they struggled to tame the earth without a ready supply of men to help. Henry said labour in New Plymouth wasn't as cheap as in England, so some landowners were learning the hard way that back home it hadn't been them who had turned a profit from their land — it had been the men they'd underpaid. This was why there was always a willing buyer for the produce Henry piled into the wagon.

'Oh, I forgot the flax,' Henry said. 'Wait here a moment.'

Bales of harakeke always made a good trade. Matāria turned

towards the sea. Te Rā shone high in the sky, his rays falling over the waves. Tangaroa's domain looked especially inviting today, except for that giant ship full of soldiers, which seemed even bigger now than when she'd watched it arrive from up the hill — and more sinister, with even taller masts. It was an open wound on Tangaroa's body — it disrespected him by its very presence.

Matāria turned away; she'd seen enough of that vessel for one lifetime. Looking instead over the rocky motu, her gaze fell on the island of Motumahanga. The whalers had called it Saddleback, as it resembled a strange, disembodied horse's back floating in the water. When Matāria first heard the name as a child she had not seen a horse. The whalers came to and from Ngāmotu by boat — they had not yet discovered the paths north and south. They named the island after this foreign creature. As a girl, Matāria had assumed horses must be huge and jagged. When she finally saw one, she experienced two contradictory emotions that wrapped tightly around each other: relief that the horses standing in front of the cart were much less terrifying than her imaginings, and disappointment that she had been so wrong.

Motumahanga was the farthest of the islands. Closer to shore and under the shadow of Paritutu was the island of Mikotahi, pointing to the heavens like a lone nīkau shoot, just as its name said. Matāria studied Mikotahi's contours, even though they were as familiar as her own hands.

'I've noticed you gazing out there a lot, Minnie,' Henry said. He was back, a bale of harakeke in his arms. 'I often see you staring at that pointy rock.'

'I suppose I do.'

'Some of the men here were talking about living out on those islands when they were children. I must say, it didn't sound very pleasant. They look terribly barren.'

'The people of Ngāmotu have gone there for generations, and some of the whalers lived there too. They're not barren. There are caves on the far side for shelter, natural rock pools for fresh water, and all the fish a man could possibly eat.'

'You don't say? Mikotahi just looks like a rock to me. Did you live there too?'

'Kāo. I did not.'

'Then how do you know so much about it?'

'How does a person know anything? Because they've been told.'

When Matāria was a child she had heard a story about the large sea creatures that lived around the island. People spoke of massive octopuses that could hold a man under water, and sharks that would tear a person apart. Sharks and octopuses: no wonder Matāria had refused to go on the waka that morning, all those years ago, to seek refuge on Mikotahi. But how different her life might have been if she'd been on the waka of women and children sent to hide on that rock when the Waikato had invaded.

She didn't want to think about it. Matāria turned away from the sea but Henry didn't pick up the hint. 'Kuru was talking about living there for a short while as a child, along with Atarangi and most of the other adults we know.'

'Yes, they did. I'll tell you about Mikotahi another day,' she said. 'It's a story for the fireside, or while lying on the sleeping mat in the dark.' Or, Matāria thought, anywhere she wouldn't have to look directly at whoever she was speaking to. Some things are best said when you can let words flow freely without having them mirrored back in another person's eyes.

Henry put his arm around her shoulders. 'Only if you want to.'

'One day,' Matāria said. 'As my māmā always told me: *Haere whakamua, hoki whakamuri.* We go forward, but we look back. The past is in front of us — even if it causes pain — because the past has set the conditions for the present. A husk of maize will only grow where the land has been tilled and the seeds have already been planted.'

'What if the seeds were planted by the wrong person in the wrong place, and going back to the same ground means uncovering bad seeds?' Henry said. 'Seeds that were better left buried?'

'Did your mother tell you that?'

'No. Her advice was limited to advising me to learn my letters and find a respectable trade.' Henry chuckled. 'That and to keep out of my father's way when he'd been at the alehouse.'

'Your talk about bad seeds — is this something to do with that man you saw? Farrington?'

Henry shook his head. 'No, I was merely pontificating about seeds. And maize — or kānga. And tilling the land.'

'But . . .' Matāria's voice drifted off. 'Never mind. We can talk about it some other time. Maybe the same time I tell you about Mikotahi.'

'My stories are much less interesting than yours. My only regret is that I can't stretch that metaphor about seeds any further. I thought it might have been a fertile ground for puns.' Henry threw back his head and laughed. 'You get it? Fertile ground . . .'

Matāria smiled. 'Yes, I get it.'

This was as much as Henry ever gave her about the past. And wasn't this the very thing that had drawn them together in the first place: two people with history that hurt? The difference was that Matāria always intended to share her inner self eventually. *Haere whakamua, hoki whakamuri.* Matāria worried that if Henry continued to walk forward without looking back he would end up stuck, which was why she needed to tell the story of Mikotahi. But not today.

Henry smiled back at her. 'Thank you for pretending to find my jokes funny. It's the best possible way to thank me for bringing you home that chair you love. I know you are secretly spending your days composing songs about its dog feet.'

'I am not. It's going to be firewood. I shall warm my hands on the flames and feel joy.'

'So you claim,' Henry said. 'But I think you'll still be sitting on that chair when you're an old lady, surrounded by dozens of grandchildren. There will be so many Minnies and Henrys and Edwins and Betsys they will confuse everyone they meet. And you will be happy, Minnie White. Mainly because you'll be in the company of your descendants, but also because of that chair.'

How Henry loved to speak nonsense. It never failed to surprise Matāria how comforting those glib phrases could be when delivered with a cheeky grin and sparkling eyes.

Henry busied himself with the horse's bridle to ready the cart for use. The people of the papakāinga prided themselves on having not one but two carts, although most people still walked everywhere and did their own carrying. But Matāria needed the cart more than most: it hurt to walk, and, without proper rest, her leg would ache so badly it kept her awake at night.

When she'd first felt the rip in the back of her calf, scurrying away after a beating, she'd not been able to bear weight for weeks without wanting to cry out in pain. But while the screams had echoed inside her head, they did not leave her lips. She stifled them, for no one had any use for a woman who couldn't walk. And after she was freed, Matāria's fear of being recaptured had kept her walking, walking, walking, all the way from the Waikato. What was it Atarangi had said? The injured kōtuku will die in the wild. How fortunate she wasn't a bird. A bird might have sung a song of pain and exposed itself for what it was: broken.

Kuru strode out of the papakāinga gates. His face was pink,

sweat ran down his brow. Around his waist hung a large stone mere, the weapon their people had used to defeat their enemies for generations.

'We'll need that cart to help Wiremu Kīngi when you're back,' Kuru said to Henry in English. 'We're going to start moving supplies to his men.'

'What, already?' Henry said. 'What sort of supplies?'

'Rifles. Blankets. Food they can eat without needing to light a fire. Any tobacco you can get us.'

'I know there are more soldiers in town now but I didn't realise conflict was imminent,' Henry said. 'Isn't there going to be a meeting to discuss it?'

'I don't know anything about a meeting, but a runner arrived just now,' Kuru said. 'The boy had run all the way from Pukeariki papakāinga and had been to all the villages north of the Whaiwakaio River before that. He said Kīngi had it from a man sent by the German missionary that Governor Browne is not going to change his mind about taking the land.'

'How is it Kīngi got his news from the missionary? The government ought to be talking to you directly.'

Kuru shrugged. 'We get most of our news from the missionaries. Or from you, Henare Mā.'

'It's not right.'

'If I was to stop and think about all that was wrong, Henare Mā, I would be too angry to speak.'

'Perhaps I should go and visit Father Schmidt myself. Find out more from him directly.'

Kuru turned to Matāria and spoke in swift Māori. 'Your husband is useful, but tell him not to meddle — he has my authority to communicate information, but nothing more. And that German may preach peace, but when war is declared, whose side will he be on? Don't forget he had my cousin exiled for being a witch doctor. These white men might be good to us, but they are not one of us. A flower sheltering under a rimu is not a tree. The same is true for your husband.'

Henry nodded sagely, not understanding what had been said.

'Henry means well,' Matāria said, also in Māori. 'And he has Māori children. He's not like those missionaries. He is one of us.'

'Matāria, be careful with your words,' said her brother-in-law. 'There are many here who think *you* are no longer one of us either. Remember?'

Matāria turned back and looked at Mikotahi. *If only.*

Haere whakamua, hoki whakamuri.

She spoke to Henry in English. 'That's a good idea, Henry. Please call on this German missionary, but only to find out what he knows. Nothing more.'

'Yes,' said Kuru. 'And let me know what you learn.'

'I can buy you more supplies at the store as well,' Henry said, pleased to be included in the conversation again. 'Just tell me what you need. I have some wages left from the odd jobs I did the other day.' He looked at Matāria and winked. 'What I didn't spend on the chair, that is.'

'You and your fool chair,' Kuru said.

'Well, we'd best be off,' Henry said. 'We're going to get Matāria's pass first, at the border fort, so she can travel freely in the settlement.'

Kuru faced Matāria and switched back to Māori. 'You're going to swear allegiance to the Queen of England?'

'I have to. I can't travel into the town otherwise, or through it. We might need to go north.'

'Why would you do that? Do you think you can join the battle with your bad leg?'

'What do you mean?' Kuru had misunderstood her — she was

talking about escaping, not joining the battle.

'I mean there is no way to travel north for us Māori anymore,' Kuru said.

'I need that pass. It might be important. It's worth trying, surely?'

'Queen Victoria has never even visited Aotearoa. Why should we swear allegiance to her to move freely around our own place? Our land?'

Matāria lowered her eyes. Kuru was an important man in the papakāinga but she would stand firm: 'I feel the mamae too, Kuru. It makes my heart heavy with pain — I feel our tūpuna weeping — but I'm scared that without the pass I won't be able to leave quickly if we have to. I need to be able to keep my twins safe.'

'Didn't you already leave once? How can you claim to be of this place if you're willing to dishonour our ancestors by pledging support to a foreign queen — only so you may leave again?'

'Auē! I didn't leave last time. I was taken, Kuru. *Taken.*'

'I—' Kuru began, but Matāria's emotions outweighed protocol and she cut him off.

'What if my children are taken as slaves?' she said. 'I know the missionaries say the British no longer keep slaves, but other white people do. I've heard stories about America — there are many slaves there, the missionaries told me all about it. What if my children end up enduring what I had to live through? I couldn't bear it.' Her voice caught in her throat. 'Tūmatauenga is coming, in a new form. And I don't know his rules.'

Kuru clutched the stone mere tied at his waist. Like all mere, it was perfectly honed to break a man's ribs and bludgeon his skull. 'None of us know this Tūmatauenga,' he said. 'He is a stranger to us all. Just like our parents didn't understand the war that descended upon us when we were children, with its muskets and cannons.'

'I *need* the pass. I don't *want* it, but I need it, Kuru.'

'I get away without one by riding the horse through the bush and taking the roads towards Taranaki. Atarangi doesn't need one either. There are no checks between here and the kānga, or anywhere else she might need to go. She says she would rather be arrested than dishonour your parents by—'

'Enough.' Henry crossed his arms across his body. 'I don't understand half of what you're saying, but I can guess its meaning. We all need to be able to travel freely around New Plymouth, and now Māori are being arrested for not carrying a pass.'

Kuru kicked the dirt with his bare feet. 'Auē. What terrible decisions we are being forced to make. No wonder Ranginui is crying so much, even though it is summer. And the rains will only get worse, I'm sure of it. Yes, Henare Mā, go and get Matāria that pass. And remember Atarangi's flour this time.'

Kuru gripped the mere so tightly his knuckles turned white. He turned and walked back towards the papakāinga, not once letting go of his weapon.

CHAPTER ELEVEN

FRANCES

Frances sat on the bench outside the general store, inhaling the scent of the town: woodsmoke, the cesspits, the tang of blood from the nearby butchery, all mixed with the sharp freshness of the bush behind the store. So many sounds also swirled around her. From the road came the thudding of hoofs, the rumble of cart wheels and the clucking of two chickens darting away from a young boy chasing them with a stick. Frances flinched as the boy ran through a fresh pile of horse manure, which splattered onto his trousers. She hoped the boy's mother employed a washerwoman.

Other sounds filled the air: the steady chopping of wood from the lumberyard down the way and men yelling to one another as they built the nearby blockhouse. Only two nights had passed since she'd last been here but already the blockhouse had sturdy walls. Not long now and it would be finished, and New Plymouth would be that much better protected.

The sounds cut in on Frances's thoughts about Clementine and George. She decided she needed to check Clementine's correspondence to see whether the letters held any clues she had missed. She would do that as soon as she got home and changed into a dry dress. And what about now? She could not return home any earlier than George had dictated. Nor could she wander off on her own, or Mother, returning from her conversation with the women of the Floral Society, would be alarmed by her absence. She might as well go into the store and ask when the mail coach was expected. Frances pulled herself to her feet and brushed down the front of her skirt, and more surreptitiously patted her damp rear. All she could do was hope nobody would notice.

She scanned the public noticeboard, which had changed since she had last looked: a man was offering a watch repair service on Saturday mornings; a farmer was selling a young bullock; a box of window glass had arrived from Wellington for sale. And the postal coach from Auckland had been delayed — it wouldn't be here for at least three more days. No letters from Clementine today, then.

About to turn away, Frances noticed at the bottom of the noticeboard was another new square of paper. She bobbed down to read it. There was to be a public meeting to discuss 'the unfortunate native question'. The Native Secretary and Land Purchase Commissioner, Donald McLean, was travelling to New Plymouth especially. Next Saturday at four o'clock, McLean promised to communicate to the people of New Plymouth what the government planned to do next about the natives. *How interesting*. George would likely go, and so would the Archers. Mother would surely join George — she wouldn't miss the opportunity of a gathering, regardless of the meeting's purpose. Perhaps Henry would also be in attendance.

Of course he would. *Everyone* would. Frances would see him there, having ensured her skirts were perfectly dry. Her heart raced. What an exciting prospect, for Frances genuinely wanted to hear what McLean had to say. She would not have to feign interest, so would be far less likely to raise Mother's suspicions.

She headed into the store. Behind the counter, Mr Thorpe, the shopkeeper, was stroking his large moustache — the kind George was attempting to grow. He bowed to her in greeting. Beside him Miss Thorpe sat on a rocking chair, sewing. She stood up to welcome Frances, adjusting her white muslin cap and grey dress. Frances couldn't tell how old she was — somewhere in that murky middle age between old and young. Clementine would have described Dora Thorpe as being too old to be a debutante, but too young to be a helpless spinster: she was possibly around Frances's age, maybe slightly older. Miss Thorpe mended garments for a small fee — a respectable and busy trade given the number of single soldiers in the township.

Well, Frances considered it respectable; Mother, on the other hand, thought Dora's sewing was evidence of The Thorpes' lower class. One day Frances would love to point out to Mother that Dora had more new dresses than Frances, including one with a lace trim. Indeed, all the merchants seemed to have more money than the Farringtons. She would also like to share her observation that the more useless a person was in terms of building this new settlement, the more Mother seemed to respect them. But of course she would never say such a thing out loud.

Beside the counter sat a box of sweet potatoes. Frances stopped to look. They were lumpier than normal potatoes, with purple skin visible through the crusted earth. There was a time when she wouldn't have noticed the difference. Before Father died, she rarely saw uncooked food — everything she ate was prepared by the cook. What would Father have said if he'd been alive to see Frances feed chickens and milk a cow? Would he have disapproved of George's abject failure to do anything with their livestock apart from chase them around the paddock until the beasts got fed up, turned around, and charged at him?

It was a moot question. If Father were alive, Frances would still be in London, blissfully ignorant of the nuanced differences between a potato found in England and a sweet potato grown in New Zealand. Or, perhaps not. Not given what Father had done with his money: ruin was ruin, dead or alive. Perhaps the blame for Frances having an intimate knowledge of potatoes lay completely at his door.

Mr Thorpe followed her gaze. 'The kūmara just came in this morning,' he said. 'Quite delicious, if you ask me, particularly eaten with fresh peas.'

'Oh,' Frances said. 'How lovely.'

Dora Thorpe chipped in. 'You won't find those back in London — not even at Covent Garden. Not fresh and harvested by the Māori in any case.'

'Indeed, Miss Thorpe.'

'Please, Miss Farrington, call me Dora. I have been meaning to say that, ever since our conversation last week about fabric.'

'And please call me Frances.'

The two women bobbed a curtsey at each other. *There*. They were now one step closer to talking about matters that weren't strictly in the realm of small-talk. Luckily, Mother was outside, still bothering the women of the Floral Society, so Frances was left in peace to commit this no doubt unforgivable social transgression.

'Very well, Frances,' said Dora. 'I must say, I don't like what these soldiers being here means for us. But their worn socks and torn shirts keep me busy.' Dora dug around inside her work bag and pulled out some brown woollen socks. 'Look at how unravelled these are. It's no wonder those regimental men seem so serious all of the time. Their feet must get terribly wet in the rain.'

'Indeed,' Frances replied. *Indeed* was what Clementine said when she didn't have anything clever to offer, and Frances had picked up the habit. It bought one time but did need to be followed by something more substantial. So much had been stripped from who Frances had once been in society, making her unsure now who she was, and often words seemed to fail her. She thought back to what Dora had said earlier. 'You are quite correct that I would never see a sweet potato in London.'

'I went to London once myself, not long before we came here in the early forties,' Dora said. 'As you know, most of us here are Devon folk, though we do get people from London on occasion. In fact, now I think about it, one of our friendlier customers hails from there. Last I saw him, he said that not a day goes past and he doesn't give thanks for being here instead.'

Perhaps not everyone misses London as I do, Frances thought, but she dared not say so out loud. Her yearning for the place of her upbringing was too raw to be anything other than a private thought. The Thorpe siblings were early settlers and, like the other pioneers, had an air of grit and toil about them. Frances couldn't tell if they had earned their aura of industry from quite literally building a town from nothing, or whether it was a quality they had possessed all along, and was what had caused them to seek adventure in the first place.

Regardless, she would not push her views on the Thorpes, as those who had come out on the early boats could become quite defensive about these things. Dora seemed amiable; it would be unfortunate to get her offside. Dora was also one of the few women Frances had met here who was both unmarried and anywhere near her age. The idea of Dora becoming a friend was too ambitious — Frances wasn't the sort of woman who made friends — but it was nice to be on amicable terms.

'This man must have had a good experience here in New Plymouth,' Frances said.

'You may know him,' said Dora. 'He's quite distinctive because he sometimes wears a native cloak, says it's warmer than a coat. We spoke of that, too.'

Mr Thorpe snorted. '*You* spoke of it, Dora. I don't believe the poor man got a word in edgewise.'

'Hmph, I don't believe that is true at all,' Dora said. 'He asked for all the latest on the soldiers, remember? We had quite a long conversation. I listened quite nicely, I'll have you know.'

Frances looked from Mr Thorpe to Dora. *Henry.* They were describing Henry.

'Oh,' Dora said, 'I needn't have wasted my breath describing him. I can see him through the window right now.'

CHAPTER TWELVE

MATĀRIA

Matāria and Henry travelled in the cart up the muddy road. There were many people walking on the road today — most of them from this part of Ngāmotu, carrying food and other supplies. Some were headed towards the papakāinga, others in the opposite direction. A dog darted out of the cart's path, turning to snap at the horse's heavy hooves.

'Get out of the way!' Henry yelled. The dog looked at Henry before scampering into the nearby trees. 'Go on, then!' Henry called after it. 'Go and join your mangy brethren in the bush!'

Henry steered the horse around a corner. Directly ahead of them was Taranaki, the top of his brown head peeking over some dark grey clouds. Henry raised his chin in the mountain's direction. 'He's shy today. Isn't that what you always say?'

'No, I was going to say he's hiding his face, tired of looking over everything. Just imagine. What if we could see what Taranaki sees? How useful would that be?'

'It would! We could see what the powerful people get up to when they think no one is looking. All sorts of debauchery, I bet!'

'What I *meant* was that Taranaki could see the best way to leave Ngāmotu. He'd know which part of the bush to travel through.'

'It would be useful to be an all-seeing mountain for planning purposes, I'll give you that, Minnie. And, on second thoughts, I'd really rather not see other people in their undergarments.'

'How can you think of undergarments when we're facing an imminent war and don't have a clear escape path?'

They lapsed into silence, until Henry said in a quiet voice, 'I have to think of such things because if I don't find distractions, things to amuse me, I'll be overcome by terror. What use will I be then?'

Matāria squeezed Henry's hand and he squeezed back.

'We'll find the stars,' she said.

'We will, Minnie. I know it.'

They passed the German mission station near the beach — a wooden school-house with two smaller buildings behind it. Betsy and Edwin went to school here, with some of the other children from the papakāinga. Atarangi disapproved, saying that, had the babies she'd had to Kuru lived, she never would have sent them to such a place. If anything, that made Matāria all the more resolute that her twins should attend. They needed to maintain their English — Henry said so — and learning to read and write would make them wise. With wisdom, they could both live good lives: a profession for Edwin, and a happy situation for Betsy, whatever that might be.

She turned to Henry. 'When will you talk to Father Schmidt?'

'Maybe tomorrow. What did Kuru say about him? I couldn't follow.'

'He was telling you not to meddle,' Matāria said. 'He is angry with the missionary for getting so involved in our affairs. Also, he says Father Schmidt drove the healer away, not long before we arrived. Tai was his name — Kuru's cousin.'

Henry snorted. 'I've heard about Tai. He was claiming to heal people with magic.'

'It wasn't magic. Tai sought to alter the mauri of the sick, and that isn't the same as magic — especially not the dark magic in the settler stories.' Matāria had spent many hours explaining to Henry that she didn't see the world in terms of holy versus evil: tapu and noa were not the same as good and bad, and Hawaiki and Rarohenga were not Heaven and Hell. Unlike many husbands, he admired her for challenging his way of seeing the world, but he still didn't quite understand. Maybe he never would.

Henry shrugged. 'The other men said people were sick, and Tai made them worse. Whatever he did wasn't working.'

'Tai couldn't stop the disease, that's true. Nothing could. One boy went to the settler doctor and had slugs put all over his body. He died also.'

'No one can stop disease once it's set its course, so Kuru's cousin should never have claimed he could,' Henry said. 'That's why Schmidt cast him out. Schmidt's as pompous as can be, but he means well.'

'Let's not talk about this anymore. We have to focus on the war — that's enough to think about.'

'You've got that right.'

The horse and cart approached the small wooden mission buildings on the low rise of grass: the only European buildings down by the Ngāmotu foreshore.

'I remember when that land was empty,' Matāria said.

'It must have been so different.'

'It was. New Plymouth is such a busy town. *Too* busy.'

'Not compared to London. It is very small, in fact.'

Matāria shuddered. 'If New Plymouth is small, with all its shops and houses and soldiers roaming everywhere, I'd probably hate London.'

'Maybe, or maybe you'd find it interesting and exciting, especially as you'd be experiencing it for what it is. Not looking around and seeing all it is *not*.'

Matāria turned over Henry's words in her mind. Of course she saw the layers of landscape that had existed before; she couldn't help it. History was all around her, just hidden from sight if you didn't look hard enough. But it was interesting that Henry had brought up London again — he'd mentioned that place more in the past few days than he had since they met. It must be playing on his mind.

'Tell me more about London, Henry. Tell me about Farrington, also.'

'London has a large tower, a filthy river and some old churches. I've not much else to say,' Henry said. 'Farrington's a dastardly crook though. That man will do anything to get what he wants, moral or not. Not many people know what a bad man he is. But I do.'

'A crook?'

'Yes, not that anyone would believe me.'

A chill crept up Matāria's spine. 'Are we safe here with him in town? Is he . . . dangerous?'

'He won't hurt us. He's a coward — with a ridiculous moustache.'

'But what did he do? Was it in war?'

'No. Not war.'

How horrible, Matāria thought. Maybe he had killed someone. When she was a child, she had seen many killed: her parents; her aunts and uncles; members of the papakāinga. Some died with quiet dignity, but others did not. As a slave, she'd seen other slaves put to death when they were old or feeble — some murdered; some left to the elements, begging for water and food. Life and death were directly intertwined, and Te Pō lurked in every space Matāria had ever existed. Everything that gives life can cause death — water, air, food, the ahi kā fires that mark their territory. Death is a constant line connecting the present with the past. It is the way it has always been, and how it will always be. But to cause the death of another person not in a time of war? That meant a great and ugly battle was being waged within a person, and was so much worse.

Henry looked at Matāria. 'Don't worry, Minnie. The man's an ass. He's nothing to us. Nothing.'

'I hope you're right.'

Hope — that useless word again. Henry drove onward, following the road into town. They passed the old pā site at Moturoa and travelled alongside the coast, eventually reaching a border fort at the edge of the town, where they were greeted by the sharp sound of metal being hammered.

The new blockhouse guarding the border was a small building behind an outer wall of split rimu logs, placed side by side and pointed at the sky. It had no windows, only a row of square rifle holes cut into the logs on either side of a heavy wooden door. Outside the wall was a deep trench where two pigs wallowed in the mud.

The smell of woodsmoke filled the air but there was no one in sight, not outside the building, or around the nearby tents. *How strange.* Matāria decided to stay in the cart, just in case, and urged Henry to do the same.

'Don't worry, Minnie,' Henry said. 'I'm not going to leap to the ground like an over-eager warrior and rush into danger. I'll stay up here and ogle from on high. Like the mountain, but without a cover of cloud over my face.'

'Good afternoon!' Henry called out. 'Is anyone there?'

The pigs looked up at them. 'Oh ho, pigs,' Henry said. 'Do you have a master? Or do you have free rein of this place?' The pigs scuttled away.

Matāria realised she could see some eyes through one of the rifle holes. Moments later, the door swung open and a young man strode out, looking up at Henry. He had on the white trousers and blue tunic worn by the soldiers, although this young man's garments were far too big for him. He reminded Matāria of a little boy who had borrowed his father's cloak and didn't yet have the mana to wear such a thing. A boy with a rifle.

'It's just me, sir. Can I help you?'

'I want to get my wife a pass, so she may have the papers to travel freely in the township.'

The young man's gaze swept across Matāria's body and settled on her face. 'Your wife, sir? This woman?'

Matāria stared directly ahead, unsmiling.

The soldier jiggled nervously on the spot.

Henry reddened. 'Yes. My wife. Minnie White. She needs the papers and is prepared to swear allegiance to the Queen.'

The young man shook his head. 'I'm sorry, sir, but I don't have the authority to sign no papers. All the others are gone south, all except the builders — there's been a Māori raid on a farmhouse, see. I can't give you anything today.'

'But Minnie needs her papers.' Henry raised his voice. 'She can't travel into town without them.'

'I can't help you, sir. Come back in an hour — the sergeant will be back then, and he'll make sure you're seen to.' He looked at Matāria. 'Come back later,' he said slowly, as if talking to a child. 'Me no help you.'

'Thank you very much,' Matāria said.

The young man burst out laughing. 'Oh, you speak English! We never know with you natives. Some of you speak English as well as me, and some only yabber away in the native language. Ain't that right?' He winked at Henry.

Henry glowered. 'I think you'll find Minnie speaks English as well as you.'

The young soldier stopped laughing and went back to jiggling on the spot. 'Ah, yes. Ahem. Yes.'

Henry pointed at the back of the cart at the kūmara and kānga and other goods. 'Can we go through today without the pass? I have to go to the store — I have goods to trade.'

'Look, I'll tell you what. I'll let you through. But you need to come back here later and get the paperwork all cleared with the sergeant. You'll come back, won't you?'

Henry gave a mock salute. 'We will. Good day to you.'

The young man waved them past. 'Good day.'

Neither spoke until the blockhouse was out of sight. Then Matāria turned to Henry. 'What if I get stopped and asked about my pass? People are being arrested for not carrying them.'

'I know. I don't like this either, but we can't turn back now. We're already halfway to the store. And do we dare return to the papakāinga without your sister's flour?'

Matāria nodded. She had been dreading swearing allegiance to the Queen, yet now she wished she'd done so. How confusing to both want and not want a thing at the exact same time.

'Let us just get Atarangi's flour and go home,' she said. 'Fast.'

'So you won't be encouraging me to sing a sea-shanty as I drive through the town? Perhaps I should sing a nice military tune instead. Perhaps "The Grand Old Duke of York".'

'No singing. No joking. Just speed.'

'Of course, Minnie. I'll move so fast they won't even see us. We'll be naught but a blur.' Henry patted her on the thigh. 'Don't worry, my love. No one will ask. I've never seen a Māori woman asked for her papers, not in all my journeys into town. Even the Hickety Pips have a sense of common decency. All will be well.'

They drove down the hill and into New Plymouth. Houses spread in all directions, most made of wood, many encircled by fences made of thin wooden stakes. Some were barely larger than a hut at the papakāinga. Others were larger: long, low structures, with windows far above the ground, nestled under strange, pointed roofs. Matāria had always thought that European houses made no sense; surely those high ceilings meant being inside was that much colder?

In contrast to the blockhouse, this part of the town was bustling with people. The sound of giggling children echoed around the street as boys in short trousers pushed around a wagon wheel. A dog chased behind them barking. Beyond the children was a two-storey public house with a gaggle of soldiers joking and talking outside. Their cart passed the beginnings of another blockhouse: the building still had no roof and there were gaps between the logs in the wall. It would be completed soon, though, and would look almost identical to the blockhouse Matāria and Henry had passed earlier. *What do they want another one for?* Matāria thought, even though she already knew the answer to that question. She'd seen the boatload of soldiers arrive, after all.

A boy's cry interrupted her thoughts: something about a newspaper for sale. Horses trotted up and down the road, most mounted by men, others pulling carts. Nearby, a large group of older women chatted loudly about flowers. It was all so noisy and busy, how could Henry think otherwise? If it weren't for Taranaki peeking out from behind his cloud, this place would feel completely unfamiliar.

Henry stopped the cart outside the store and leapt out, grinning back up at Matāria. 'I'll be quick.' He gathered up the goods from the back of the cart. 'I'll sell this lot and talk to Mr Thorpe about what's going on in the township. He'll know what's what. Then we can go home and tell Kuru.'

'I'll wait in the cart,' Matāria said. Up high, where she could see danger coming.

'I'll be so swift you won't even have time to miss me. I promise.'

CHAPTER THIRTEEN

FRANCES

Frances pivoted so she was standing with her back against the box of kūmara, and faced the door. Henry stepped inside.

'Oh!' Henry looked startled. 'Frances! How do you do?' His eyes darted from Frances to each of the Thorpes and back to Frances. 'Your brother — is he here also?'

Frances fussed with her cuff. She'd spent two sleepless nights trying to decide what to say to Henry, and all he wanted to know about was her brother.

'No,' she said. 'He has taken the cart to run errands. It is just me here today. And Mother, although she is outside somewhere.'

Henry raised an eyebrow. 'Ah.' He looked even more dishevelled than he had the other day: his hair was a mess, his shirt was wrinkled and he had dark shadows under his eyes. And that nose — she was sure it was much bigger than she remembered. He was carrying two flax baskets of what might have been maize, but Frances couldn't quite tell. So he *was* a farmer — her hunch had been correct.

Stop staring, Frances, she admonished herself. *Collect your thoughts. Say something intelligent.*

'Indeed,' she said. 'Indeed.'

Henry shook his head. 'I can scarcely believe you live in New Plymouth. I never would have expected you and your family to leave London.'

'My sister Clementine is still in England. She married and has five children now. So it's just George, Mother and myself.'

'Clementine married, but you did not?'

'Indeed.' Why he had asked this excruciating question in such a direct manner? His face gave nothing away.

'I remember Clementine well,' Henry said. 'I hope she found contentment.'

'As do I. I have not seen her for many years.'

Henry looked closely at Frances. 'Where do you live? In the township proper, or somewhere nearby?'

'George bought a farm just south of here, down towards the giant rock.'

'Paritutu.'

'I beg your pardon?'

'The giant rock. It's called Paritutu — that's the Māori name. Pari means cliff; I don't remember what tutu means, but I really ought to find out.'

'Oh. I think I've been told the name before, but forgot. These local names are so hard to remember, don't you think?'

'They're not really, once you try.'

Frances hadn't even said fifty words to Henry; how had she got it so wrong already? She was desperate to redeem this conversation and find out what happened twelve years earlier. A lecture about local place-names was hardly the conversation Frances had hoped to have; she wished she had not encountered Henry in the company of others.

Behind the counter, Dora laughed loudly. 'Oh, how very delightful,' she said. 'You are both from London and not strangers at all! Isn't that just lovely? I love a good coincidence.'

'Yes,' Frances said, 'such a coincidence. Although, given the size of New Plymouth, I only wonder that it did not happen earlier.'

Dora polished the shop counter, the smell of beeswax filling the air. 'As I've said to you both before, London really is so noisy. Isn't it nicer here? So much more restful.'

Henry twisted his mouth in an exaggerated expression of contemplation. 'Compared to London, yes. Though perhaps not for much longer.'

Mr Thorpe gestured at Henry. 'If I can get a word past my sister, I'll wish you good afternoon, Henry White. How can I help you today? You have more maize and kūmara to sell?'

But Henry didn't reply. He was now gazing expectantly at Frances, who felt herself blush. He hadn't looked at her like that in over a decade. Perhaps all the time spent making herself look presentable was paying off. *Of course he should be looking at Minnie like that, not me*, she thought. Perhaps Mother had been right all along: perhaps Henry White was a cad.

Henry motioned to speak.

'Yes?' Frances said, to encourage him.

'Er . . .' Henry pointed past Frances at the counter.

Oh. Frances felt ill. That was what he wanted — to get past her so he could talk business with Mr Thorpe. Frances was standing in the way. She ducked her head and shuffled aside.

'Nice to see you again, Thorpe,' Henry said to the shopkeeper. 'I need another sack of flour today, thank you, and some more tobacco.' Then he added casually, 'Heard any news?'

Frances had been dismissed. She mumbled her farewells, closed the door behind her, and sank onto the nearby bench. The nerve of Henry, lecturing her about a giant rock while not taking time for proper conversation. But she wasn't giving up now that she had come all this way . . . She would stay here and intercept Henry as he left the store. She needed some answers.

In the distance still, she could see Mother talking to the women from the Floral Society, arms waving in the air. Behind the women, young soldiers came and went from the public house, most wearing a uniform the same shade of blue as Frances's dress. Closer to the store was a Māori woman in a dress the colour of burlap. She was climbing down from her cart awkwardly. Unlike most other Māori women Frances saw, this woman wore no jewellery, not even one of those green pendants around her neck. The woman limped towards where Frances sat. She had striking features: large eyes, full lips. The woman had ignored almost all rules of propriety and fashion in her dress — she did not wear a bonnet or a cloth cap, and her hands were bare. Nor did she have stays under her dress, let alone a crinoline to keep her skirts wide. Yet the woman still looked elegant. How could that be?

The Māori woman stopped in front of Frances, looked towards the general store and tapped her foot. Studying the woman out of the corner of her eye, Frances was conscious that she had not seen many natives up close like this. George said they were smelly, but this woman wasn't — she smelt better than George, who bathed even less frequently than Frances. The woman flinched and reached down to rub her calf.

'Would you like to sit down?' Frances asked, shuffling along on the bench.

The woman looked at her as if seeing her for the first time. *Oh dear*. Frances had frightened the poor creature, who probably didn't speak a lick of English. Frances pointed at the seat beside her. 'Sit down?' She gestured at the woman and the seat in turn. 'You. Sit. Sore leg.'

The woman lowered herself onto the bench — as far from Frances as she could.

'Me Frances,' Frances said, pointing at her own chest. 'You?'

The woman turned to face her. 'Good afternoon. My name is Matāria. How do you do?'

Frances cringed. The woman spoke perfect English and probably thought Frances was some sort of ape, talking in grunts like that. 'You speak English!'

'So do you,' Matāria said.

Frances felt the redness creep up her neck and over her face. *How embarrassing*, being scolded by a native woman for being ignorant. She hunched her shoulders and looked down at her hands. 'I apologise. I'm very sorry.'

'Don't apologise,' Matāria said sharply. 'You weren't to know what I could or could not understand. A woman should never apologise when she has not done wrong, as it makes her appear meek. Sometimes the waves wash the driftwood away on its own; the sand plays no part.'

'You're right — I shouldn't have apologised,' Frances said. 'I'm sorry.'

'You just apologised for apologising.'

Frances laughed; she couldn't help herself. 'You're right again. So this would not be the best time to apologise for apologising for apologising?'

'No. Not only would that make you appear meek, but it would confuse me.'

'I'd also confuse myself,' Frances said. 'Especially today. I'm not having a very good day, you see. Or a good week, in fact.' Or a good decade, she almost added, before deciding against it. No need to be melodramatic.

Matāria stared at the new blockhouse building. 'I understand.'

They lapsed into silence, although Frances had so many questions for Matāria. How had she learned English? Why was she here, and what was wrong with her leg? She didn't know where to begin, so she said nothing, examining Matāria as subtly as possible.

A flash of movement caught her eye. Frances looked up to see George crossing the road towards them with two soldiers. The three strode in unison, arms swinging. All wore serious expressions — if George had not been among them, Frances might have been more than a little intimidated. She hated to think how Matāria must feel.

Frances stood as her brother approached. Matāria did the same.

'George,' Frances said. 'I thought you had some errands to run. You were going to be another hour at least.'

'I shall be, if not longer. You will have to wait. These men and I have business to attend to.' George looked at the other men and nodded. 'I'm joining the Taranaki Rifle Volunteers. I'm not the same as one of these regimental men, of course, but we in the volunteer militia will do our bit to help solve the native problem.'

'We will be glad of your help,' said one of the soldiers.

'I hope you shoot as well as you drink,' said the other. 'And handle a rifle better than you play cards!'

'Of course!' George replied. 'I am an excellent shot.' He pulled at the edges of his moustache, threw back his head and laughed loudly. Frances stole a glance at Matāria, who was standing perfectly still: so still that Frances wondered for a moment if she was even breathing. How horrible it must be to listen to George joking about shooting her own people.

'George.' Frances motioned in Matāria's direction. He clearly hadn't noticed a Māori in their presence; perhaps now he would be more careful with his words.

George looked at Matāria and winked. 'Don't be scared. I won't shoot *you*. Just the troublemakers.'

'Yes,' a soldier said. 'Only Kīngi and his ilk. Not the ladies.'

The men guffawed. Matāria's mouth twitched but she remained silent.

'You won't even give us a smile?' the other soldier asked. 'Can you not take a joke? Are we not amusing?'

'She's probably stupid,' the first soldier said. 'Or doesn't know English.'

'Or both.'

'I'd wager both,' George said.

Suddenly Matāria looked George in the eye. 'George,' she said. Her voice was low. 'George Farrington?'

George stepped backwards. 'Yes,' he said. 'That's me. What of it?'

One of the soldiers whistled. 'She fancies you, Farrington. Got a way with the native ladies, do you? I'm sure she'd teach you a thing or two.'

'I'd not pay to lie with a woman like that,' the second soldier said. 'But I'd do it for free.'

Frances gasped. These men should not be speaking like this in front of a lady. *Two* ladies. Matāria might be a Māori, but she still deserved common decency. Frances crossed her arms across her body. 'George, let's fetch Mother and leave.'

George ignored her. He stared at Matāria, fists clenched.

Matāria stared back. 'I do not fancy you, George Farrington,' she said. 'I would rather lie with a pig. But I know who you are and what you did. I see you.'

George's mouth dropped open, displaying a row of crooked teeth. 'What? What are you talking about?' He turned to the other men. 'The woman is definitely mad. She's hysterical.'

That's what he said about Clementine, Frances thought. Her arms and legs tingled. Matāria had spoken out of turn but she was not hysterical. In fact exactly the opposite. She possessed a calmness Frances admired.

One of the soldiers pushed Matāria. 'You apologise. You do not speak to a white man like that. You say sorry. Right now.'

'No.' Matāria's voice was hoarse but clear. 'I will not apologise. I did nothing wrong.'

George raised his hand as if to strike her. 'Apologise!'

'No,' Matāria said.

Frances lunged forward to stand between Matāria and the men. 'Stop. Stop this now.'

George's voice was low. 'Move out of the way, Frances. What has come over you? Listen to me. *Move.*'

'Yes,' one of the other soldiers said. 'We need to check this woman's pass to move freely in the town. That's why we're here.'

'It seems to me that you are here to make trouble,' Frances said. 'This woman has done nothing wrong. Leave her alone.'

'Move, sister. We will check this woman's pass, by force if we have to.'

'I don't understand why you are acting like this, George!'

George's voice was loud now. Spittle flew from his mouth as he spoke. 'Move. Out. Of. My. Way.'

Frances looked from George to the soldiers. Her bravery seeped away, leaving a strange, hollow feeling laced with self-loathing. She stepped back, and suddenly saw Henry rushing towards them. Henry's face was bright red, his mouth in a tight line. Mr Thorpe trailed close behind.

Frances tried to meet Henry's eye. He didn't notice: his attention was on Matāria.

'Minnie!' he yelled. 'Minnie!' He pushed George out of the way. 'You leave my wife alone, George Farrington.'

Wait — what? Frances's mind scrambled to understand what Henry had said.

He spoke again, even louder this time. 'Leave her alone, you brutes. Leave my wife alone!'

CHAPTER FOURTEEN

MATĀRIA

Why had she drawn attention to herself? Matāria went back through the events in her mind to see if there was anything she could have done differently. She had been left waiting far too long on the cart, eventually deciding to climb down after a group of women kept shooting her nervous glances. It hadn't been sensible to remain up there: she could see everyone, but everyone could also see her. Being so conspicuous wasn't safe, not without her pass. If only she hadn't left the papakāinga today. *If only*: an even more useless phrase than *hope*.

Walking the short distance to the store, Matāria had surveyed her surroundings. This was as good a place to wait as any, she had thought. Henry was only inside the shop should she need him. A settler woman sat on a wooden bench — she would have been handsome if she weren't so pale and her eyes so sunken by weariness. The woman had pointed from Matāria to the seat; Matāria had sat. There was something about direct instructions that made them hard to ignore, even when the person giving them looked as though Tāwhirimātea would blow her over with a single breath.

As the two women spoke, Matāria had assessed this Frances woman. She wore a dress as blue as Tangaroa's domain, with delicate folds that had reminded Matāria of waves hitting the shore. *Beautiful.* The woman's gloves were light grey — apart from one small brown smear, they were the gloves of a woman who never had to work with her hands. Frances obviously didn't ferment kānga or gut tuna before smoking them for trade, nor had she ever been owned by another person. And yet Matāria could see that Frances had once had a light in her that had been dulled, like the moon on a cloudy evening. This woman was a slave to something.

Then the soldiers were crossing the square directly towards her. Should she have run and hid in the bush until Henry was done? If she slipped between the ferns and squatted behind that rimu, these men would not find her. Papatūānuku would draw Matāria into her leafy fold, where she could lie like a tuatara until the men were gone. But sneaking off into the bush would have seemed suspicious. And Henry would have come out with his sack of flour and wondered where she was. He would have worried.

Hurry up, Henry, she had thought. *Hurry.*

But the men were right in front of them. Matāria had made the wrong decision — running away would have been better.

Then the settler woman had stood and called this man, her brother, by the name George. Time had stood still. *George.* This man, whose uniform was at odds with the others, was called George. Was he George Farrington?

From there, the conversation had passed in a flurry of angry words, throughout which, two thoughts danced in Matāria's mind. The first: she would not apologise to those vile men when she had done nothing wrong. She would not be the weak dog, and these men were not the strong dogs. They were insecure men in fancy uniforms — nothing more, nothing less. And the second: where was Henry?

Henry had finally dashed from the store and pushed George out of the way, but the men hadn't listened. One of the soldiers had pulled Matāria to her feet and another had shoved her; the pain had shot up her bad leg.

'Come with us,' the first soldier had said. 'Walk.'

'Are you certain this is necessary?' the shopkeeper had asked. 'Gentlemen, must we really take these measures?'

'Get back inside your dusty old store,' George had replied. 'Don't interfere in matters that are not your business.'

Another push. Matāria had turned around and looked for her husband. 'Henry!'

'I'm here, Minnie.' Henry had jostled past one of the men and strode alongside her. 'I'm not going anywhere.'

One of the soldiers had laughed. 'You're right about that. You're under arrest too.'

Matāria had walked as quickly as she could but her leg made it difficult. Her heart was pounding. And here she was: Matāria was the injured kōtuku and this was the wild.

Betsy, she thought. *Edwin*. What would they do when neither of their parents returned home?

CHAPTER FIFTEEN

FRANCES

Frances watched Matāria being led away by the soldiers. George trotted self-importantly behind.

'Hurry up,' said the solider who had Matāria by the arm. 'Walk faster.'

Henry was being escorted by the other soldier, his face dark. 'Slow down. She's got a bad leg.'

The men didn't listen; however, Matāria didn't seem in pain. She walked with a limp, but with her head held high. If Frances didn't know otherwise, she might have thought Matāria was leading the men rather than the other way around.

Before they turned the corner, Henry turned and yelled towards where Frances stood. 'Thorpe! My cart. It's standing over there. Return it to the papakāinga for me — please.'

'I'll look after it!' Mr Thorpe called back. 'I'll keep it safe for you.'

Then Henry, Matāria and the men were gone. Frances was stunned. Henry's wife wasn't a Grecian goddess with porcelain skin and fair hair — she was someone else entirely. Frances had never considered herself much of a catch, but it was still a shock that a Māori woman, a lame one at that, was superior in Henry's eyes.

But why should it be otherwise? Her presumption of being better was just as foolish as her mother looking down on Mrs Archer: uncharitable at best, and downright nasty at worst.

Speaking of which, George had shown a real nastiness today. Had he always been like this? Her brother's sense of humour was never particularly kind, and he lacked Albert's amiable nature, but that was simply George being George.

'Well,' said Dora Thorpe. 'That was wholly unnecessary.'

'I agree,' Mr Thorpe said. 'Poor Matāria wasn't bothering anyone.'

'Not at all,' Frances said. 'She was only sitting on that bench, talking to me.'

Dora sighed. 'I've not heard of any Māori women being arrested for not having a pass before. How terrible that Matāria should be the first.'

'I don't like this new pass rule,' Mr Thorpe said. 'Many Māori people don't have them yet and it's making trading much more cumbersome. We've lived alongside these people for years and not come to blows — they were very kind to us when we first arrived, weren't they, Dora? I don't see why it has to change.'

'I've a good mind not to darn those men's socks. As for George Farrington—' Dora gasped. 'Oh, sorry, Frances! I don't mean to talk ill of your brother like that. How rude of me.'

'It's quite all right,' Frances said. It *was* ill-mannered of Dora to speak so, but the fact that Frances agreed with her prevented any feeling of resentment. Dora grinned at Frances, relieved. Frances gave a small smile back — she was always reluctant to smile, as she was self-conscious about her crooked teeth.

Mr Thorpe chuckled. 'As long as Miss Farrington doesn't say rude things about *your* brother, Dora.'

'Never!' Frances said. 'I would never say an impolite word

about you.' Frances realised a moment too late that she might have been overly enthusiastic on that point. She blushed. 'I mean . . . you know . . .'

Mr Thorpe smiled, while Frances looked at the store's verandah boards, wishing she could take back what she'd said.

Dora swiftly changed the subject. 'I ought to get back to my darning. We hope to see you again soon, Frances. We could always take a turn near the coast one day, perhaps look at some of the native plants down there. I know the women of the Floral Society call them ugly, but I find them very pretty in their own strange way.'

'Oh,' Frances said. 'Yes, I would like that.'

Dora's grin was even wider than before. Frances couldn't help but notice Dora's teeth were just as crooked as her own, yet they didn't diminish the brilliance of her smile.

Dora gave a curtsey and went inside. Mr Thorpe stayed put. Frances had never seen him outside his store before. He was taller than she'd realised, and slightly younger.

'I don't like the way events are unfolding,' he said. 'Last year Henry White used his connections with the local Māori people to find men to build this store to replace the old one. And look how he and his wife are treated now. Poor Mrs White, taken away like that, with her bad leg too.'

'Do you know Henry well?' Frances asked.

'Not particularly, and I have met his wife only a handful of times. But we have transacted business on many occasions and I have every reason to wish him the best. I probably don't know him as well as you do. You were acquaintances in London?'

'Yes, we were.' *Acquaintances*. What a terrible demotion — and for reasons she still did not understand.

Mr Thorpe nodded. He had such a kind face.

'What a terrible business that was just now,' he said. 'These soldiers don't love New Plymouth as I do. They come in from England or wherever they've been posted previously. They'll fight, then leave as soon as this is all over and done with. Those still alive, that is. I worry about what will be left in their wake.'

'As do I.'

'I'd best go back inside. Do accept Dora's invitation, Miss Farrington. It would be nice to see you again.'

Mr Thorpe bowed to her and left. Did he actually want to better make her acquaintance, or was he simply being polite? Surely, if it were a true invitation, Dora or Mr Thorpe would have named a time and place, not issued a vague invitation that now required Frances to follow up. Yet both Thorpe siblings had been so warm — the invitation had felt genuine.

Her thoughts were interrupted by a familiar but unwelcome voice. 'Frances!'

Mother was crossing the road, her skirts bouncing with every step. Her face was flushed, her lips were in a tight line. She stood facing Frances with her hands on her hips.

'I thought you were going to join me and the women from the Floral Society when you were finished in the store,' Mother said. 'You were supposed to walk over and find me — we were just around the corner over there. Then you would not have been caught up in all that hullabaloo. I was so worried about you, Frances. So very concerned.'

'Hullabaloo?'

'You know what I mean. I just saw Mrs Richmond who had it from Mrs Perry who spoke to one of the soldiers a block from here.'

Mother's face was pale and her hat askew. 'I knew that Henry White was trouble. I knew he would have put my darling Frances in the path of danger.'

'I'm sorry, Mother.' Frances studied her feet, ashamed of herself for upsetting her mother. 'I didn't mean to frighten you.'

As soon as the words were out of her mouth, she jerked her head back up. Wait a minute! Mother had in fact *not* asked Frances to join her and the other ladies. Frances had done exactly what Matāria had pointed out — apologised for something that was not her fault. She would tell Mother as much. Right now. But as Mother's eyes darted about, Frances could not tell if she were sad or cross. Maybe speaking up right now would be unwise. Yes, she would wait until her mother's temperament appeared more even. Right now she needed to distract Mother from what had happened.

'How were the women of the Floral Society?'

Mother's face transformed and she clapped her hands. 'Oh! I am going to buy seeds to plant in the garden. It has been decided. I'll have the finest garden in all of New Plymouth, and when it is grown, I shall invite the women from the Floral Society to admire my handiwork. We shall have tea and cakes — served by Kitty, if she's not in an impertinent frame of mind, that is.' Mother shook her head. 'Actually, no, not Kitty: that girl is altogether too uppity, not to mention likely to go gallivanting off at some stage to get married in her home-made crinoline of reeds. When the women of the Floral Society come calling, I shall have a much better maid. I might also invite Mrs Archer, but only if she agrees to change her ways. She would want to come, though. Mark my words.'

Frances's head throbbed. Sometimes listening to Mother felt like being pelted by rocks. Frances wanted some silence to think over all she'd seen. She needed to be on her own.

'Perhaps you ought to buy those seeds now,' she said. 'Before George gets back and it's time to return home.'

'Yes. We are of one mind. How delightful.'

Mother spun around and strode towards the store. As soon as she was gone, Frances looked back at the now-empty bench where she'd sat with Matāria. Minnie. Matāria or Minnie? It didn't matter: both versions were Henry's wife, and a woman being led to prison by George, with Henry in tow.

Frances still had time to wander up and down Devon Road to see if there was anything interesting to look at, but she no longer felt the inclination. She sank down into the bench. No, she wouldn't go for a stroll. Not now. She would sit right here and wait until it was time to go home.

CHAPTER SIXTEEN

MATĀRIA

Matāria's leg throbbed, worse than it had in months. She was too proud to tell the men she was hurt, but she needed them to slow down.

'Not so fast. Her leg is sore,' Henry called out from behind her. *Dear Henry.* He might have a tendency to drink too much liquor and bring home an unwelcome chair, but he always knew what she was thinking. Him drawing attention to her injury was far better than her doing so herself. He knew how to help.

'You should have thought of that before your wife strutted around the township without her pass,' one of the soldiers said, the younger one who had pushed Matāria earlier. He barely came up to Henry's shoulder, and his moustache was nothing more than a sparse cluster of hairs. Matāria had always thought there were two types of people in the world: those who gain respect, and those who take it from others because they cannot earn it for themselves. This young soldier was clearly one of the latter. 'You shouldn't have disobeyed the Governor's orders.'

'We went to the border fort on the way here in order to get one,' Henry said, 'but there was no senior officer present. The soldier we spoke to said we could go to town on condition we returned later in the day, which we had every intention of doing.'

The young soldier scoffed.

George winked at him. 'I suppose they all have excuses like that.'

'You haven't heard the half of it. Most of them claim the land is theirs anyway, so why do they need a pass?'

George laughed. 'If it was theirs, they'd do something with it.'

The soldier continued. 'They're not like us, these people.'

Matāria inhaled sharply. 'That's true. We are strong and noble,' she said, before she could think better of it, 'whereas you are swine.'

She knew she shouldn't have said it. But if she came across as weak, these men would take pleasure in asserting their power over her. They would push and push and push, until they got bored and tossed her aside like a plaything. If she were strong, they would try to break her, but they might also respect her a little. It had worked with the men who'd kept her as a slave. In any case, she had no choice. The only thing in her control was how she reacted to these men. If she didn't hold herself in a way she could feel proud of, she had nothing.

George spun around to face her. 'Don't call me a swine! Do you hear?'

'But it's true.' Henry's voice was forceful. 'I remember what you did back in London.'

'You keep quiet, Henry White.'

'You shan't silence me this time, Farrington.' Henry's face was red. 'I'm no longer a young boy who can be bullied and sent away.'

George measured Henry through narrowed eyes. 'Is that so? You were an impoverished scoundrel back then, and today you're nothing more than a man being led towards a gaol cell. I can't see much difference.'

A third soldier had joined them, an older, more imposing man. He laughed nervously, running his hand through grey-flecked hair.

His uniform had more adornments than the others', and his boots were so shiny they reflected the light. 'Perhaps we should walk in silence. We do not wish to escalate matters further.'

'It's not *me* who is escalating matters,' George said. 'Henry White is responsible. He's a scoundrel, I give you my word.'

'Nonetheless,' the older man said, 'let us walk without talking.'

George and the young soldier shared a look, but neither said anything.

They marched in silence past another public house, past some houses. Eventually they reached the large stone church with its high roof, sitting at the base of a steep slope: St Mary's, she thought it was called. A place where the settlers gathered to pay homage to their god. Around the church was a Pākehā urupā of wooden headstones, recording the details of those who lay beneath the dirt. Henry told stories of large cemeteries back in London, filled with stone tablets and statues, but these settlers hadn't been here long enough to collect dead in the same way. They would in time, especially if war came. And the more settlers laid to rest here in the ground, the less likely the remaining ones would ever leave, because to do so would be to abandon their loved ones, lying in Papatūānuku's long embrace.

'Around the corner,' one of the younger soldiers yelled. 'Come on, walk faster.'

Matāria bridled, but did as instructed. In front of them loomed Marsland Hill, a large, flat mound covered in long, rectangular military barracks. In addition to the wooden buildings were rows and rows of triangular huts made of white fabric — tents, Henry called them. The tent tops pointed to the sky like the sails of a European vessel. They seemed very flimsy, insufficient to keep out all the rain that had fallen recently. No wonder the soldiers always seemed so angry: they didn't even sleep in proper dwellings. Matāria's hut at the papakāinga was more sturdy. All the better that these tents were thin; Tāwhirimātea might blow them over, forcing the soldiers away. Then Te Ātiawa would be left in peace.

The older soldier now walked beside her. George started to say something, but the man glared at him and George closed his mouth. Matāria smiled inwardly.

'This way.' The soldier led Matāria along a narrow, muddy path between two huts. A pungent smell wafted into her nostrils: a mix of waste, mud and the rancid, tangy scent she recognised as liquor. Matāria could see sentries marching up and down in front of the rows of tents, rifles slung over their shoulders. She looked down and watched her footing as they passed a small enclosed area where the odour was particularly strong. This must be where they do their business, she thought, or at least where they deposited it. It wasn't far from where some soldiers were eating, sitting in a circle. The men chewed on hard crusts of bread, oblivious to the fact that they were so close to waste and the urupā outside St Mary's. How disgusting. No wonder the essence of this place was so dark and unclean.

The grass had been trampled by dozens of boots. Before Matāria had left Ngāmotu, this site, Marsland Hill, had been Pukākā Pā — named for the kākā the old people said were once plentiful in the bush nearby. The hill had been taller; the British had flattened its head to build their barracks at the top. Kuru once said the soldiers had taken away so much soil, the hill was now shorter by the height of two men. But it was still high enough to offer a view of the ocean from the summit. The British had that vantage point now: they could see everything. Except kākā — they were long gone. As was Pukākā Pā, cut off at the forehead and cloaked in a mauri of murky gloom.

They arrived in the middle of the barrack grounds. Horses neighed in the distance. Soldiers loitered outside the tents; some stopped to stare, others whistled. A small number looked away as if they didn't like what they saw.

'Minnie.' Henry reached towards her when they stopped briefly.

She grabbed his hand. 'Henry.'

'All will be well, Minnie,' he said. 'I promise.'

A soldier pushed them apart. Matāria steadied herself by landing heavily on her sore leg.

Kia toa, Matāria, she thought. She needed to be strong.

'Come on, keep walking!' the young solider yelled.

'Silence!' the older soldier barked. 'I said to walk in silence.'

Matāria walked as tall as she was able, looking across at Henry. What a good man he was.

Eventually they stopped in front of a low stone building with small windows. The makeshift gaol.

CHAPTER SEVENTEEN

FRANCES

Frances stepped into her bedroom and closed the door. The late-afternoon sun fell over her bed. She sat on the chair by the small table and stared out the window. The Māori women Frances had seen from the cart that morning were now returning from over the hill, arms full of maize. The two children with light-brown hair skipped alongside, chattering to each other.

Halfway down the rise, the women stopped, laid down their maize and closed their eyes. One of the women led the others in a Māori chant — a sombre ritual of some sort, a religious ceremony even. The boy and girl joined in. Frances had met the local missionary, a German, and heard about his efforts to convert these people. This ritual on the hill could be evidence of his good work, and Frances might be witnessing a prayer.

Leaning towards the glass, Frances surveyed the group. No, they were not holding their palms together — this was not a prayer. And this wasn't even a religious place — it was nothing but a barren hill, overlooking the sea and a field of maize on the other side. The group stopped chanting, gathered the maize and continued down the hill. The women walked quickly, the children skipping to keep up. They looked so happy. *How lovely it must be to have so little to worry about*, Frances thought.

She needed to re-read her letters from Clementine. Frances reached under the bed and pulled out a small metal box. Sitting on her bed, she opened it with a creak; the long sea journey had not been kind to the hinges.

Inside sat a pile of letters tied with string. At the top were the three letters she'd received from Henry twelve years ago. The edges were worn, the seals long fallen off. Frances knew every word of his messy scrawls off by heart; there was no reason to read them again, especially knowing what she now knew. The first promised to call on her the following Thursday should she welcome it. The second said he would like to take a turn with her around the park and have a particular conversation with her. She pulled them out of the box and cast them aside.

Underneath Henry's letters were a handful of visiting cards, pamphlets and other mementos from London. She read the cards: once-familiar names printed in beautiful, swirling text usually accompanied by a picture of a floral arrangement. People did not have the same habit of paying calls and leaving *carte de visites* here as they did in the old country. The farmhouses were too far apart and the roads too primitive for calling to be much undertaken, and horses were usually wanted for more important work.

Even in New Plymouth, the habit had fallen out of favour. The houses were far too small; it was impossible to pretend to be out when there were no more than half a dozen rooms, usually all on one floor. Besides, leaving a card felt ridiculous when calling on an acquaintance and being told they were feeding the swine or tending to the garden or any of the other chores women in the colony often had to perform themselves. Mother saw this as further evidence of how backward things were in the colonies, but Frances didn't miss coming home to find that no one had visited because of their family's reduced circumstances.

She pulled out the black-edged memorial card from Father's funeral, which was not long before she met Henry — their courtship had occurred between Father dying and her learning the truth about what her favourite parent had done. *Oh, Father.* Frances had such fond memories of him: walking through the woods with him and Albert; interesting conversations in his library; his low chuckle whenever something amused him. Most of all, she thought of her father's calm presence, which balanced out Mother's moods. Oftentimes, Frances only needed to hear Mother's voice to feel anxiety descend. Her father had the complete opposite effect on her . . . but he'd left them in financial ruin.

Frances felt as if Father had died twice: once on the date noted on the memorial card; a second time when she'd learned about the debts. All that remained in her memory was a tangle of thoughts and a vague sense that she hadn't known him at all. Much like Henry, now that she thought about it. She turned the card over: she did not want to be reminded of Father today.

At the bottom of the pile were Clementine's letters: all the correspondence Frances had received from her sister since Clementine left home. She spread them out on the bed. There were not many. The top two were sent to New Plymouth, the first dated not long after Frances left England, arriving three months later. Clementine spoke about her five children.

'They grow up so fast,' her sister had written. 'Other women express a certain mournfulness when their younger children are grown. Not me. I do not mind at all. Not being either with child or having a babe to care for has been quite remarkable. I feel I can think properly again. It is liberating.'

Last time Frances had read this letter, she'd assumed Clementine was revelling in being able to amuse herself once again with painting and reading, and hoped her sister's mental reawakening would mean more regular correspondence. But it seemed to mean something completely different now.

She continued reading Clementine's tidy handwriting: 'I do regret having sleep-walked for much of the past decade. But I cannot dwell too much on that. My children are at an age when they are with tutors much of the time and I, once again, have more time at my disposal. All I can do is use it as best I can. These other women who regret the passing of time must have had more help with their children than I had — or been blessed with fewer of them. I cannot think of any other way to reconcile their different views on the matter with my own.'

Frances read to the end of the letter. Clementine signed off as she always did: *Take care of yourself, dear sister, and please give my regards to Mother.* No mention of George.

Frances reached for the next letter and skipped to the last line. It said the same. She thumbed through every last letter from Clementine, studying the final solicitation of each one. They were all variations of the same theme: Frances was implored to take care of herself or be well, and to give Clementine's regards to Mother. Clementine did not once mention George.

A feeling of foreboding came over Frances. This was so odd, Clementine not passing on regards to her own brother. Why had Frances not noticed this before? Feeling unsettled, she read the final lines once more. The earlier letters were signed off *Be well, dear sister.* The more recent letters tended to say *Take care of yourself.*

When had the change happened?

When Clementine first married: *Be well.* In the years immediately following — a series of letters that focused on whichever child Clementine had most recently borne and whatever pregnancy she was experiencing at the time: *Be well.* The change occurred in late

1856, just prior to George buying the land in New Plymouth and making arrangements for them to move. *Take care of yourself* then became a feature of every letter sent since — letters that were few and far between.

She pulled her blanket around her shoulders. Perhaps Clementine had been anxious about the prospect of their going so far away, or there was some other perfectly reasonable explanation for this shift in tone.

Yet another thought danced around Frances's mind, one that could not be ignored: had something happened?

CHAPTER EIGHTEEN

MATĀRIA

The sun was not yet high in the sky; it was 'mid-morning', as Henry would say. At least, that was Matāria's best guess at the time — she didn't actually know because there was no window between her and the wider world. The only light to the cell came from a rectangular hole in the door. Every now and again she'd see a pair of eyes peering through that hole, and she'd meet them with her own: the essence of kanohi ki te kanohi. The eyes give clues about what a person is like, whether their laugh is genuine or their love real. But not these eyes looking through the hole in the door — they stared from the shadows and could not be read. Sometimes the gaze was followed by a voice, though the words were not directed at Matāria, but to someone else nearby.

'The native lady isn't doing much, sir,' the voice said.

'You're doing a good job of taming that filly, but you've still got a way to go,' another voice said later.

Matāria tried to stop listening after that, as words unheard accord the speaker less power. Whoever was connected to those floating eyes could cast their thoughts into the cold breeze of Tāwhirimātea and have them blown far away. They would not worm their way into her head.

But oh, to see the sun, or even the sky! Birds would usually give a clue to the time of day but she couldn't hear any of those either. Just the soldiers, talking, singing, shouting as if they were in the same cold, dark room as her. Sleep had been impossible: even if the cell had been quiet, how could she sleep when she was here and didn't know where Henry had been taken? Henry: he kanohi taiaha, eyes like on a taiaha, looking from both sides of an argument, keeping on good terms with both factions. Did that make him conciliatory or two-faced? Or merely stuck in the middle? And if her husband was he kanohi taiaha, where did that leave her?

It was light when she'd been thrown in here. Sometime later, when she assumed it was night and Te Pō had descended, Matāria spent hours prowling around her own personal Rarohenga. There she saw the pain in her legs like flashes of light, and was haunted by the kākā, which had long ago left this pā. Her tūpuna came and warned her of bad times to come. They were followed by her future mokopuna, haunting words falling from their lips.

'You are the puna in between the tūpuna and us, your mokopuna,' her grandchildren said. 'You are the spring of water. Yet you are in this place. Where can the puna flow now?'

'I'm trying,' she said. 'I don't want to be here.'

But no one was left to hear her — only the ghost of one lone kākā remained. Matāria felt as if she were yelling into the wind. Her mind twisted and turned in dark corners, weaving an intricate kete made from both reality and dreams. Dreams that were interlaced with the strong stench of the chamber pot in the corner that she couldn't avoid using, but which no one had come to empty.

In the middle of the night all her common sense had disappeared, leaving a confusing mix of anger and fear that ricocheted around her head in a series of ugly imagined conversations: with the soldiers, with George Farrington, with Henry. With herself.

Perhaps it was heading towards the middle of the day now. Or maybe it was still early in the morning. She wished she knew. Knowing would help her feel less confused.

Her thoughts returned to her children. Betsy and Edwin must be so frightened, even more scared than Matāria herself. She imagined what might have happened the previous evening. Atarangi would have taken them back to the papakāinga after their day collecting kānga. Betsy would have had a big exciting story to tell Matāria: something pushing at the edges of truth. She'd have run to the hut, face red with the exertion, Edwin trailing close behind. Matāria pictured them both rushing through the gate and up the hill to their small home. They would have burst through the door, yelling in their excited voices.

The hut would have been empty.

Did they search the papakāinga for Matāria? Atarangi would have been cross, her irritation slowly turning into worry. Atarangi and her children may still not know where Matāria and Henry were. News didn't always travel quickly in and out of the township — not without a runner boy, or someone else sent on a particular errand. It was possible Atarangi and the twins were still ignorant.

Me moe au, she thought. She needed to sleep. She lay down on the wooden pallet and closed her eyes. If she could just get some sleep, she could collect her thoughts: only then would the wall between what was real and her worst imaginings return. Her head and heart and puku would better link together without the distraction of fatigue. When that happened, Matāria could decide what to do next.

Not escape from this cell, of course. This was where she would remain for the time being. No, her decision would be in aid of her inner self. As a slave she had taught herself how to keep despair at bay. Guiding stars could be found in your own head only when you were calm and receptive to tohu. One day in the Waikato she'd spied some dirt so dark it reminded her of the black sands of Ngāmotu. Over that dirt walked a kākā. From that day onward, Matāria knew that she would one day walk home. The knowledge had seeped into her bones and made her strong, even when she was being beaten or degraded or worse.

She opened her eyes again and gazed around the cell. No tohu here; no messages to show the way. There were no guiding stars waiting for her in this cell, just a locked door and an over-full chamber pot. Which only reminded Matāria that she had lost her freedom. Again. But at least this time she hadn't been taken to the far-off Waikato. She was still on the lands of her tūpuna: under the watchful eye of Taranaki, near the giant rock Paritutu.

Matāria clutched her chest; her heart beat loudly. Was that fear she felt, or anger? Maybe neither, or perhaps both — she couldn't tell. Perhaps the two emotions were not so far apart.

A sound wafted in from the adjacent cell — a man singing a waiata about long journeys to nowhere. The man's voice was rich and full of anguish: it captured Matāria's pain, yet didn't make her sad. Instead, it cheered her up slightly, because she now felt less alone. Her breathing slowed.

'Ko wai koe?' she called out.

The singing stopped. 'Who are *you*?' the man responded, his voice gravelly and low.

Matāria felt herself shrink with shame. She shouldn't have asked the question in such a direct manner. Her circumstances had caused her to forget how she ought to speak to those she did not know. She apologised to the man for being rude and recited her pepeha.

'Ko Taranaki tōku maunga, ko Waiwakahio tōku awa, ko Te Ātiawa tōku iwi.'

Wherever she might be, whoever might try to violate her, these were — and would always be — her mountain, river and iwi. She recited a brief whakapapa and then said: 'Ko Matāria tōku ingoa.' Henry could never understand the purpose of the pepeha. It amused him when Matāria met another Māori and it was the first thing they said to each other. He would never quite grasp the fundamental difference between contacts and connections, and how knowing where someone was from helped you understand who they were.

The man responded with his own pepeha. Unsurprisingly, they were related — same maunga, same awa, same iwi. The same links back to Tamarau and Rongo-Ue-Roa, the ancestor of all of Te Ātiawa, and, before them, to Ranginui himself.

'Ko Tai tōku ingoa,' he concluded.

Tai — the freed slave, Kuru's cousin. The man driven away by the German missionary.

Matāria pressed against the wall that separated them. 'Matua Tai. You're the healer. I've heard talk of you. Some say you were treated very badly.'

Some also claimed that Tai deserved it, as Henry had pointed out, but it didn't seem appropriate to mention that right now. An animal in chains does not need to be kicked to learn it is trapped.

'I think the gods were making mischief when I was born,' Tai said. 'I have walked this earth for almost fifty years, yet still I have no place.'

Matāria thought back to when the Waikato invaded. 'You were older than I, when I was taken as a slave. I thought they killed all the older boys.'

'Not me. I am a teina of a teina of a teina, probably back all the way to when Tamarau had no wife. Even the Waikato knew I had no mana.'

'Not everyone can be a rangatira. And you whakapapa to this place, the same as me.'

'No.' Tai's voice sounded as if he were further away than the other side of a wall. 'Nowhere is my place. I was a slave. Then I was free, but my whānau did not want me anymore — they said I was unclean. And here I am now, in gaol.'

'I was a slave too, Matua Tai, but this is still my home. This whenua is still mine, even if my whānau didn't want me back either.' Matāria's eyes watered; she had never been brave enough to say that out loud before. Tears rolled down her cheeks. The events of yesterday, being imprisoned, having no sleep: it was suddenly all too much. She began to sob.

'They did not know how to receive us — me, my husband, my twins,' she said. 'Even my sister Atarangi struggled. She struggles still. I am not a sister to her, I think. I am just a bad smell.' *Much like this bucket.*

Matāria remembered Atarangi's glare as she looked from Matāria to Henry the day they first arrived at the papakāinga. How Atarangi had judged Betsy and Edwin, her eyes resting on their lighter hair and skin. Matāria gave herself a shake. She could not cry here; what if the soldiers saw? Especially that young one — Matāria was sure he owned at least one set of the eyes she'd seen peering through that hole in the door. She would not give them the satisfaction.

'I do not mean to make you weep,' Tai said. 'Don't be sad, sister.'

'I am sad,' Matāria said, 'but that does not mean I am weak. I will not cry again today.'

'And I will sing,' said Tai. 'If the soldiers tell me to stop, I will sing under my breath.'

They fell into companiable silence.

'Atarangi,' Tai said eventually. 'The wife of my cousin Kuru?'

'Āe. And he was upset when you were cast out and told to leave the region. Did *he* not want you?'

'Kuru was not cruel, but nor was he kind. When I returned, he moved in that grey place where a person is not judged bad through their actions but through their lack of actions. Kuru didn't send me away — it was that German missionary who turned everyone against me. But Kuru stayed silent when it happened.'

'We confuse them, those of us who came back. Our experiences are so different from theirs. They don't understand our lives; they don't *want* to.'

'No. We were not there to help bury the bodies of those slain by the Waikato, nor clean the red blood from the earth. We were not part of the waka fleet that came back from Te Whanganui-a-Tara. But we had our own burdens to bear.'

Tai and Matāria shared their stories. He had been taken in the aftermath of the battle of Pukerangiora. He'd tried to leap off the cliff like so many others that day to deny the Waikato the chance to take their lives or capture them, but he had been caught.

'They kept me for food for their journey home,' he said, 'but I got too thin. None of them wanted to eat me, so I was made a slave.'

And he had been arrested this week for the same reason as Matāria: not carrying a pass. After his release he planned to voyage south, all the way to the head of Te-Ika-a-Maui.

Matāria asked why.

'The war will be in the north. It will be too dangerous to go there, not knowing what paths will be open. And when I travelled that way through the bush I encountered many wild dogs, even more than you see in the trees around Ngāmotu. I even saw one that was as fierce as Irawaru. Your children would not be safe.' Māmā had told her the story of Irawaru, who had been a man before Māui transformed him into a dog.

'I had hoped to take my husband and children up north. There is a kind missionary we once stayed with — we had thought to return.' Matāria's shoulders slumped. 'That was why I wanted the pass. That's why I came into the town yesterday.'

'I fear you're too late.' Tai's voice was soft. 'Going south would be better. There are many settlements there now, both Māori and settler. I plan to follow in the path of the whalers. Maybe when I'm all the way in the south I'll find some pounamu. Or rather, some pounamu might find me. Once in my travels I met a Ngāi Tahu man who told me about the mauri of the pounamu and the journey it must take. I'd like to be part of that journey. I need all the help I can get.'

'Will you walk or take a boat?'

'Who'd let me on a boat?' Tai made a guttural sound. 'I am told you walk to Paritutu and keep going out of the Te Ātiawa rohe and south along the coast. I will see our whanaunga from Taranaki Iwi, and later Ngāti Ruanui and Ngā Rauru. You walk and walk until Taranaki is beside you, and keep going until he is so far back you have to squint to see him. Then he will be gone from view.'

Matāria nodded. She knew about that road but had never herself taken it. 'Aren't there settler farms on that road? Is it safe to pass? I think Father Schmidt had a mission station down that way before he came to New Plymouth.'

'Who knows?' Tai said. 'But I have to go south. I have nowhere else to go, and it is time for me to try making a living elsewhere.'

'And heal people as well?'

'No. Not anymore.'

'That is probably a good idea, Matua. May you find somewhere to settle in peace, wherever that might be.'

'Will we *ever* find our place, sister?' Tai's voice was mournful. 'I know you say the land is your place, but we're on our land right now and we are not free. Our people are on the brink of losing even more; soon they may have nothing. And what of people like you and me? Will our people ever welcome us? Will we always be in the space between?'

The space between. Tai had put into words what Matāria had felt ever since her return but never able to articulate. 'Āe. Maybe the space between is where the likes of us will always remain. But I want better for my children.'

'You must find a way, then, of finding them a place. And once you have done that, you must find out how to follow them, and not come back.'

Matāria looked towards the door. She needed to leave this place — this cell and this rohe. How much she wished Henry were here with her.

'My husband is called Henry,' she said through the wall. 'Henare. At the papakāinga they call him Henare Mā.'

'Mā for his skin? You married a white man, sister?'

'He is both a white man and a man with the name White,' Matāria said. 'Have you seen him? I don't know what happened to him after I was put in here. Do you know where he is?'

'There was a settler man in here this morning. Yellow hair, large nose. I had seen him before, around where Kuru lives. I have seen him handing out tobacco to the men. But we had not met.'

'You saw him? Where?'

'He was being led past my cell, towards the door. He didn't look happy. He was looking this way and that — maybe trying to find you. Then a soldier pushed him away.'

'Where? Where were they taking him?'

'I don't know. I'm sorry, sister.' Tai's voice was mournful. 'I wish I could help but that was all I saw.'

Matāria put her head in her hands. Henry was gone.

CHAPTER NINETEEN

FRANCES

The days passed. Frances sat in her bedroom at her small table, pen in hand. *Dearest Clementine*, she wrote.

Movement outside the window caught her eye. She looked up to see Kitty dash past towards the stable boy. Frances couldn't hear what they were saying, but their conversation was punctuated with large hand gestures and scowls thrown at the house. She hoped it wasn't directed at her. The maid had been sharp with Frances earlier — Frances had been so distracted thinking about the public meeting taking place that afternoon, she'd forgotten to collect the eggs. And the full milk pail had hurt her arms so she'd put it down too roughly then slopped half the milk on the ground. Frances had felt so guilty she'd agreed to make the bread, and had even managed to do so without having to ask for advice — a first.

'This bread smells good,' Kitty had said, surprised. 'You're getting better at kneading the dough.'

'Thank you.' Frances felt so much pride she was able to momentarily forget her aching arms.

'I have finally taught you something useful,' Kitty said. 'I should be paid for being a tutor as well as a maid.'

Frances had laughed at the maid's joke. Unthawed, Kitty had

stalked away without looking back. And now, outside the window, Kitty spoke rapidly to the stable boy, her posture tense. Eventually the two of them walked briskly around the side of the house and out of view.

Turning back to the blank page, Frances positioned her pen. The words did not flow. Should she tell Clementine about the bread? She could describe how delightful it was to mix seemingly unrelated foodstuffs and, with some skill, transform them into something that tastes so delicious. Would Clementine understand the tiny jolt of joy Frances got from looking at the cooling bread, and thinking: *I did something worthwhile today*?

No, she couldn't write that. Clementine wouldn't understand. She might be shocked to learn Frances was baking at all, let alone taking pleasure in the result. Frances put down the pen and gazed back out of the window, this time at the grassy hill behind the house. The Māori women were up there again, standing in a circle, heads bowed. The same boy and girl stood on either side of one of the women. After a while they stopped their chanting, gathered the maize and trudged down the hill.

The children trailed behind them, the girl's feet dragging along the ground, the boy's shoulders hunched. They had been lively last time she'd seen them, but today they seemed listless. Sad, even. Poor things. Spending their days cutting maize could not be easy.

Some of the women of New Plymouth lamented the lack of discipline in the Māori children. They complained at length how the natives were a malign influence on their own offspring, encouraging them to forgo their studies and instead swim in the swift rivers and climb trees, even discarding their clothing in warm weather. Frances had no firm views on the matter; the young colonials often appeared healthier and happier than children in London, and the Māori children seemed content enough. But not these two. Not today.

She looked back at her paper and sighed. If only her pen would write the most perfect, eloquent words, without Frances having to decide what to say first. And she was running out of time — they would leave for the meeting before long. Frances had thought about little else since she woke — her only reprieve had been concentrating on baking bread. Numerous catastrophic scenarios ran through her mind, for there was so much that could go wrong should Henry and George meet again. If Henry and his wife were even out of gaol, that was.

She also had a sense of foreboding about the native question, reflecting an uncomfortable shift in her own thoughts on the matter. Before she had watched Matāria being led away, Frances's views resembled the way she'd felt in London about the Crimean War. She had often spoken to people who had a close interest in the events in Russia: a brother who was fighting; a sister joining Florence Nightingale's nurses. But she herself had no opinion on the conflict because it did not affect her day-to-day life. It had been someone else's fight, nothing she needed to get too closely involved with.

She looked at the spot where the Māori women and two children had stopped before they disappeared over the hill. This was not like the Crimean War at all.

Frances smoothed down skirts of her blue dress, donned in anticipation of the meeting. Her face and neck were clean, her hair smoothed and caught in a net at the nape of her neck, with only one curled tendril let free. There was no evidence of chickens or cows or baking on her hands. Frances had dressed early on purpose, so she ought to be able to concentrate on writing this letter.

She ran though the questions she wanted to ask Clementine. Has our brother participated in any dastardly, underhand tricks that you are aware of? You say I must take care of myself. Am I in danger? George said you visited him prior to our departure for New Zealand, but you did not see me during this visit. Why, dear sister? Why?

She put the pen back down. She simply could not write those words dripping with drama and intrigue. They belonged in one of those magazine serials she used to read in London. If she had it all wrong, Clementine would think her childish and melodramatic.

A frightening thought snaked its way into Frances's head. If she *were* in danger it was not safe to send a letter containing those questions. While those new envelopes that sealed themselves were in greater circulation now, they were not stocked in Mr Thorpe's store, so all Frances had was her wax and old-fashioned seal — which was too easily broken. Mother was known to open others' letters if it amused her to do so, including those intended for sending. The serials Frances had enjoyed reading had taught her one thing: if one is in danger, it is best not to alert others to that fact.

But she had to write something. She picked up the pen again and wrote in her tidiest handwriting, carefully rounding each letter, just as she had been taught.

I have so much to tell you since I last wrote. You will never believe who I saw, right here in New Plymouth. Henry White, in the flesh! For the first time since that day in the park, all those years ago. How long ago that feels, that strange sliver of time between Father dying and us learning of his debts. When I thought I had found a man who would ask for my hand in marriage.

But there is no reason to go over that old ground now, dear sister. I only wished to tell you that I had seen Henry again. I can also confidently say that my feelings for him have greatly diminished upon reacquaintance. While I still yearn to know more about the circumstances of his leaving, upon meeting his wife (yes, sister! He is married. To a native woman, no less!) all thoughts of Henry and Frances and our happily-ever-after life are gone, especially as I surprised myself by admiring his wife's character. Of that particular union, I also wonder if it is she, not he, who is the more noble of the two. But I cannot know for certain until I understand the circumstances of his departure.

Frances read over what she'd written. It was a good start. She would next enquire about the health of each and every one of Clementine's children and that of her husband — it was only polite to do so. Only then would she try to find a way to ask Clementine indirectly if she knew of anything untoward about George.

A knock sounded on the door. Frances turned, just in time to see it swing open.

Mother appeared in the doorway, hands on hips. Her hands were caked in dirt — she'd come from her garden in front of the drawing room. Her face was pink.

'Frances,' she said.

'Yes, Mother?'

'What are you doing?'

'Writing to Clementine. Our conversation earlier reminded me that a letter was long overdue.'

'Hysterical Clementine,' Mother said. Her tone was soft; it was almost as if she were talking to herself.

'George called her that too, but I don't remember Clementine ever being particularly hysterical.' Frances put down the pen. 'She was always the mistress of her own emotions, I thought. Remember when we learned the true extent of Father's money troubles? Clementine was the rock we all depended upon, the backbone of our family.'

Mother shook her head. 'George is a good judge of character. I know he misremembers details about Albert on occasion, but that is because George was just a boy when Albert was wounded. As an adult, George is never wrong.'

'He is never wrong?'

'Never. It is not in his nature. He even said this morning he'd known all along that Mrs Archer wasn't a good friend to me. If only he'd shared his observations sooner — I've implored him to do so next time, as his understanding of human character is so infallible.'

'But this is Clementine, Mother. Your own daughter.'

'George does not lie.' Mother's voice was hard. 'I know this to be true. George is a good judge of character, and he tells the truth.'

Frances looked back down at the page in front of her. Perhaps writing wasn't such a good idea after all. She couldn't hold an idea in her head long enough to articulate it, and now that Mother had caught her in the act, her words were likely to be read before they were sent.

'Enough about Clementine,' Mother said. 'I am not here to talk about her.'

'Why *are* you here?' Frances was careful to keep her voice light.

'I have been working on my garden,' Mother said. 'I must turn the soil before I can plant those seeds I bought. The women from the Floral Society will be so impressed.'

'I am sure you will create a very handsome garden, Mother. Much better than my vegetable patch.' In fact, she thought, Mother had little idea about gardening, so any success with the flower garden would likely be good luck rather than good management. She immediately rebuked herself for being uncharitable. Why should her mother have any idea how to garden? She had employed gardeners for most of her life. The fact she was now embracing such work as though it were perfectly normal for a lady to lift a spade was to be applauded. Frances was proud of her mother for trying something new.

'I think you've not been turning the soil correctly,' her mother said. 'There's an art to it, you see. Perhaps you ought to watch me so you can learn. That way, your vegetables will grow.'

'I am sure it's as simple as that.' Frances bit her tongue. Mother was warming up for something, she could tell from her expression. Flattery would possibly distract her, so was worth a try. 'I am sure your garden will be a sight to behold. Simply glorious.'

Mother's face turned a shade pinker. *Hmmm*, thought Frances. There was a fine line between flattery and mockery, which she may have just crossed. Then Mother wailed loudly, the sort of guttural sound befitting a bereavement or similar great loss.

'It will not be any of those things if *you* have anything to do with it.' Mother pulled a kerchief from the small pouch she wore around her waist and dabbed her cheeks. 'Do you know what I found, Frances? I am quite upset by your lies. Quite upset indeed.'

Frances sat very still. What could Mother have possibly found in the garden to upset her so? Frances didn't want to walk into a trap. And she hadn't done anything wrong.

'I . . . I don't know what you're referring to, Mother, I'm sorry.'

Mother waved the kerchief in the air. 'Peach stones! So *many* peach stones in the garden outside the window — some buried, others thrown there with wanton disregard. *You* ate the peaches, just as I suspected.'

Frances recoiled. 'I don't like peaches.'

'That is *exactly* what someone lying about stealing peaches would say. And I cannot turn the soil with all the stones there. You must come and pick up the stones yourself, Frances. You simply must.'

'Mother, you seem so upset. Why don't you sit in the drawing room and have a cup of tea?'

'No!' Mother dabbed her eyes. 'I don't want tea. I only want those horrid stones removed from the soil.'

'You could ask Kitty to do it.'

'I refuse to ask Kitty. She's being very sullen at present, even more uppity than usual. Unless *you* were to talk to her about it . . . ?'

'No, I couldn't possibly.' Frances had barely scraped her way back into Kitty's good graces after baking the bread.

'Then it must be you, to collect the stones, Frances. There is simply no other option.'

'But I did not put them there. I don't like peaches and I don't want to touch peach stones that have been in someone else's mouth,' Frances said. 'That . . . that disgusts me.'

'I *know* it was you,' Mother sobbed loudly. 'I am so upset, Frances. I know I hide it well, but I am. I came here hoping you would cheer me up by agreeing to help, but . . . oh! You have had the opposite effect. Why will my daughter not seek to comfort me? Why?'

'I'm sorry, Mother.' Frances bowed her head. There was no point arguing when Mother was in one of these moods. Matāria was wrong. Apologising wasn't weakness; sometimes it was common sense. 'I'll clean up the stones for you.'

Mother stuffed her kerchief back into her pouch. 'Thank you, dear Frances.' She turned and shuffled out of the room.

Frances looked back at her letter. She picked it up. *Rip*. She tore it into long shreds, and then ripped those strips into small squares. Maybe she would try again later.

For now, she had peach stones to pluck out of the garden.

CHAPTER TWENTY

MATĀRIA

The outer door beyond Matāria's cell was being unlocked. She rolled over on her wooden pallet and looked towards the small hole in the door. It had been a long day. Tai had been released the previous evening, calling farewell to Matāria as he was being led away. Matāria had wished him well. Perhaps one day he would find what he was looking for. Perhaps Matāria would as well. One day, but not today — her focus was on getting out of here and back to her children. Maybe a sense of belonging was too much for her to hope for. It would be enough to be free.

Along with the pallet for sleeping, her cell contained her boots beside the door; an empty bowl that had once been filled with lukewarm potage; and a chamber pot that needed emptying, even more than before. Matāria had used it as little as possible, until the feeling in her stomach changed from discomfort to pain. Even when she was a slave she'd been allowed to slip into the ferns when she needed, and never had to sleep so close to where she defecated — let alone eat. Having no control like this made her wonder if she really was a wild animal that deserved to be here.

That's what most of the soldiers seemed to think. Since Tai had gone, it had been harder to ignore their conversations. There was one going on out there now, though this time it was too quiet to make out. More often, though, they didn't seem to care if she heard, so Matāria had spent many hours listening to their kōrero. Some of the guards were like George Farrington: brash men yet to learn that loud opinions were not a sign of strength. They bragged about all the rebellions the 65th Regiment had suppressed: in India, in Canada, in other places that Matāria had never heard of.

Others had long, wistful conversations about their homes in England. Matāria tried to imagine the wives and children they talked about, left behind in places with names unfamiliar to her tongue. The men seemed to miss their families terribly. *Then go back to them*, Matāria had thought at first. *Go home and leave us alone*. But then she realised these men could not leave. They were prisoners in a way, too; they had to remain here, fighting for land they'd never inhabit themselves.

Footsteps sounded outside her door, the key rattling in the lock. Matāria sat up as the door swung open, making her wince at the sudden light. The older soldier from the first day stood in the opening — the nice one, who was neither cruel nor mocking, who had also brought her food and blankets. Did not being mean make him nice? Matāria was too tired for such thoughts. All that mattered was that he was standing in front of her in an open doorway. His arms were empty — no food or blankets this time. What did he want?

The man's eyes swept around the room, deliberately avoiding the chamber pot in the corner. Matāria stood, blocking his view of it. This man would not see her shame — it wasn't her fault no one had emptied it. She patted her hair, which was coming loose from the coil twisted at the back of her head.

'Mrs White,' he said. 'I come bearing news.' His face was neutral; it wore no hints of whether this news was good or bad. 'I have received word. You are to be released immediately.'

Matāria bowed her head. She was going home — to Betsy, to Edwin. To Henry. She could leave this place at last.

'Thank you, sir.'

He stepped aside. 'You may leave now.'

'Right now?'

'Yes. At this very moment.'

'Thank you, sir.'

Matāria reached for her boots and put them on. They felt tight across her feet; her toes pushed against the leather. *It doesn't matter*, she thought. The discomfort couldn't slow her down. She tied the laces and pulled herself back up. She took one step past the man, then another. Her leg felt heavy and tender, but nothing could stop her. She headed down the wooden passage towards the open door. Soon, a breeze tickled her face. The air was fresh — not as crisp as the wind from the sea or heavy with the scent of rain, but it was enough, especially as, with every painful stride she took, she was further from the stink and darkness of her small cell.

'Mrs White?'

The soldier's voice behind her was low. Matāria turned to face him. 'Sir?'

'You will need to walk, I'm afraid. You have not yet sworn allegiance to Her Majesty. But I don't think anyone will check. There are too many of your people on the streets today for anyone to bother. That native place near Mt Eliot is being emptied.'

'What place?' Did he mean her home? Had her family been sent away?

'One of those pā where you people live.' The man motioned towards the far distance. 'It's close to the centre of New Plymouth. Near the port and the Governor's residence. Far *too* close, some say.'

'Pukeariki,' Matāria said. The man wasn't talking about Matāria's papakāinga, but another one close to where the Huatoki flowed into the sea. The place the great chief Te Rangi-apiti-rua used as a pā many generations ago, and where the people of Ngāmotu had lived ever since. Māmā used to tell stories of collecting hāngi stones from around there as a little girl. And now the people were being thrown out. Henry had warned they might do this. 'What's happened to the papakāinga at Pukeariki?'

'We've given the order for everyone to leave. Today. Men are mobilising to move the inhabitants as we speak.'

'But the people have lived there for generations — at least a hundred people live there now. Where will they go?'

The man shrugged. 'I have no idea,' he said. 'The authorities have not given them any direction that I am aware of. They simply want them outside the town's boundaries. I wager they'll demolish the place before long, and use the land for something else.'

Mātou, Matāria thought. *Not rātou.* The man had said 'they', when he really meant 'we'. *We'll demolish the place.* Nausea overwhelmed her.

The soldier spoke again. 'Do you need some water before your journey? I can fetch you some. It's fresh from last night's rain.'

She shook her head. She would not accept anything from this man. And she knew all about the British and their water — it made many people ill, which was why they drank so much fermented as ale or boiled in endless cups of tea. 'No. I will leave now.'

'Well, go to the border fort and get your pass at the first opportunity.' Then he dropped his voice so that Matāria might have missed his words entirely if she hadn't been standing so close. 'Don't give the likes of George Farrington an excuse to arrest you again. He clearly dislikes your husband.'

Matāria looked the man squarely in the eyes. 'Thank you, sir.'

She made her way over the muddy path and through a cluster of white tents. Two young soldiers jeered at her as she passed.

'I'd pay for a piece of that.' The man was polishing his bayonet. It glistened under the sun's rays. The sun was past the highest part of the sky; it was much later in the day than Matāria had realised.

'Why?' the other men said. 'She can't even walk properly. And she'd probably eat you afterwards. Or give you the clap.'

'Or both!' a third man yelled out.

'Oi.' Matāria recognised the voice of the soldier she'd just been speaking to. 'Wash your mouths out, the three of you. This isn't the docks. Would you speak like that if your mother was nearby? Or your wife?'

Matāria limped as fast as she could, not waiting to hear what the men would say next. They could yell whatever they wanted; their words would disappear on the wind. A crisp wind that licked her face, reminding her that she was outside once more. It was time to find her way back to Henry and her children.

CHAPTER TWENTY-ONE

FRANCES

Frances kneeled in the dirt and groaned: she'd already spent far too much time out of doors today doing chores. And she'd had to change back into her brown dress for this was messy work. She studied the area in front of her. So much mud — and so many peach stones! She should have worn her old gloves so she didn't have to touch these repulsive, wrinkled lumps with her bare hands. Lumps that had been in someone's mouth. *But whose mouth?* Frances shuddered. This task was degrading enough without lingering on that particular detail.

She plucked a stone out of the soil. And a second. And a third. A sliver of peach flesh was attached to the hard core of the third stone. Nausea surged through her. Horrid things, peaches. She turned the earth and found four more, some fresher than others. Eventually there were at least a dozen of the beastly things in a small pile.

A conversation was taking place in the drawing room. Although the window was supposed to have six small panes of glass in it, there were only five: the pane in the bottom right was missing and she could hear the voices clearly. Frances didn't know how it had been broken, nor did she ask, as the damage was a sensitive issue in their household: Mother wanted it repaired, but George said the local glazier had taken against him, so would not come.

'I'm not going to tell Frances,' she heard George say. 'She will learn about it in due course.'

'But the letter—' Mother replied, her voice low.

'Frances wasn't expecting a letter, so is none the wiser.'

Mother exhaled loudly. 'But Clementine—'

'Hush, Mother.'

Frances stood up and peered through the broken window. 'Tell me what?'

Mother and George turned towards her. Mother raised her hand to her mouth. 'Oh my! You gave me such a fright, creeping about like that.'

George leapt to his feet and rushed at the window. 'What is wrong with you, Frances? Sneaking about and eavesdropping on conversations that do not concern you.'

'You were talking about Clementine.' Frances leaned against the window ledge. 'You were talking about my sister.'

'What of it?' George said. 'It's none of your business.'

Mother turned her head away from George. Her face was drained of colour, her posture stooped as she quietly stroked the tassels of her mourning shawl, looking as if she were going to faint.

'Mother?' Frances asked. 'Are you all right?'

Mother shook herself, sat up straight and squinted at Frances. 'The only thing that makes me unhappy is you standing in my freshly turned soil. My poor flowers! If they fail to bloom on account of the dirt being trampled, I shall tell the women of the Floral Society it was because I have a daughter who insists on listening in on other people's conversations.' Mother sobbed. 'What a betrayal indeed!'

'I was collecting the peach stones, just as you told me to!'

George snorted. 'Then you ought not have put them there in the first place.'

‘I already told you, George. I do *not* eat peaches.’

‘Says the hysterical spinster standing in a garden, peering through a window like a thief in the night.’

Says the man who promised to replace the glass, but did not, Frances thought. George had a hard glint in his eye — there was no point in continuing this conversation and risking upsetting Mother further. She would ask about Clementine’s letter later.

She looked at her feet, planted firmly in the soil. Beside them were the stones in a small pile. Just look at her. What a sight she was. She dropped back down to her hands and knees and collected the peach stones in her apron. Now she would have to change her frock and tidy herself up once again to go to the public meeting.

A thought occurred to her. *Henry*. If he were there, she could ask him what he knew of her brother and sister. It was worth a try. After all, she had no one else to ask.

CHAPTER TWENTY-TWO

MATĀRIA

Matāria walked down Marsland Hill towards the distant sea. Her boots rubbed against her heels and her leg hurt, but she would not stop until she was far from the gaol cell: away from the young soldiers with their crude words, away from the large white tents, and past the church at the base of the hill. One foot in front of the other, down, down, down; the bad mauri of the barracks weakening with every step.

Pausing at a corner on which stood some cottages, Matāria turned back to face the hill. Behind it was blue sky, and in the distance stood Taranaki, on display for the first time in weeks. He was the same as ever: the jagged peak that resembled the tooth of a shark; the hills at his base; the rocky slopes covered in caves where the bones of some tūpuna had been placed, long before Matāria was born.

A pleasant tingle crept up her arms and legs, settling in her chest. Pukākā Pā had lost the top of its head but Taranaki was still there. A whakataukī came to her, one spoken by the iwi also named Taranaki, who lived further around the coast: *E kore a Taranaki e ngaro, he harakeke tōngai nui nō roto Waiwiri.* Matāria felt the truth of the words: Taranaki would not be lost; it was strong like harakeke. A saying that had even more depth when Matāria remembered their flax was being stripped and sold for rifles. For the first time in days, Matāria's head felt as clear as a cool stream.

She considered which route to take. Ahead lay Devon Road, but there were far too many settlers milling around. Matāria was too conspicuous with her limp, as well as her face: she didn't need a moko kauae to tell the settlers who she was. Nor did she want to walk past all the earthworks and the building of blockades. There was one other route from here: through the few remaining trees in the bush. Taking a sharp left into the undergrowth, she pushed her way through the ferns, stumbling over roots and branches.

Her mind kept going back to Tai's mention of the wild dogs in the bush, which sounded larger and fiercer than any Matāria had herself encountered. But she was a grown woman, she should be able to fend off kurī — although she'd rather not be tested. She couldn't let herself dwell on this, otherwise every creak of a tree would sound like a growl and every shadow would have sharp teeth. The fear would make her forget that she was as strong as harakeke. Fear would slow her down. *One step at a time,* she thought. *One step. One more. It's just a shadow. And one more.*

Splinters of sunlight fell on the earth. Above her, a tūī sang: a message from Papatūānuku to keep going. From a nearby branch, the tūī's mate joined the waiata. Matāria's breathing was laboured, but her heart felt lighter. Taranaki and these tūī were tohu guiding her path. Henry said tohu didn't exist, that a rock was a rock and a bird was a bird and there wasn't any more to the matter. That was probably why he felt so maudlin at times: a world where nothing had a mauri must be such a colourless place. For Matāria, especially today, the tohu reminded her she was back in nature, safely hidden in the bush, and soon she would be home.

She came to a wooden building and peeked at it through the leaves. It was a house. The settlers were very clear about whose property was whose: she knew neighbours couldn't wander close to others' homes, that crops belonged to whoever grew them, and a house could only be entered by invitation — even if you had been welcomed there before and shared food. Henry told her there were even more rules person must follow; Matāria didn't know what they were, but thought it best to keep clear of this house regardless. Squatting down, she squinted past the wooden building and into the distance. A familiar bench came into view: she was across the road from the general store.

Waiting for the passers-by to move on, she peered through the window of the house she was hiding behind, curious about the clutter of possessions the settlers had — items that must have been part of Henry's life before he took up with her. Once, through an open door, she had seen a table holding tiny stuffed birds under a glass dome, and still didn't understand what purpose that object might have had. The missionaries had a strange painting of a lamb with a cross on its back, and a waka huia for jewellery. They had another treasure box with tiny bottles of tinctures inside which Matāria had loved to dust so she could lift the glass stoppers and sniff the unusual contents.

But the missionaries' house was plain compared to some she had spied: like this one, brimming with heavy curtains, lace fabric draped over furniture, vases and figures made of some sort of shiny stone, lamps and cards. These settlers often had so many belongings they had to fit in extra furniture to accommodate them, such as a mantelpiece, which Henry hoped to build her one day, as well as dressers, cabinets and bookcases, trunks and cupboards, and many other items she wouldn't even know how to name. Wagons had been increasingly teetering into town packed with such unwieldy household goods. Quite what the settlers did with them all she did not know — the chairs included.

After a while all seemed quiet, so Matāria edged out of the

shadowy bush. The sun was gone: clouds had woven a mat over the grey sky, and Taranaki was back in hiding. Matāria looked up and down the street and sighed. She had no choice but to follow the road now until she reached the coast, including passing by the exact spot she'd been arrested. Her boots were heavy and hot; a blister was forming on her largest toe where it rubbed against the leather. She could take them off, but then she'd have to carry them, which would be a nuisance and would also draw attention, given that settlers were horrified by the sight of bare feet in the township. It was deemed almost as bad as being bare-headed. As Matāria had no hat, she should avoid making things worse. She just had to keep going as she was. After all, she had walked all the way home from the Waikato, which had taken many months. This walk today was nothing.

She noticed that the blockhouse now had a roof, and split logs were erected in a solid row for a fence with a line of small holes for rifles to point through. It had only been a few days; the labourers must have been hard at work. The settlers barely even glanced at the new building — did they not understand what it meant? They went about their business as normal, the women in their large round skirts, colourful shawls and bonnets. A few, carrying buckets and parcels and one leading a gaggle of noisy children, were in plainer dresses similar to Matāria's own. The settler men also varied: there were those in long coats and tall hats, those dressed like Henry in shirtsleeves and waistcoats, and the soldiers buttoned up in their uniforms. Matāria sank back as the Hickety Pips marched past, breaking stride only to avoid piles of horse manure. They were walking towards the ocean.

Kāore, she thought. They weren't going to the ocean but towards Pukeariki Pā. Matāria crossed the street to where there were fewer people, though plenty of eyes still tracked her every movement. The hairs on her arms stood up in warning: *you are being watched*. But no one said anything to her.

A steady stream of carts and wagons full of settlers overtook her, all travelling in the same direction: towards a cluster of buildings up ahead. What was going on? Not that it mattered to Matāria; all she cared about was not being stopped again and asked for her pass.

Then a cart rattled alongside her and pulled to a halt. Matāria looked down at the street and limped on, as swiftly as she was able.

'Excuse me,' a woman's voice called out. 'Excuse me!'

Matāria kept her head low, pretending she hadn't heard. If she didn't respond, the cart might go away. Oh, to be back in the bush with the tūī again. She felt so exposed out here.

'Mrs White, isn't it? Henry White's wife?'

Matāria stopped and turned around slowly.

A man and a woman sat in the front of the cart. The man had whiskers that might once have been black but were now peppered with grey. The woman had brown hair parted under her bonnet and wore a grey gown trimmed with white. She had a face that might have seemed kind if Matāria didn't see danger at every turn.

'Good afternoon,' the woman said. 'I am so very pleased to see you again.'

Beside her, the man gave a nod of greeting. 'It wasn't right that they took you away.'

Matāria checked their faces: it was the man who worked at the store, and the woman was his sister. She'd met them before, with Henry. Not that she could remember their names right now.

'I am so pleased to see you,' the woman said again, bending towards Matāria. 'We were so worried about you.'

'I took Henry's cart back to where you live,' the man said. 'Just as he asked. I took it down to your little village by the sea—'

The woman interrupted her brother. 'We can take you home too, if you'd like that. We have just shut up the store to attend the public meeting, but could take you home first. It would be no trouble.'

Thorpe. Their name was Thorpe. A name Matāria could not translate into Māori. Their eyes were filled with pity and the woman kept talking. *Dora*. That was her name: Dora Thorpe.

'I must say, it's quite warm today, is it not?' Dora said. 'The sun appears to have taken leave of us, yet the air is still warm. We have this meeting to attend shortly to hear about all of the drama swirling around at present. We couldn't believe you were arrested by those beastly men. Oh, how awful that was to watch! I have more than half a mind to say something at the meeting. But we will accompany you home now. You don't look at all well, and I don't mind being a little late. Not one bit.'

'Yes.' The man said.

Matāria had walked too far and slept too little to properly follow Dora's stream of words, but she did understand one thing: if Dora had truly wished to take Matāria to the papakāinga, she would not have said it would make them late. She would have simply made the offer and let it stand. Matāria didn't need a tohu to tell her that this woman's words were as empty as air.

'I am well, thank you. I can walk.'

Mr Thorpe turned to his sister, then back at Matāria. 'Are you quite sure?'

Matāria nodded. 'Thank you for your kind offer, sir, but I can walk.'

Both brother and sister stared at her. Neither spoke.

'Thank you.' Matāria said again.

'Very well, Mrs White,' Mr Thorpe said eventually. 'Safe travels, and please give my regards to your husband. I hope to see him back at the store in due course.'

Matāria watched them rattle off in the same direction as the other carts. She should have accepted their offer: her leg hurt and she would have got home to her children so much more quicky. She would have avoided being stopped for her pass. Matāria rubbed her leg. This tiredness was making her doubt herself. No, she'd done the right thing — demonstrated her strength. She had shown that these settlers could have their public meetings about her whenua but she was still strong like the harakeke.

I should have accepted the offer.

I did the right thing in demonstrating my strength.

I should have accepted the offer . . .

Further down the road, she realised she was following a crowd of people, more than she could count. What was more, they were not just any people, but *her* people, from the Pukeariki papakāinga. Their long line was trudging towards her own papakāinga at Paritutu. Men and women lugged sleeping mats, blankets, and kete bulging with kai. Children darted up and down, weaving in and out of the hunched adults. Beside them, a cart carried old people and small children, squashed so tightly they would not have been able to fit another person. One of the old women looked to the skies and wailed.

'Auē, auē!'

Beside her sat an old man, tears silently streaming down his face, looking as tired as Matāria felt: the deep weariness that seeps into your bones and permeates your wairua.

'Hurry!' someone yelled from the line. 'We need to get that cart back to Wiremu Kīngi, full of supplies.'

'We're going as fast as we can,' someone else yelled back.

'It's not very far.'

'It is when your arms are full.'

Matāria caught up with a woman she recognised: they had been children together, all those years ago.

'Tēnā koe,' Matāria said shyly.

'I know you,' the woman said. 'You're the teina of Atarangi. The slave.'

Matāria felt the words punch her in the stomach. 'I am no longer a slave.'

'You are free now.' A statement, not a question.

'Āe.' Matāria thought about the cold prison cell on Marsland Hill: the hard bed; the chamber pot; the constant chatter of soldiers outside her room. 'I am free now.'

'You went away,' the woman said.

'I came back.'

The woman gazed at the sea. 'So did I, on the waka from Te Whanganui-a-Tara with your sister. And look at me now: being forced to leave my home yet again.'

'You will be welcomed at my papakāinga.'

'I only hope the British let us stay there. I am too tired to walk anywhere else, and all of our waka will now be used for war.'

'I hope there will not be a war.'

The woman shrugged. 'Is there anything we can do to stop Tūmatauenga?'

Matāria said nothing, just trudged along in the stream of people. The old woman's voice could still be heard, even though the cart was now ambling into the distance.

'Auē, auē. Auē.'

CHAPTER TWENTY-THREE

FRANCES

Frances trailed Mother and George into the hotel, which she had never entered before. Unlike the new establishment near the general store, this hotel had space for large gatherings. The central hallway from the large front door led to the public bar. This was not the place for a lady, but the meeting provided the perfect excuse to see where many men — and a few disreputable women — spent so much time. While the furniture looked comfortable, the strong smell of ale, pipe smoke, sawdust and mutton fat were far from appealing.

A second door at the end of the verandah opened into the assembly room, where dances were sometimes held, as well as other occasions of particular importance, such as today's meeting. Bright naval ensigns hung from the walls and rafters, as did withered ferns that the staff had yet to take down from the last dance.

Mother made her way to the group of chairs that had been set aside for the ladies, but the room was tightly packed and all the seats were occupied. 'Oh, bother. We ought to have got here earlier.'

'This is your fault, Frances,' George said. 'You kept us waiting.'

How unfair, Frances thought. After the morning she had had, she was not going to let this go.

'Mother and I stood by the cart for at least ten minutes before you arrived,' she replied, enjoying the unexpected surge of defiance. 'It was *you* who was late.'

'You ought to have called out. How was I to know you were ready? Am I to read your mind, as well as provide for you both?'

'My point is that if you were late, you can hardly place the blame on me.'

'Calm yourself, sister! And keep your voice down. This is not the occasion to get hysterical.'

'I am perfectly calm, and my voice is barely above a whisper—'

'I am sorry, George,' Mother cut in. 'We ought to have spoken up.' She pointed at a group of women standing in one corner. 'Look over there! Mrs Archer is already here, talking to my new friends. I wager she's saying unpleasant things about me. I had best put a stop to that nonsense immediately.' She hurried across the room.

'I'll stand at the back,' Frances said to George. 'Over there, by the wall.' The distance from her brother might improve her mood. It was a cruel irony that she had felt perfectly calm before being accused of not being so.

George grunted and turned his back, striding towards some men gathered around a stocky gentleman at the front. The man had whiskers down each cheek and dark hair swept to one side. His coat was well made, his upturned collar spotless. This must be the Native Secretary, Donald McLean.

'I'm George Farrington.' Her brother's voice carried to where Frances stood as he bowed slightly towards McLean, reaching out his hand. 'I am pleased to make your acquaintance, sir.'

'Good afternoon,' McLean replied in a thick Scottish accent, shaking George's hand perfunctorily before looking past him to the man with whom he'd been conversing before George had interrupted.

Leaning against the wood-panelled wall, Frances observed the latecomers arriving, noisily greeting those already present. Standing alone and unnoticed, she felt as if she had accidentally strayed into a space she'd not been invited to enter. Her mother and brother, while they had not been welcomed with open arms, were at least acknowledged.

The people Frances recognised were not those her mother would want her to associate with: the butcher and his wife and older children; the man who tethered horses outside the store, who was always polite, even if he did smoke in the street; the chandler and his wife; the old woman who ran the dame school; the seamstress sitting alongside the hatter. No sign of Henry. Nor of Matāria.

In fact, now that she thought about it, there were no natives present at all. That was probably not surprising. What was surprising was the number of people here Frances didn't know. She noticed a cluster of men and women with plain clothes and sun-kissed faces. They must be farmers from further outside the township. *Real* farmers, possibly even some who'd had the misfortune to experience the recent Māori raids. The sort of farmers who broke in George's farm before he bought it, toiling on the land day in, day out with their wives and children: draining swamps, clearing scrub, chopping down trees. Dressed in what was probably their best, they sat expectantly.

McLean inspected his pocket watch and walked to the front of the room, unfolding a piece of paper. A man put a glass of ale on the table beside him, and McLean was quick to take a sip.

It was getting stuffy: several men were puffing on pipes, and too many people were crammed in too small a space. The main reason Frances had come had been to see Henry, and he wasn't here. For all she knew, he might still be in gaol. Had she fallen so low that now she mixed with convicts? She had never known anyone who had been imprisoned. George had refused to tell her what had happened after Henry and Matāria were led away the other day, but Frances assumed they were not held for long, and surely not convicted. After all, neither had done anything wrong. Her eyes combed the room, but there was definitely no Henry. *Was* he still in prison?

'Frances!' A women's voice cut through the noise. Dora Thorpe wove her way between crowds of people, waving and grinning her toothy smile. 'I'd hoped to see you here. May we join you?'

Mr Thorpe appeared three steps behind his sister. He bowed shyly at Frances. Frances smiled back, but kept her mouth firmly closed.

'How do you do, Miss Farrington,' the store owner said.

'Good afternoon, Mr Thorpe,' Frances replied. 'How do you do?'

Dora rolled her eyes and laughed. 'You two are a fine pair of conversationalists, aren't you? I shall leave you to your *how do you dos* and find a glass of water before the meeting starts.'

'Have you had a pleasant day?' Mr Thorpe asked Frances.

'Oh, yes.' She knew she ought to offer more to carry the conversation forward, so she said the first thing that came to mind. 'I baked some bread.'

'Oh?' Mr Thorpe said. 'How accomplished. I hadn't realised you did such things. I thought . . .' He stole a glance at Mother, in a group of well-dressed women.

'That I am a gentleman's daughter, and that, as such, I would never fall so low as to be found with flour on my face and my hands in the dough bin?' As soon as the words were out of her mouth, she wished she could retract them.

'No, not at all,' Mr Thorpe said. 'Forgive me, I expressed myself poorly. I was merely remarking on how admirable it is that you can bake. It is a *good* thing, Miss Farrington.'

Frances blushed. 'Yes, it is satisfying to feel useful, I find. Neither my sister nor I were taught anything so practical as baking bread when we were in London.'

'Ah, is that the sister that writes to you?'

'Well, she has only written two letters since we arrived. But she is so busy, I must not complain.'

'But . . .' Mr Thorpe's voice trailed off.

'But what, Mr Thorpe?'

'Oh, never mind, Miss Farrington. I cannot recall what it was I meant to say.'

They lapsed into comfortable silence. A kindness radiated from Mr Thorpe's entire being: it was in his eyes, his upturned mouth, the way he turned his body towards Frances and even bent slightly towards her. A warmth crept over her body. It wasn't the heady excitement she'd felt with Henry when she was younger — the feeling that they two were the only planets in their very own universe. This was different. *Safe.* Mr Thorpe made her feel safe.

That reminded her: *Henry*. Frances looked around the room again. He still wasn't there. Mr Thorpe might know more. 'That man and woman who were taken away outside your store — Matāria and Henry White. Do you happen to know what happened to them?'

'I do,' Mr Thorpe said. 'I returned Henry White's cart to the village by the sea, just as I had promised. Then, on the way here, not one hour ago—'

Dora Thorpe reappeared, interrupting her brother. 'Have I missed anything?'

'I was just about to tell Miss Farrington about seeing Mrs White as we were on our way here.'

Dora's shoulders slumped. 'I scared her away with my natter. I try not to talk so much, I really do. She looked quite put out after I talked to her. I was most unwise in my choice of words. I feel quite awful about it. And she was clearly in pain . . .'

Dora Thorpe stopped speaking. Silence had fallen across the room. Frances looked from Dora to Mr Thorpe, longing for them to continue speaking about Henry and Matāria, but all eyes were now turned towards the front of the room.

McLean took a long drink of ale and raised one arm. The meeting had started.

CHAPTER TWENTY-FOUR

MATĀRIA

The group of women and children trudged along the coast towards the papakāinga where Matāria lived. Red harakeke flowers edged the path, pointing to the sky, the thick leaves of the plant splaying in all directions. On the other side of the flax bushes was the rocky shore. The ship Matāria had seen a few days ago was gone, but another just as large was now in its place. It rocked in the sea swell, masts naked. No one was disembarking; whoever had come on this boat was already ashore. And those who would be aboard when it eventually sailed away were lucky: these English boats might be the only way to leave Ngāmotu without walking.

It was a long walk for those carrying their whole life in their arms. Two women in front of Matāria had babies strapped to their backs while their older children ran through puddles nearby. Someone else struggled to shoulder an overflowing kete of potatoes and carrots. A girl about Betsy's age cried about having to leave behind her collection of flowers; a boy complained he was hungry.

Matāria found herself alongside the woman she'd known as a child.

'I'm Mere,' the woman eventually said. 'I remember us learning with rākau together, back when we were children.'

Matāria shook her head. 'I remember you, but not using the rākau.'

'You were there. You came with Atarangi. We played by the river after our lessons.'

'Are you sure it was me?'

'I am sure.'

Matāria felt cold all over, a deep chill that even the warmest fire wouldn't remove. She couldn't remember at all. If she had forgotten these details, what else had she lost? How many other details from her childhood were so thoroughly gone from her memory that she didn't know to mourn their loss?

Mere stared at her. 'You look as if you are about to cry.'

'I don't remember learning the rākau.'

'Let's talk about something else,' Mere said. 'This walk is hard enough without feeling sad.'

'Yes,' Matāria said. 'I just want to get home to my husband and children.' She pictured them in their small hut: Betsy talking loudly, Edwin watching carefully, Henry in that ridiculous chair.

Mere hugged her bulging kete to her chest. 'This is too heavy. I should have left more of my belongings behind.'

'I can take some of your load, e hoa. Give some of that to me.'

'Kāore. You can hardly walk. You can't carry my things as well. But thank you.'

'I can walk.'

'I see you limping, Matāria. If there were any space on that cart carrying the old people, I would have suggested you get in also. I see how your face pales each time you must step down a slope.'

'I would never take up space like that. I don't need it.' Matāria thought about the Thorpes' offer of a ride, but pushed it out of her mind. *What's done is done.*

Mere sighed. 'When I look at what I'm carrying it seems like so little, compared with what I had to leave behind. Yet this small amount is still so heavy. Who knows when I will see my other belongings again? There wasn't much: an extra blanket, a settler dress, another kete. But it was enough.'

Matāria understood completely. She had had to do the same thing each time she'd moved. What she left didn't add up to much, yet those items wove the fabric of a life.

'You may see those things again,' Matāria said. 'How I wish I knew what the future would bring.' She'd seen the tohu encouraging her to keep up her journey today: both Taranaki and the tūī. But beyond that? Nothing but darkness.

'Perhaps it's best we don't know,' Mere said. 'At least this way we can hold onto hope.'

'I would prefer to know. Then I can better keep my twins safe from harm.'

Mere raised an eyebrow. 'I know one thing for sure,' she said. 'That we will fight them. Ko te kōrero e kī ana: *kaua e mate wheke, me mate ururoa*.'

Matāria turned over Mere's words in her mind. Was she right? *Was* it better to die like a brave hammerhead shark than a flailing octopus? Wouldn't it be better that Betsy and Edwin didn't die at all? Matāria didn't know what to say to this woman she barely remembered.

They walked in silence — up the coast road, over the rise, down the other side. How tight her boots were; the blister would surely burst soon.

Eventually the group shuffled around the corner and Ngāmotu beach stretched out in front of them. At the end of the beach, close to Paritutu's base, was the papakāinga. Matāria's chest felt full. *Home*. Some of the children sped ahead: racing each other, laughing loudly.

The adults stood more erect, their loads lighter now the end was in sight. Matāria's leg throbbed as she limped the length of the beach and up to the gates. Outside the fence stood women she knew — those who stripped harakeke with Atarangi. They greeted the arrivals with fresh water and cooked kānga.

'Nau mai,' one of them said to Mere. 'Nau mai, whanaunga.'

'Where should I go, cousin?' Mere asked the woman. 'Where should I put my things? Where can I wash my feet? Where will I sleep tonight?'

'We'll find a place.' The woman looked at the large group outside the gates. 'We'll find somewhere for all of you.'

Mere bowed her head. 'Thank you.'

'Matāria!' One of the other women cried out. Others saw her and gathered around, speaking all at once.

'You're back!'

'We heard you were in gaol — auē!'

'How much your children missed you!'

'Go to them now, Matāria. They will be waiting.'

Matāria pushed through the crowd and up the papakāinga hill, passing those who had arrived from Pukeariki earlier. These new people spilled out of doorways and clustered in small circles, chattering about how they had come to be here today. Matāria ignored them as she made her way up to the kūmara storehouses at the back of the papakāinga. Her hut came into view.

'Betsy! Edwin!' she called. 'Henry!'

Nothing. Matāria took a deep breath and entered her hut. The bed mats were laid out; Henry's clothes were draped over the chair with dog feet. But no husband, and no children. She hurried out and looked around — towards the beach, towards the area near the fire, back at the road below.

'Henry? Betsy? Edwin?'

No response.

'Henry?'

She returned to the hut and sank into the chair. She needed to remove her boots and rest her leg before venturing out in search of her family. Her lids grew heavy; she closed her eyes. The sound of crashing waves echoed in the distance . . .

'Māmā! Māmā!'

Matāria's eyes flew open and she stumbled up. In front of her was Betsy, charging forward. Edwin was behind her. Both had tears streaming down their cheeks. Matāria stretched out her arms and wrapped them around her twins. She inhaled: they smelt like the sea mixed with the scent of cooked kānga.

The children's words tumbled over each other.

'I was so worried—'

'. . . you went away, and Pāpā went away too—'

'. . . we didn't know where you were—'

'. . . then that man came and then Pāpā came and then—'

'. . . all these new people came—'

'. . . why can't we have kānga too?'

Matāria held up her hand. 'Shhh,' she said. 'I'm back now. We'll have plenty of time for talking.'

Betsy pulled back and put her hands on her hips. 'I did *not* like you going away.'

Edwin attached his arms around Matāria's middle and held on tightly. 'No. We did *not* like it.'

'I know.' Matāria's eyes filled with tears. 'I know.'

A shadow fell over the doorway of the hut. Atarangi.

Matāria stepped towards her sister and, although Edwin clung to her skirts, held out her arms. 'Atarangi. I'm back.'

Atarangi stared, expressionless. A lump formed in Matāria's throat.

'I said I'm back.' Matāria's voice shook. 'I was arrested, and only released this morning. I've walked from Marsland Hill — I thought I wouldn't make it, but I saw Taranaki, and then a tūī—'

'I thought you might have seen a pīwakawaka rather than a tūī, for all the pain and death you bring. I wonder if a pīwakawaka has flown into your home and you have kept it a secret.'

Matāria gasped. Everyone knew a pīwakawaka inside a hut foretold a death, ever since the cheeky bird betrayed Māui and caused his death at the hands of Hine-nui-te-pō.

'I have never seen a pīwakawaka indoors,' she said. 'Never. And if I had, I would have told people.'

But Atarangi wasn't listening. 'You invite war into our village,' she said. 'I think you are cursed. You refused to get on the waka to Mikotahi when we were children, and our parents were killed. Now you and your husband make trouble, and my Kuru must go to war.'

Edwin let go of Matāria and slunk outside the hut. Betsy followed.

Her children must not believe Matāria had killed her own parents — she'd explain that to them later. Matāria herself had to believe her parents' death wasn't her fault or the guilt would crush her. She would be covered in such a dark cloak she'd struggle to see the sun's rays ever again, even on the sunniest of days. She was just a child when the invasion happened. A child who made a mistake and reaped the consequences. Over and over and over.

Matāria shook her head. 'I fear Tūmatauenga more than anyone. I would give anything—'

'No.' Atarangi cut her off. 'You keep making trouble. You went into the town without a pass.'

'I was buying your flour.'

'You were buying nothing but attention and danger. And, as

soon as he was released, Henare Mā insisted on visiting the German missionary and got himself tangled in a conversation about what we Māori must do for peace. Who is your husband to tell us what to do? Who is that missionary to preach his gospel of peace to us? They are neither *from* here nor *of* here. How can they know what is best?'

'Henry is only trying to help,' Matāria said. 'And I saw Tai, Kuru's cousin. Rather, I heard him. He was in gaol too.'

'See? He was arrested because of that man. And who knows where he will go next, as he's no longer welcome here.'

'Then tell Kuru to defy the missionary and invite Tai back. You could find a way of getting word to him, I'm sure. He's taking the road south but won't have made it very far yet. The missionary has no real power.'

'It's more complicated than that. Tai was a slave.'

'Then why is the missionary to blame? He may have lit the fire, but did he place the kindling? Did he fan the embers until they turned into flame? If Kuru will not make Tai welcome, is the German really to blame?'

Atarangi shook her head. 'Who cares about that old slave when war is so close? War that you and your husband are stoking by walking around town when you know should not. The only fire you ought to be worried about is the one about to burn your own hands.'

'We've not done anything wrong, Atarangi.'

'Then why has your husband taken a horse and gone to that settlers' meeting? A horse that could not easily be spared. Henare Mā told Kuru there were things he wanted to say to his fellow countrymen. How can speaking out do anything good? The British no longer listen. It will just make them even more vengeful—'

'A meeting?' Matāria's heart rate quickened. Perhaps this was the same place the Thorpes had also been going. 'What sort of meeting?'

'An important one we were not invited to.' Atarangi's face was pink. Her hands shook — something was wrong with her.

She's scared, thought Matāria. Atarangi was so frightened the fear was rising out of her in the torrent of rage directed at her sister. But Matāria understood.

'Don't feel ashamed,' Matāria said softly. 'I'm scared too. I'm very frightened.'

Atarangi glared at Matāria. 'I'm not frightened. I'm *angry*.' She spun around and walked out of the hut.

Matāria watched her sister go. This land was part of her, she was of this place, but she would never be invited into Atarangi's circle. She put her head in her hands. Tai was right — she'd always be in that space between. Perhaps Matāria had been wrong: it wasn't Taranaki or the tūī that had been the tohu. Maybe it was Tai all along, telling her that she should leave Ngāmotu, never to return.

CHAPTER TWENTY-FIVE

FRANCES

The crowded room was silent. Frances glanced sideways at each Thorpe. *How nice to have some friendly acquaintances*, she thought. All other eyes were on McLean, even Mother was intent on the Native Secretary.

The Scotsman studied those gathered. 'Ladies and gentlemen, thank you for attending this meeting on an issue of paramount importance to all of us.' He spoke softly; from the back of the room, Frances strained to hear what he was saying.

'Let us first go over the facts of the matter. In the early 1830s, the local Māori tribe left New Plymouth after the war with their Waikato brethren. They all fled south — to Wellington, to the South Island, to God knows where else. The destination does not matter. All that is worth noting at this juncture is that they left. Gone. They left this area completely, and gave up all rights to their land in the process.'

'Here, here!' a man yelled.

'Hmm,' Mr Thorpe said quietly. 'I'm not sure that's accurate. There weren't many Māori people when I arrived here in 1841, but there were some. And I understand those who left always intended to return.'

McLean continued. 'The local tribe were all gone. And not a decade later, many of you arrived. You built this fine township on abandoned land.'

'It doesn't seem abandoned to me,' someone yelled from the back. 'I see them everywhere, especially down by the sea, eating fish-heads and whatnot. Who are those people if the local tribe are gone? What about the dozens of them wandering around today, looking sorry for themselves. Who are they?'

McLean raised his chin. 'That's a good question. The tribe did come back — in their hundreds, once they deemed it safe to do so. They then had the audacity to pretend they'd not lost the rights to their land in the meantime.'

'It's clear then,' a woman called out, 'that it is *not* their land. So we can farm it.' Beside her, Mother nodded vigorously.

'So why is there an issue at all?' Frances recognised the questioner as the fellow who fixed clocks and watches every Saturday afternoon.

McLean turned to the man. 'Because Wiremu Kīngi is blocking the sale of the land. Te Teira Mānuka wishes to sell the Waitara block to the Governor. As you may recall, he laid a great feathered cloak in front of the Governor to symbolise the passing of the land from native hands to our own. This is as good as a Deed of Sale to these people.'

'I don't care a jot for a feathered cloak,' someone yelled. 'I want to farm that wasteland covered in naught but ferns. What we need is more land.'

McLean's eyes swept the room. 'Quite right, my good man. Wiremu Kīngi claims he is the chief and Te Teira does not have the authority to sell. But he does. I have investigated the matter thoroughly, and that is my conclusion. The sale will go ahead.'

The room erupted in cheers. Frances could hear George whooping from the front row.

A portly man stood up: Schmidt, the missionary. He wore a baggy black jacket and trousers; his thin hair was parted down the middle of his head. Frances regarded him with curiosity. She knew the town was divided on Schmidt. Some respected his work — Schmidt was generous with his time, and often helped those he considered his flock; while others judged him a pompous and interfering bore. George said the man was close to the natives and had even learned some of the language, so he was not to be trusted for that reason alone. Frances had not met him enough to have formed her own view.

The cheering died down.

'I have one question, sir.' Schmidt spoke with a heavy accent. 'You say the land was abandoned by Te Ātiawa. You claim they no longer have rights over the land. Yet Te Teira is Te Ātiawa too. How does he retain the right to sell when you claim Wiremu Kīngi does not?'

McLean stood in silence; he appeared to be deep in thought. Frances craned forward. Eventually McLean replied. 'You oversimplify my words, Father. Let us discuss this later — we can talk more in private. I can assure you of one thing, however. Te Teira has the right to sell the Waitara Block, which is why we, the government, can and will accept the purchase.'

'So the government confirms it will accept Te Teira's offer to sell?' Schmidt's voice was expressionless.

'Yes.'

'And what about all the Māori people who will be displaced?' Schmidt asked. 'Already many have had to leave their homes—'

'Serves them right!' A man sitting near George interrupted the missionary. 'I had to leave my first farm because of their raids.' The man stood up, his whiskered face red. He was one of the hardened farmers Frances had noticed earlier. He jabbed his finger at the missionary. 'They had a battle between themselves on my land and shot my sheep. I only count my blessings that it wasn't one of my children. This is all their fault.'

A group of settlers began to clap. The man set his jaw at Schmidt and sat back down.

Schmidt remained standing. 'We cannot expect these people to become more civilised if they are angry with us for taking their land,' he said. 'They will never abandon their old gods and open their ears to the True Word if they feel we have betrayed their interests.'

'This *is* in their best interests,' McLean said. 'Living in a thriving, civilised society is in everyone's best interests.'

'Whose side are you on, Father?' asked the clockmaker. 'Are you not on our side?'

'This is not a matter of sides,' Schmidt said. 'This is a matter of right and—'

'Which side are you on?' the man called, even louder than before. 'Whose part will you take, Father?'

Schmidt opened his mouth, then closed it again. He glanced at McLean and sat back down.

McLean looked around the room. 'I have examined the matter extensively and communicated with the Governor. We have decided that the colonial government buying the land from Te Teira is legitimate.' There wasn't a hint of defensiveness in his words — just quiet authority.

'That's not true.' A new voice interrupted from the other side of the room. Frances turned, along with everyone else, but she already knew who it was.

Henry pushed his way to the front, his hair falling over his face, his shirt filthy. He looked even more unkempt than when she'd last seen him.

'You are mistaken, sir,' Henry said. 'You *know* Te Teira doesn't have the right to sell that land.'

'I am not mistaken,' McLean said.

Henry pointed at the men sitting with George. 'You are all driven by greed and desire for land that is not yours. Shame on all of you. Shame.'

'Shame on you, not me, Henry White!' George leapt to his feet. 'Ladies and gentlemen, pay this man no attention. He was arrested with his wife not three days ago. His *native* wife. He wed her when no good Englishwoman would have him.'

Frances pushed back against the wall; a sharp ache throbbed in the side of her head. Why would George say such a thing?

Henry raised his finger at George. 'Leave my wife out of this, George Farrington.'

George turned red. 'Henry White should not be welcome here. I knew this scoundrel back in London. His father was a doctor and his mother a seamstress. He is not a gentleman and is not worthy to attend this gathering.'

'Watch your mouth.' The man behind George spoke out. 'My wife is a seamstress, and doctoring is a perfectly respectable profession.'

'But it is still a profession,' George replied. 'Do you not see that?'

Beside Frances, Mr Thorpe stiffened. 'Your brother . . .' He shook his head as his voice trailed off.

'Sit down, Farrington,' another man yelled. Frances recognised Mr Black, the man who sold baked goods, including those fine wedding cakes she liked to admire.

'I'm no gentleman, but at least I can slaughter my own beasts,' a farmer said to George. The man bowed slightly and smirked. 'Your Lordship.'

Henry glared at George. 'What value is your opinion, Farrington, when you think it worth cultivating what looks like a dead rodent on your upper lip?' Someone laughed loudly, and others in the crowd tittered.

George paled.

'Sit down, both of you,' a man called from near where Frances stood. 'Stop wasting our time with your petty squabbles. You sound like a pair of fishmongers' wives.'

George sat down slowly. Frances could see that he was very angry indeed.

Henry faced McLean. 'Go ahead with this purchase if you insist. But you should all feel shame. Shame at taking Māori land. And shame that you, Mr McLean, are not even granting Māori the courtesy of a meeting to communicate your findings.'

No one said a word. Henry and McLean glared at each other for a long moment, before Henry turned and walked out the door, slamming it behind him. The dull thud echoed around the silenced room.

Frances stared at the closed door. Clearly she was not going to be able to talk to Henry today.

'Are you all right, Frances?' Dora whispered.

'Sorry, yes, I am just . . . I don't even know what I am. Perhaps it is this room — it is so stuffy.'

Dora put her hand on Frances's arm. 'I understand.'

At the front of the room, McLean raised his hand. 'That man, whoever he is, is simply incorrect. And his words do not change matters. I believe that Te Teira is the correct person to sell the land. The government will begin surveying the land north of New Plymouth at first light tomorrow.'

The crowd cheered loudly, clapping their hands and stamping their feet. Only a few remained silent: Dora and Mr Thorpe; Schmidt the missionary; some others Frances did not recognise.

Donald McLean picked up the glass of ale from the table and drained the last of the amber liquid. 'There may be a war, but it is a war that we will win.'

The cheering rose even louder. Frances put her hands over her ears but could not drown out the sound of all those people welcoming war with such enthusiastic delight.

CHAPTER TWENTY-SIX

MATĀRIA

Matāria sat by the fire with Edwin and Betsy on either side of her, one under each arm. They'd crept back into the hut after Atarangi had left and had barely let Matāria out of their sight since. Edwin hadn't said much about the past few days, but Betsy had. They'd been looked after by Atarangi. They were both well fed and clean, their hair washed, their faces scrubbed. Matāria kissed the tops of their heads. Atarangi's words had hurt her deeply but she was still grateful for the care her sister had shown the twins.

The fire burned brightly, warmth radiating from the flames. Tonight the papakāinga was alive with conversations. Over the chatter, Matāria could sometimes hear the pahu being struck by the men posted as sentries at the gate. The large gong made of matai wood echoed when hit: a reminder to anyone contemplating attack that the sentries were on high alert.

Matāria had never seen so many people gathered around the fire — those from her own papakāinga, as well as her whanaunga from Pukeariki. A smell of sweat hung in the air: not everyone had been able to go down to the beach to wash before the light faded. Every hut overflowed with bed mats but there still wasn't enough space. Some of the visitors would sleep under the stars: outside the whare kai, alongside the kūmara storehouses, up against the walls surrounding the papakāinga. Others had moved into the caves at the base of Paritutu — their tūpuna had slept here, they said, so it was good enough for them. No one told them how terribly cold it could be inside the rock — it was only ever meant to be a place of refuge.

Matāria had thought about inviting someone in to share their hut but there just wasn't room, even with the chair banished outside. All she could do was ask Ranginui to keep his tears at bay until after the newcomers found somewhere dry to sleep.

Atarangi sat as usual among a group of women in a circle, their fingers tearing at the flax so quickly it was a like a blur in the semi-darkness. Their conversation carried on the breeze.

'There is not enough to eat,' an old woman said. 'We have more people than we can feed.'

'My children are hungry.'

'Tomorrow, everyone who is able will harvest the last kānga and potatoes,' Atarangi said. 'Those who can't must venture into the bushes for berries, or remain behind to prepare kānga pirau. The men who aren't readying for war should fish at the lagoon, or the sea for kai moana.'

'The potatoes are too small,' another woman said. She was older than Atarangi, her moko kauae faded to grey. Matāria knew her as a kaiako who taught younger women about the art of flax, her weaving so masterful it was as if she had learned from Hineteiwaiwa, god of weaving, herself. 'We are digging up the potatoes too soon — we should wait until the fishing season is over, as we have always done. The kānga is ready now, as is most of the kūmara. But not the potatoes. They are like little rocks.'

'They will be all right cooked properly under the hāngi stones,' said Atarangi. 'It's not our fault the British wage war at this time of year, when our crops have not been in the soil long enough. But we have no choice. We have to feed people.'

'We won't be able to provide the best sustenance to our warriors. Who can win a war on a half-empty belly?'

'We must collect the potatoes anyway. Kuru has said so.'

'We need to collect more fresh water at first light,' another woman said. 'It is all gone — our whanaunga from Pukeariki were thirsty.'

'Āe,' the kaiako said. 'We will rise early and do that.'

Matāria stretched her leg out in front of her but couldn't flex the muscle; it pulled tighter than leather. Tomorrow she would hurt even more, and so would her blistered toe. No harvesting kānga or collecting berries for her, much less potatoes. The kōtuku with a bad leg, the one that would have died in the wild, will have to prepare the kānga pirau instead.

'It's time for bed,' she said to the twins. 'We all need sleep.'

Betsy pulled away. 'But we're not tired.'

'No,' Edwin echoed, 'we're not tired.'

Matāria shook her head. 'But *I'm* tired, my lovelies. I did not sleep well last night. My bed was made of wood and the soldiers talked all night long.' She thought about her dreams of kākā, her descendants, and all the other visions that had danced behind her closed eyes. 'I had some bad dreams, too. Me moe au ināianei.'

'Don't be silly, Māmā,' Betsy said. 'Grown-ups don't get tired or have bad dreams. Just children — but not us. We're not tired children, we're normal children. Aren't we, Edwin?'

'Yes.'

'And we want to listen to Pāpā. Look, Māmā, he's standing up to speak to the men.'

Henry stood on the other side of the fire where the men gathered, Kuru among them. How wonderful it had been to see Henry when he'd returned from the meeting. But he had been upset — the meeting had not gone well. He'd rushed to tell Kuru all about it as soon as he'd embraced Matāria and made sure she was all right.

'This conversation might not be for your ears,' Matāria said. 'They are talking about Tūmatauenga and a hui your pāpā went to earlier.'

Betsy scoffed. 'We already know about Tūmatauenga, Māmā. We know he is coming, Edwin heard the women talking about it and he told me. We know *all* about it.'

Matāria turned to Edwin. 'Oh?'

Betsy answered for him: 'Whaea Atarangi told us about the old war as well. We did a karakia for our kuia and koro who were murdered after you were a naughty girl and refused to ride in the waka. We went to where they passed out of this world and began their journey up Te Oneroa a Tohe and to Hawaiki.'

Matāria's chest tightened. 'That's not how it was.'

She looked her son directly in the eye. 'Edwin?'

'Do you mean our koro and kuia didn't go to Hawaiki?' he asked.

'No. I mean yes. They did.'

Betsy interrupted. 'Then what?'

'That's not why they died, I meant. It was more complicated than that.'

Edwin had the face of someone rummaging deep within themselves to find the right words.

'Yes, son?' Matāria said softly. She put her hand on her son's arm. 'Kōrero mai.'

Eventually Edwin spoke. 'If I am a naughty boy, will you and Pāpā die?'

'No!' Her voice was shrill, louder than she'd intended. Trying to calm herself, she continued, 'We will be safe. All of us.'

From the other side of the fire, Henry's voice carried towards them. 'I'm told that, after I left, it was confirmed they'd be sending out surveyors and that Te Teira had the right to sell the land.'

Loud angry cries exploded from the men standing around him.

Kuru leapt to his feet. 'Our whānau in the northern hapū will go into the land in the dead of night and pull up the survey pegs. Without survey pegs, the Governor cannot claim the land. We will stop them.'

Henry shrugged. 'They will fight you. They said as much. It's not right, but that's what will happen.'

'If it wasn't for Henare Mā we would know nothing about it at all,' someone yelled. 'They say we should negotiate with them, but how can we negotiate when they do not speak to us? They're not acting with manaakitanga. They're treating us like animals.'

'I will pull out survey pegs,' said Mere, Matāria's walking companion.

'So will I.' Another familiar voice: Atarangi.

'It's Aunty,' Betsy whispered from beside Matāria.

'Āe,' Matāria replied. 'It is.'

'What is she talking about?'

'I'll explain later, when we're back in the hut.'

'How will you travel north of the town?' a man said. 'Are we not stuck south of the township, without our cursed passes?'

Atarangi's mouth set in a firm line. 'I'll find a way. We have horses, we have waka. Only those who lack cunning get arrested.' This was aimed straight at Matāria.

'If we pull out their pegs, war will definitely come. There will be no avoiding it,' Kuru said.

'War is coming,' someone else said. 'This is not the start of this tale. We are already halfway through.'

Kuru motioned at the area around them with his arms. 'We know this land better than they do — every stream, every hill, every path. The Waikato were stronger than us and they couldn't occupy these lands. We are still here today; our ahi still burns in this place. The

British have more soldiers, but they're not us. We can win this fight.'

The group clapped. Beside Matāria, Betsy clapped with them. Edwin was silent.

Henry looked around at the crowd and over at Matāria, meeting her eye. *Come, Henry*, she thought. *I want to discuss the future with you*. She still didn't have a pass, so they could no longer go north. Tai had made Matāria see she might not have a place here, and with every passing moment his words felt more like a sign. Henry raised his left eyebrow at her. *Good*. He'd understood. Matāria pulled herself to standing. 'That's enough, children. It's time for bed. Haere mai.' She limped off in the direction of her hut, Edwin and Betsy following.

'Will we win the war?' Betsy said.

'Of course we will,' Matāria said. 'We have to.'

'What if we don't?'

'We *will*.'

'Can I go with Whaea Atarangi to pull up pegs?'

'No, Betsy.'

'Why?'

'Because you're too young and it will be dangerous.'

Betsy shook her head. 'I can pull up pegs. I'm strong and brave.'

'Minnie!' Henry jogged up behind them and took Matāria's hand. 'If I were a betting man, I'd place a wager that war will start within the week.'

'And you're not a betting man?'

'No, not anymore. I reformed my wicked ways. No gamble could top that chair you love so dearly.'

She squeezed his hand. 'We're *not* taking that chair with us if we go. When we go. I should have put it on the fire tonight to help warm all these extra people.'

'We'll see, Minnie. Let's discuss it all tomorrow. I've been so sick with worry about you I've barely slept, and I can't string two thoughts together.'

Matāria nodded. 'I'm tired too.'

She walked towards the hut between her husband and son, Betsy skipping around them: her little whānau. They all needed a good night's sleep because none of them knew what would happen next.

CHAPTER TWENTY-SEVEN

FRANCES

The news came with Mrs Archer, but before she arrived Frances had been sitting in the drawing room beside Mother, who had already traversed flowers, the weather and George's talents as a farmer. Mother also talked at length about how inconvenienced they were by having to replace Kitty, who had resigned from her position three days ago.

'You're not the worst,' Kitty had said to Frances as she waited to be collected by a friend. Kitty's belongings were stuffed into a sack beside her.

'I wish you weren't leaving,' Frances had said.

'It is all because of your brother,' Kitty said. 'If he had only—'

At that moment Kitty's friend had arrived and she swiftly departed the farm without looking back, leaving Frances none the wiser. She had asked Mother, who promptly changed the subject. No one told her anything: she was so sick of it.

'I always knew that girl was ill-bred.' Mother fanned her face. 'She was always acting above her station. I should have known she was trouble as soon as I saw her fashioning that crinoline for herself, as if it mattered what she wore. Well, you and I shall be busy, Frances. I work like a slave as it is; it'll be even worse until we get another girl.'

If we can get another girl, Frances thought. 'Yes,' she said instead. 'Indeed.'

She would ask about Clementine now — it was the perfect time. Mother wasn't in a particularly bad mood — there had been no further mention of peaches, or Henry, or how slighted she'd felt by one of the women at the town meeting. There was even a touch of pleasure in her lamentations about Kitty leaving, as it gave her something new to complain about.

'Mother . . .'

Something caught her eye out the front window: a woman was hurrying up the path. It was Mrs Archer, walking briskly, face bright red, dressed in her usual visiting attire: a plaid silk dress with large skirts, a dark blue knitted shawl and a straw bonnet.

'Oh, look,' Frances said. 'Mrs Archer is coming.'

Mother squinted out the window. 'Fancy that. A visit from Mrs Archer herself. I know exactly why she has come: to gloat that I have lost my only servant, and to find out the sordid details so she can tell the other women all about my misfortune. Mark my words.'

Frances stood up to greet their neighbour. 'I suppose we shall soon find out.'

'Horrid woman,' Mother continued. 'How dare she come here. She was extremely impolite the other day, telling me George was too sharp with the girl. Mrs Archer has no idea whatsoever of how useless Kitty was or how hard it is to manage a certain sort of servant. Besides which, it is none of her business.'

A knock sounded on the door and Frances hurried to open it.

'Good day, Mrs Archer.'

Mrs Archer had beads of sweat rolling down her forehead. 'Good day, Frances.' She dabbed her brow with the back of her hand. 'I apologise for the imposition, but I have some news I want to share with you right away.'

'Of course.' Frances shook Mrs Archer's hand. 'Won't you come in?'

Mother stood as Mrs Archer entered the front room. 'How pleasant to see you,' she said, bowing stiffly. 'To what do we owe the honour?'

'Please, Mrs Archer, sit,' Frances said, since her mother did not.

Their guest sat in the nearest balloon-back chair. 'I have much to tell you. As soon as I catch my breath.'

'Frances will fetch you a cup of tea and a slice of cake.'

Passing the empty meat safe on the cool side of the house, Frances walked quickly to the small kitchen. It was a nuisance to get to in the rain, but far enough away from the house for the courtyard to act as a barrier in the case of a fiery accident. A large open fireplace took up one wall and was almost as tall as Frances herself. She noticed the flames needed stoking again, and the pile of wood by the door was getting low. George would have to see to that; Frances drew the line at wielding an axe.

Against the other wall hung a row of shiny metal pots and pails below several shelves of crockery. The butter churn took up a corner of the room, and Frances realised with a jolt that it would now be her job to turn it. The scoured table was covered in an array of cooking instruments, utensils, bowls and plates, as well as jars of pickled cucumbers, elderberry syrup and preserved fruit.

In her haste to leave, Kitty had left quite a muddle, though when Frances took the sugarloaf from the dresser, she was pleased to see that order reigned there. The sacks of oatmeal, rice and potatoes were half full, Frances noted; however, judging by the hole gnawed in the hessian, the flour needed to be moved out of reach of whatever rodent had helped itself.

Alas, she would be spending a lot more time in here now, not to mention doing all the other chores, most of which were far less pleasant than baking bread. But right now she had refreshments to prepare and could only be grateful that Kitty had baked a cake before her departure, and that Mother had not eaten it all in the interim.

Once the water had boiled over the fire, Frances carried the loaded tray through to the drawing room, where Mother and Mrs Archer were smiling at each other from their respective chairs. Frances listened to their conversation as she poured the tea.

'I could have sworn you were cross with me,' Mrs Archer said. 'Why, you barely spoke to me at the town meeting.'

'Bah! I scarcely spoke to anyone — all my time was spent listening. Of course I was not ignoring you, dear friend.'

'Oh, I am relieved,' Mrs Archer said. 'I thought I heard you refer to me as a battle-axe when you were speaking to the other women. I must have been mistaken.'

'Of course I would not call you a battle-axe! You misheard me. I may have been talking about how, if there were to be a battle, we needed to sharpen our axe. Nothing to do with you at all!'

Mrs Archer's eyes were bright. If Frances didn't know better, she'd think their neighbour was mocking Mother.

'I am glad we have that settled,' Mrs Archer said. 'Now, let us get to the business that brings me here today—'

'Why would I be cross with you, my dear friend?' Mother cut across her. 'I have simply been out of sorts recently.'

Frances, now seated, took a sip of tea, careful not to meet Mother's eye.

'I don't doubt that for a moment,' Mrs Archer said. 'Anyway, my son just this hour came back from town with some information I wanted to share—'

'Your son is now engaged to be married, is he not? It is the talk of the town!'

'He is — to the lovely Anne Grant. They will marry as soon as these problems with the Māori people have blown over. I like her very much.'

'The women in this town are quite dismissive of George, you know. It makes no sense to me whatsoever, especially as he is a landowner. Someone must be spreading dreadful lies about him. That's his suspicion, for there can be no other explanation. I wager it's that scoundrel Henry White. Why, you heard with your own ears how he slandered George at the meeting.'

Mrs Archer sipped her tea. 'How vexing that must have been for George. Now, to update you on what I have learned—'

'Speaking of vexing, did you hear what Mrs Halcombe said to Mrs Burrows at the most recent meeting of the Floral Society? Mrs Burrows told me that Mrs Halcombe was very dismissive of her native lilies. It was *quite* the drama, and even more so when we later learned their husbands had fallen out over the upkeep of that orchard they'd bought together.'

'Oh? I had not heard that. They are both perfectly pleasant to me when I see them. I am surprised they would turn against each other like that.'

'Well, you don't know the half of it, then. I am in fact growing a flower garden myself, and am planning a garden soirée for the ladies of the Floral Society. I have decided to invite Mrs Burrows instead of Mrs Halcombe. Of course I could not invite both of them. If I did, drama would most certainly ensue yet again.'

Mrs Archer's voice now contained a hint of irritation. 'I am certain you could invite them both, and they would be polite to each other in company — if, indeed, we are even in a position to host garden soirées any longer. Which brings me to what my son said—'

'Oh, no.' Mother shook her head. 'I couldn't possibly invite both Mrs Burrows and Mrs Halcombe. That simply would *not* do. I have a nose that discerns the scent of drama better than most. And my garden will be so lovely, it would be such a terrible shame for discord to spoil the event.'

Mrs Archer placed her teacup on its saucer. She met Frances's eye in what might have been a wink.

'Yes,' Mrs Archer said. 'It would be a shame.'

'What brings you to visit us today, Mrs Archer?' Frances asked. 'You seemed to have walked in quite a hurry. I imagine you have something to tell us?'

Mrs Archer turned to Frances with obvious relief. 'I have news from my son. He was in the township where he saw the notice.'

'What did he see?' Mother asked. 'Tell me! I've been dying to hear your news ever since you arrived.'

When Mrs Archer spoke again, her voice quivered. 'Apparently Māori radicals have removed the survey pegs in the block everyone is arguing about. That troublemaker Wiremu Kīngi is refusing to apologise, so Lieutenant Colonel Murray has made a declaration of martial law.'

Mother gasped.

Mrs Archer continued. 'The Rifle Volunteers and the militia have been called up for active service — including my son.'

Mother wailed. 'Oh, my! That means my George will have to fight. How *horrid*. Oh no!'

Frances's head filled with a cascade of thoughts so intense she struggled to focus. Eventually, one bubbled to the surface. They were at war.

CHAPTER TWENTY-EIGHT

MATĀRIA

The news of martial law reached the papakāinga after Niko met the German missionary while setting eel traps at the lagoon. Father Schmidt was known to walk around the area in the mornings: praying, singing, contemplating whatever sorts of things he ruminated upon while alone.

'This might be war, boy,' he had apparently said in broken Māori. 'You'll want to keep your head low, that's my advice. We are in a state of martial law. Go back to the pā and tell your people what I have told you. I do not dare go myself as some of your elders are angry with me.'

Niko was a swift runner, much faster than most, and he ran back to the papakāinga with the news. Some liked to joke that he learned to run from having to dart away quickly after making his trademark cheeky remarks.

The news spread quickly. Matāria had been sitting outside the hut, threading slices of cooked mamaku pith onto flax strings to dry, so it would be ready to take for sustenance when they fled. Henry crouched beside her, smoking his pipe. When they heard, they looked at each other; Matāria knew the alarm on Henry's face mirrored her own. They didn't speak — there was nothing to say, not without learning more. Around them, people stood in small clusters: talking, yelling, crying. Underneath all the frantic and confused words, several questions emerged.

'Is martial law the same as war?'

'How can it be war with no battle?'

'If it is war, why has no one told us?'

'Are we safe?'

But no one knew the answers. This wasn't like during the Waikato War, when Chief Kaihua promised to attack Te Ātiawa at the next full moon, and did just that. The rules of engagement with these British soldiers were unclear. Matāria's stomach was tight. Henry stared into the distance, grooves furrowing his forehead, reluctant as always to admit the depth of his concern. Just as she'd never admit to him how badly her leg hurt today.

Nearby, Betsy and Edwin played with the scrap ends of some sawn timber. They lined them up and made the wooden chunks collide.

'Crash!' Betsy cried. 'Bash!'

'Boom!' said Edwin.

'What are you playing?' Matāria asked.

'War,' Betsy said, pointing at the pieces of timber. 'This is one side and these are the enemies. This side is winning, though. They have more rifles.'

Edwin raised an imaginary gun at her. 'Lots more rifles. More than sixty-seven.'

Matāria turned away so they couldn't see the sadness in her face. Of course they were playing war. How could they not? It had lurked in every shadow for months, and now it was out in the daylight.

Kuru hurried towards them. His eyes were wide and he twitched his fingers, radiating a mix of fear and excitement. What did he want?

'Ata mārie,' Matāria greeted him.

Kuru nodded at Matāria and turned to address Henry, speaking in English. 'Henare Mā, I have a favour to ask. Can you ride to the store to learn what you can? We need to know what is happening.' Kuru spoke so quickly his words tripped over each other.

'Of course. I'm always happy to prove I'm more than merely the man who provides tobacco and chairs. I'll go right away.'

Matāria frowned. She didn't want Henry to get into any trouble but she knew he was the best person for this task. Those who knew him understood he was a white man living at the papakāinga, but to everyone else he was just another European labourer going about his business.

Henry turned to look at her. 'What's wrong, Minnie?'

She turned away. Henry didn't need to know her fears; she could deal with them on her own. 'Nothing,' she said. 'It's nothing. Go now.'

Kuru's shoulders relaxed, his fingers stopped twitching. 'I know that look from Atarangi,' he said to Henry. 'They say *nothing* but they really mean *something*. Kei te pukuriri ia.'

'You're right — but she'll tell me eventually. She always does.'

Matāria growled at the two men. How could they make jokes at a time like this? She understood men sometimes covered their feelings by making light of a situation, but there was nothing remotely funny about martial law. 'I can hear you two talking about me,' she said. 'I'm sitting right in front of you. And I'm *not* grumpy.'

'I know that look as well.' Kuru winked at Henry. 'Atarangi gives me that one too. Kei te pukuriri rawe atu ia.'

Henry opened his mouth to laugh, but caught Matāria's eye. 'Right. Well. I'll head off now and find out what I can.'

Kuru became serious again. Matāria could sense a deep anger in him, humming just under the surface. It evoked in Matāria a similar feeling to the one she got right before Rūaumoko rolls over in Papatūānuku's belly, making the earth shake: a danger that you sense in your entire body before your mind knows what to fear.

'Āe,' Kuru said, his voice controlled. 'Keep your head down and your ears open. And ehara koe i a ia.' Thanks given, Kuru trotted down the hill and out of sight.

Matāria stood to walk with Henry down to the stables below the papakāinga, where the horses were tied.

'Who wants to come and see the horses?' Henry called back to the children.

'Me! Me!' they cried. Betsy and Edwin threw down their game, leapt to their feet and skipped ahead of their parents. The twins' clothes needed a wash, their hair needed brushing, but they were clean, well fed and happy, in spite of the looming war.

'I want to go on the horse with Pāpā,' Betsy said to Edwin. 'But I'd rather go in a waka.'

'Me too,' Edwin said. 'Then we can see all the sea creatures and watch all the fish. Fish don't have rifles.'

'But we don't have to worry,' Betsy said. 'Remember? We have six hundred thousand guns.'

'I thought it was sixty-seven.'

Betsy flicked her hair. 'It doesn't matter, both are enough.'

Henry and Matāria exchanged a glance.

They arrived at the wooden lean-to, which could stable five or six horses, although only two remained today. A boy inside was shovelling manure. Henry barely registered the child's presence, but Matāria greeted him. Henry didn't yet understand that, at the papakāinga, all tasks were important. Unclean horses were not fit for use, so even this manure collector was a vital part of Te Ātiawa's ability to fight.

Edwin tugged at his mother's arm.

'Yes, darling?'

'Is . . . is Pāpā coming back?'

'Of course I'm coming back!' Henry said. 'Soon. In fact, you'll barely notice I'm gone. It shall be so fast that, when I return, you will turn to you sister and say: *What is he doing back already*?'

Edwin smiled at his father, but Betsy put her hands on her hips. 'You didn't come back quickly last time.' Her eyes narrowed, just like her aunt's. 'You were gone for a day and a night and another day, and Māmā was away even longer than that. And now she can't walk properly.'

Matāria put her hand on her daughter's shoulder. 'Pāpā will be back soon. And I can walk as well as ever. I'm just tired.'

Henry shrugged dramatically. 'But I *did* come back, did I not? And now I have something much more important to discuss. Edwin, Betsy: which of these fine steeds shall I ride?'

'The brown one,' Betsy said, her earlier question forgotten.

'The grey one,' Edwin said.

'Whichever is more tame,' Matāria said.

Henry laughed. 'The grey one it is.' He mounted the horse and grinned down at Betsy. 'I'm sorry I didn't go with your choice, darling. But, as your Māmā has reminded me, I ought to choose the safer horse, and I dare not disobey your Māmā. I am brave, but not *that* brave.'

Matāria put an arm around each of her children and the three of them watched as Henry rode down the path towards the town. He passed a group of women returning from the direction of the potato crops, and then he was gone.

'Pāpā will not die in the war,' Betsy said loudly.

'And he has a kind horse,' Edwin said.

As they walked back to their hut they saw a familiar figure standing watching.

'Whaea Atarangi!' The children rushed to her, taking a hand each. Atarangi smiled. 'Kia ora kōrua, Boy and Girl.'

Atarangi looked at Matāria, the smile dropping from her face.

'Has Kuru gone to join Wiremu Kīngi's men?' Matāria asked her sister.

Atarangi turned back to the twins. 'I saw you two playing an exciting game outside your hut earlier. Do you want to run back to it?'

'Yes!'

'Me haere, kōrua,' Atarangi said. 'Kia tere!'

The twins spun around and raced away. As soon as they were out of sight, Atarangi stepped away from Matāria. 'Kuru is going nowhere that you need to know about. You're not to be trusted. You've spent more time away from this area than in it, and your husband is as white as his name. He tangata pono kē ia? Henare Mā might not be honest at all.'

'You went away too. To the south with all the other Te Ātiawa. Most people here went away and came back. Why am I different?'

Atarangi's face darkened. 'It was *completely* different. I was with our people.'

'It's not as if I had a choice!' Matāria said. 'And Henry is trying to help us — he tangata pono kē ia. He's going to the store to find out what's happening. Kuru asked him to go.'

'He reports back a lot of information, that is true. But, as I said to Kuru last night, how do we know what he shares to get that knowledge?'

Matāria glared at her sister. Atarangi stared back. When Matāria had faced down George Farrington and those soldiers, anger and indignation had pulsed through her body so much she had tingled. That day, Matāria had felt as if she were made of metal. Yet, facing Atarangi, her own sister, she felt weak. Rather than finding something within herself to fight with, all Matāria experienced was a great sadness about all her deficiencies. The space between that Tai had described grew even larger in Atarangi's presence, threatening to swallow Matāria whole.

Before she could collect her thoughts, Atarangi was gone.

CHAPTER TWENTY-NINE

FRANCES

The conversation in the Farringtons' drawing room had moved on to the domestic arrangements necessary in the face of war. Mrs Archer had decided to drive into New Plymouth to buy some goods from the store as soon as their horse was free.

'I'll need maize, sugar and oats, as well as some potions for my various ailments,' Mrs Archer said. 'My son will be fighting in the volunteer militia, so he may not be able to help at home. You will be in the same position, I imagine. We women need to help one another.'

'Of course we do,' Mother said. 'Who knows what danger might lurk in the shadows, ready to pounce? Why, if you were to be attacked and scalped, I might even be the very last person to see you alive.'

Mrs Archer rose from her seat and stood by the door. 'I do not believe the Māori people engage in scalping — this is not the American west. But I take your point. I really must be off. Thank you for the tea and cake,' she said to Frances.

'How would we know whether these people partake in scalping?' Mother pressed on. 'Frances's old beau, Henry White, knows their ways. The very man who made a fool of himself by speaking at the public meeting the other day. I understand he has married one of the native women. Fancy!'

Frances felt heat creep up her neck and over her face. The drawing room felt smaller than before. She opened her mouth to speak but her tongue felt tied.

'Oh!' Mother said, looking at her. 'I hope I have not spoken out of turn, but we don't have any secrets from our dear friend Mrs Archer, do we, Frances?'

'Indeed,' Frances said softly.

Mrs Archer looked at Frances, her eyes kind. 'I've known Mr White ever since he arrived with his wife,' she said. 'The late Mr Archer didn't have a bad word to say about him — they often had an ale together down at the public house. And Mr White is hardly the first Englishman to wed a Māori woman: there are more around than we could possibly count, going back longer than I've lived here, and then there's that Mary Bishop who proposed to, and wed, a Māori man. That was years ago, but I am still not sure if New Plymouth society has completely recovered!'.

'Well,' Mother said, 'your husband clearly did not know Henry White very well. My George does, though. He could tell you a tale or two about the odious ruffian.'

Mrs Archer's face was expressionless. 'And I am certain there is no gentleman in all of New Plymouth who could find a bad word to say about your son.'

'Exactly,' Mother said.

Frances concentrated on her hands resting in her lap. Her need to get away from Mother gnawed like hunger.

'I must be off,' Mrs Archer said again, more briskly.

Frances leapt to her feet. The request was out of her mouth before she'd had the chance to think it through. 'When you do venture into town next, Mrs Archer, may I please come with you?'

'Yes of course,' Mrs Archer smiled. 'Of course you may, my dear. I'll come and collect you tomorrow, the moment my son no longer requires the horse for more important business.

'Thank you.'

As Mrs Archer retreated down the front path, Frances waited for the inevitable onslaught. Mother put her teacup down with such force the tray rattled. 'I do not see why you must go gallivanting around the countryside with Mrs Archer tomorrow. If George is absent as well, I do not know what I will do.'

'I will not be gone long, Mother. Two or three hours at most.'

'What if the rebels come and attack while you are all gone? Kitty is no longer here to defend me. Although I dare say that uppity girl would not be much use even if she were present.'

'They will not attack our farm,' Frances said with more confidence than she felt. 'Now, I need to take the teacups to the kitchen and work out what supplies we require from the store. There is also dinner to prepare, and much to tidy after Kitty left so quickly.'

Mother shook her head. She was hunched and pale. 'I need you here, Frances. If you go, I shall be all alone. If I am alone, I shall do nothing but worry about this impending war . . .'

'You could plant your garden — all the peach stones are gone.'

'I don't *want* to tend my garden while you and the horrible Mrs Archer are in New Plymouth together, like the best of friends.' Mother plucked a crumb from her bodice. 'You must brush your hair beforehand. Then, when you are scalped, it will be a tidier trophy.'

'Mother!'

'*Hmph*. I do not like the idea of you joining Mrs Archer. I don't trust that woman.'

'We women must stick together, as she said. I thought it was very neighbourly of her.'

'I would sooner stick myself to a serpent. Sit down, Frances. No, don't sit, fetch me another cup of tea. Then you may sit.'

Frances decided to seize the moment. She steadied herself on the back of a chair and turned to her mother. 'The letter that came from Clementine — the one you and George spoke of. I have not seen it myself yet. May I read it? Is my sister well? Is something the matter?'

'Stop!' Mother waved her arms in the air, her eyes wide. 'Leave me be! I wish to be alone; you talk too much. Can I never have a moment of peace? Go to your room. Or the kitchen. Or anywhere.'

'But, Mother, I asked a question—'

'Go!'

The two women stared at each other. Neither spoke.

'Go.' Mother's voice was quiet this time. 'Please.'

Frances moved towards the door without saying a word, leaving Mother in the drawing room, sitting with her head in her hands.

CHAPTER THIRTY

MATĀRIA

The sun was high in the sky when Henry returned, newspaper in hand. He looked tired, his eyes sunken. Word travelled around the papakāinga before he could tether his horse. Within minutes, dozens of people had gathered.

'Kōrero mai, tell us what you learned,' called one of Kuru's friends.

'What does martial law mean?' someone else asked. 'What did you hear, Henare Mā?'

Henry waved the newspaper in the air. 'Whakarongo mai!' he said in heavily accented Māori, and in English: 'Listen! I have the latest newspaper! I shall read it to you all this very instant.'

Those gathered fell silent and even the sentries standing near the pahu couldn't take their eyes off Henry. Near the gong sat the children, huddled together. Edwin and Betsy padded their way to the outside of the group and sat down: two heads covered in light brown hair near an ocean of black. Betsy was dressed in her usual smock that fell to her knees, but Edwin only wore a strip of fabric tied around his waist, like many of the other boys in the group. Matāria noticed he'd removed his shirt. Perhaps he was too hot, or perhaps he simply wanted to fit in.

'That's my pāpā,' Betsy mouthed to Niko, who sat beside her.

'Fishhhhhhh,' Niko mouthed back.

Betsy turned her back on him. Edwin did the same. Niko looked at his feet: he knew he'd gone too far — again. There were twice as many children as usual, Matāria noted, because the children from Pukeariki were there too, gazing at Henry with big eyes. Matāria couldn't imagine how exhausted these children must be after being forced by soldiers waving rifles to abandon their homes.

Matāria went to stand behind Henry — they'd earlier agreed she would translate into Māori as needed. Many in the papakāinga spoke some English, but the language used in the newspaper was complicated, even for her. Yet this was the best information they had until messengers arrived from other papakāinga with instructions on what to do next. Or until Kuru returned from wherever he'd gone.

'Proclamation of martial law,' Henry read in English. 'Militia to be called out.'

People looked at one another as a shudder of fear pulsed around the group.

'What does that mean?' someone called out. 'He aha te kupu "proc-lama-tion", Henare Mā?'

Matāria opened her mouth to translate. What was proclamation in Māori? 'Pānui,' she said eventually, although that wasn't quite the right word. Proclamation felt like a kupu with much heavier undertones than the word for announcement or notice.

'Te pānuitanga,' she said. That would have to do.

'It means we're in the realm of Tūmatauenga,' someone else said. 'With an enemy prepared to fight in all seasons.'

Henry kept reading. 'It says here that a land survey was commissioned, but it was "resisted by some eighty natives without arms".'

Shouts rang out from the crowd.

'Tino pai!'

'Didn't realise my arms had fallen off!'

'We'll show them how well we can fight with our invisible arms . . .'

Matāria saw Mere and Atarangi exchange a look. Had they been two of the eighty? Surely not — the surveyed land was too far away. But Matāria didn't feel she could ask.

'Keep reading,' someone yelled.

Henry skimmed the paper, then threw it on the ground. 'This makes no sense. It didn't when I first looked, and I understand it even less now. It doesn't say what martial law means — only that the militia are being called out and some more stockades are to be built around the town.'

'What did you learn from talking to people?' It was the same man who had yelled out earlier — Kuru's friend.

'This is what I know.' Henry spoke in a loud voice. 'You still need a pass to enter the township, but I know from recent experience that going to the border fort might not help you get one, so it could be a wasted outing. You will also need to stay away from the blockhouses. New Plymouth is bursting with idiots, twitching for a fight. And yet another boatload of soldiers is coming, and more weapons are on their way for the soldiers.'

Matāria felt numb. The murmur of voices became louder and louder. The two sentries returned to the pahu. Atarangi and Mere approached the man who'd asked the question, and the three of them were soon deep in conversation. The children leapt to their feet and ran off, Betsy and Edwin on the outskirts of the pack, but not close enough to be anything other than followers. Two children remained: Niko and a young girl from Pukeariki who had been sitting next to him. She looked very tired. The boy and the girl were similar, Matāria noticed — cousins, perhaps. The girl lay down, curled herself up into a ball and closed her eyes.

Henry interrupted Matāria's thoughts by laying his hand on her arm. 'Sorry I didn't find out any more, Minnie.'

'It's more than we got from the missionary,' Matāria said.

'It's not right, me having to be the one to share this information. I don't like it. I'd wager old Schmidt feels the same.'

'Kuru shouldn't have asked you. Asking things of other people does nothing but pass a burden from one to another. And it exposes weakness.'

'No, I don't mean that at all,' Henry said. 'Kuru can — and should — ask me such things. It's not weak to ask for help; a single person cannot do everything for themselves. My problem is that we are not receiving news directly.'

'Perhaps Wiremu Kīngi knows more. Someone could ask him?'

'You overestimate my countrymen. I imagine your cousins in the other papakāinga are doing exactly the same as we are — reduced to combing the newspaper and reading information that makes no sense, even to someone who learned English from birth.'

Out of the corner of her eye she saw Niko gently prodding the girl next to him, who sat back up, a confused expression on her face. A woman approached her and ushered her away. Mātāria was glad the girl was being taken somewhere for a rest. She obviously needed it.

Turning back to Henry, Matāria said, 'To beat the same scrap of fibre again, we need to decide what we are going to do. I don't want to wait until war is on our doorstep.'

'I agree. We need to find a way to leave. Soon.' He looked around: at the people standing in clusters talking animatedly; up at Paritutu. 'We'll come back, though. When the war is over. I know this place is important to you.'

Matāria thought again about what Tai had said. 'Maybe we won't come back. Maybe I'll never find my place here. I am of the land — I always will be. But am I really of these people?'

Henry looked surprised. 'If that is what you wish.'

She glanced over at Atarangi, who was still talking to Mere, some of the other women nearby.

'Perhaps it is.'

'We could try and catch one of the postal coaches going to Wellington or Auckland. They're still running — I saw the notice outside the store.'

'They wouldn't let me on the coach five years ago, long before martial law was declared. I don't see my chances being any better now.'

'We can take a horse and cart south.'

'Whose cart? We don't own one ourselves, and the people here need theirs. And we couldn't feed a horse for more than a day. A hungry horse won't pull a laden cart far.'

'Then I will go to the shipping office and ask about boats. We may be able to get passage, maybe to Auckland, or Christchurch in the south. I hear it's growing as a town; there will be opportunities for us there. We might even obtain a passage to Australia.'

'Australia? That's . . .' she paused to find the right words. 'That's on the other side of the ocean. It's too far away.'

'Surely anywhere is better than here? And if we can't get a boat . . .' Henry's voice trailed off.

'We will walk. We walked here. We can walk away. If we have to leave the path used by settlers, there will be trails along the ridges of the hills and along the shore. We can find them. We'll need to be mindful of high tide and watch the moon, but it can be done.'

'But your leg, Minnie—'

'My leg is barely hurting at all today. It's getting better.'

'It's barely hurting? Really?'

'I can hardly feel it,' Matāria lied. She looked past Henry at

Paritutu and the rocky islands in the vast expanse of ocean beyond Ngāmotu beach. Her eyes misted over.

'I'll ride back to the store tomorrow and buy supplies,' Henry said. 'I've still got some earnings. We'll be fine, Minnie. I promise.'

'I'll start packing our things. Those that will fit in a kete, that is.' She thought about Mere walking here yesterday. 'We need to take as little as we can.'

Henry winked at her. 'So we're not taking our beautiful chair?'

'We're not taking your chair!'

Though that reminded her: she should find room for the sewing case the missionary's wife had given her. It was small and its cloth wrapping was not heavy. Whenever she produced it to sew on a missing button or repair a tear in Henry's shirt, the twins were captivated by the colourful thread, the fine metal needles and the tiny pair of scissors. She had learned sewing when they stayed with the missionaries. It was a skill not denied any woman, though she had discovered that fine ladies only did embroidery. Perhaps it was like flax weaving — not for the likes of her.

Someone ran past them — a runner boy arriving from the north. Not far behind was Kuru on his horse. A cry went up as people rushed to greet them. Henry and Matāria went to join them to hear the news but Atarangi blocked their way, standing with her arms crossed across her chest.

'This information is not for you, Henare Mā,' she said. 'We don't know that you're not a traitor.'

Henry's mouth dropped open. 'But Kuru—'

Atarangi held up her hand. 'No. We are about to hear things about future battles. It is not for your ears, for you do not belong here.' She turned to Matāria. 'Either of you.'

'What are you talking about?'

'You married Henare Mā. That marks you as different.'

'Other wāhine Māori have married and lived with white men, Atarangi. It's been happening ever since the whalers came. Some of our men have even married white women — look at Wiremu Tahana and his settler wife! I am not the only one, and my children are hardly the only tamariki with mixed whakapapa.'

'Your hair does not flow freely and your husband built a chimney in your hut. You don't wear our ornaments, and you sit in a chair rather than squat in the dirt. Sometimes you speak with the dialect of the Waikato. You are not like us.'

Not like us. Matāria closed her eyes and waited for the sadness to descend, but instead she was overtaken by a bubbling, scalding anger. Atarangi could speak rudely to her — she'd come to expect no less — but not to Henry. Especially not so soon after her husband had done Kuru's bidding. And if neither Henry nor Matāria belonged here, what did those words mean for their children? She was furious. Her eyes flew open.

'You dishonour our tūpuna,' she said. 'Especially our parents. This is my land, just as much as it is yours. Your interests in it are no greater than mine.'

'It is completely different. And you got our parents killed by refusing to get in the waka to Mikotahi. Their deaths were *your* fault.'

Matāria flinched. Henry drew himself up to his full height. 'Please do not speak to my wife like that. You are good with our children, and I am grateful. But I do not like the way you speak to Minnie.'

'Minnie.' Atarangi spat the word out. 'You and your *Minnie*.'

Mere, who stood nearby, intervened. 'We have another war to worry about now,' she said softly. 'We all suffered when the Waikato came, but that was a generation ago. This is now.'

Atarangi recoiled as if she'd been slapped. 'Mere, it was Matāria who brought Tūmatauenga!'

Mere shook her head. 'Te Teira brought Tūmatauenga with his dishonesty. The settlers brought Tūmatauenga with their greed. The settler government brought Tūmatauenga by ignoring the wishes of our paramount chief. And we welcome Tūmatauenga because we will not let them win.'

Tears pooled in Atarangi's eyes. 'My māmā . . .'

'My māmā died too, Atarangi,' Mere said gently. 'As did my brothers — in battle, or as slaves. Others were kai tangata. My heart bleeds to think of their disrespected bodies; it will continue to bleed for as long as it beats in my chest. And look at what else we lost. It was so much more than people. Our carvings went into swamps during that war — where are they now?'

'Lost,' said Atarangi.

'They are lost to all of us,' said Mere. 'All we have are the stories of how beautiful the carvings were, particularly the mata kupenga — such an elegantly drawn net, everyone says, but the only place we can see it now is in our dreams. But mostly we lost whānau. So many Te Ātiawa left Ngāmotu and never returned. They may not come home for generations: they light their fires in Te Whanganui-a-Tara now, or in Te Wai Pounamu. The war of our childhood was bigger than you and Matāria, Atarangi. It was bigger than all of us.'

'But—'

'We look back at our losses and acknowledge the hurt. But we have enough pain to bear as it is. We must move forward.'

A tear rolled down Atarangi's cheek, then she spun around and rushed away. Mere nodded at Matāria and followed her friend.

The sound of weapons being sharpened echoed across the papakāinga. Henry and Matāria stood hand in hand and watched Atarangi go. Matāria's heart ached. Atarangi would never welcome her back.

CHAPTER THIRTY-ONE

FRANCES

The following day Mrs Archer collected Frances as promised.

'Tell that woman I am too indisposed to see her,' Mother had said before Frances left. 'Tell her I have taken to my bed.'

'Are you unwell, Mother? You're paler than usual.'

'I am *terribly* ill. With Kitty gone and you so busy drawing water, boiling up the clothes and cooking, I must now dust *all* the furniture, otherwise we will live in filth. I do not have the constitution for such toil. And those chickens! They haunt my dreams. I cannot live like this, Frances. It is not right. It's not right at all.'

'I fed the chickens, Mother,' Frances said. 'And collected the eggs. I also made some sauces that, I am pleased to say, did not have the consistency of clotted cream, unlike my earlier efforts.'

Frances had surprised herself by enjoying cooking their dinner the previous evening, and also found deep satisfaction in polishing the furniture until it shone. Fetching water, on the other hand, made her arms ache. That was when she missed Kitty most.

'You should not be doing a maid's work,' Mother said sadly. 'Your father would roll in his grave.'

Frances didn't respond.

Mother gasped. 'I just thought of something. Will you be back in time to prepare my supper? I will starve like a beggar if not.'

'I shall be back in good time to boil some potatoes, the same as yesterday. And I can poach some eggs as well, if you would like me to.'

'Such a dull meal. Do we still have no meat? Oh, how I would love to eat a dish of stew with some vegetables!'

'We have no meat, Mother. It is too expensive with so much of it going to the soldiers. We may not have meat until George is able to slaughter our pig, which would give us plenty to eat, and some to sell.'

'What about vegetables? We have those?'

'I was only able to retrieve three carrots and one cucumber from my vegetable garden, and we ate those yesterday at luncheon.'

'Surely there are more now, ripe for the picking.'

'There are not. But I will look in the general store for more interesting things to eat — if we can afford them.'

Mother made a huffing sound. 'I suppose that will have to do. Although, if you take too long with Mrs Archer, I shall be forced to eat the slop you use to feed the animals. So do not take too long.'

Frances was relieved that Mrs Archer was too polite to acknowledge, on being given Mother's excuses, that Mother was quite visible standing behind the curtain in the drawing-room window, watching as Frances pulled herself up into the cart. Mrs Archer twitched the horse's reins.

'You drive yourself,' Frances said, impressed.

'Needs must,' Mrs Archer shrugged. 'Relying on men is all well and good while they're here and willing to help, but it's not a very good strategy when they're not. This cart won't drive itself.'

They passed George in one of the front paddocks. He was wearing his volunteer militia regalia and high boots, which he'd hardly removed since acquiring them. Frances had seen him admiring himself in the mirror and twirling his moustache.

'I am sure the women will find me irresistible,' he had said, catching her looking. 'And Father would be so proud!'

In the paddock, he waved a long stick in the air, slashing invisible enemies in the sky.

'Take that, native!' His voice carried to the cart. 'And that!'

Mrs Archer chuckled. 'You have quite the family.'

'Indeed I do.'

'Do you sometimes wish you lived somewhere else?' Mrs Archer said softly. 'I mean, there is little here for a woman of your education. Our closest relatives are not always the best companions.'

Frances shivered; it felt as if Mrs Archer had seen her naked — exposed, vulnerable, completely as she was. She turned to look at the older woman, whose eyes remained on the horse walking calmly in front of her.

'I try not to think of it like that,' Frances whispered.

'It is nothing to be ashamed of,' Mrs Archer said. 'I myself felt the same in my youth. That was why Mr Archer's entry into my life was so timely. Marrying him allowed me to move away and be free of my own family. I must confess, in the beginning it was a large part of his appeal.' She chuckled. 'How lucky I was that love followed.'

Frances felt winded. Henry would have been to her what Mr Archer had been to Mrs Archer. So many of her fantasies over the years had been about the life they'd build together. It was what Frances had yearned for the most: being the mistress of her own home; not having to ask for permission to do simple things; not being criticised for having strong emotions, however unladylike they were. A lump formed in her throat. She should have given up on Henry and married someone else before the extent of Father's debts were revealed. But how was she to know? She stared at the sea in the distance, bringing her thoughts back to where she was: a spinster at the mercy of her brother and mother.

'I have no fortune to bring to a marriage. I did once, but that was many years ago.' But then, she thought, it had not been enough to convince Henry . . . What hope would she have now of attracting a suitor, both penniless and twelve years older?

'You're still young, Frances. And New Zealand is different from England — many men look for a woman who can help them keep house in a more practical sense, rather than a woman who comes with money. I understand from your former maid that you are a quick learner, so good things may happen for you yet.'

Frances smiled.

They sat in silence. Frances was deep in thought, while the other woman hummed to herself. A quick learner: what a gratifying compliment from Kitty. Frances had also learnt a lot since Kitty had gone. Why had she made such a fuss about picking up peach stones? It now fell to Frances to empty Mother's chamber pot each morning — that was so much worse. Mother of course gave no thought to the fact that, for it to be ready for use each evening, someone had to empty and clean it. Frances was determined, though, that Mother should continue in this blissful ignorance. Mother had sunk far enough without the indignity of thinking about who emptied the chamber pots.

They had caught up to several other wagons, all travelling in the same direction. Some were piled with furniture: tables, chairs and packing trunks stacked precariously high. Settlers seemed to be moving into New Plymouth from the farmland south of the city with whatever they could carry. Frances watched aghast as a wooden box slipped off one of the carts and spilled its contents in front of them. Knives, forks, plates and cups all fell into the mud.

'Oh dear. They were in such a hurry to move they didn't even stack the cart properly,' Frances said as they passed by.

'They must be terribly frightened.' Mrs Archer turned to the man and woman scrambling to pluck their treasures out of the mud. 'Can we help you?' she called.

The couple turned towards Mrs Archer. As they did so, a small wooden table slid off the cart and landed in the mud. Dread swelled in Frances's chest. She lived in the countryside too — not as far out as these people, but still outside the township and the protection of the soldiers. Perhaps Mother was right to fear attack. Should they be moving too?

'No, no. Do not mind us,' the man said, voice gruff. 'It won't take us a moment. But thank you for the offer nonetheless.'

'My best tea things!' The woman started to weep, plucking her china out of the mud. 'I cannot bear it. And now the pig has escaped too.'

With a look of commiseration and a flick of the reins Mrs Archer drove onward, past the border fort, past men digging ditches, along the coast and into the township spread out below Marsland Hill. Scores of soldiers marched up and down the road in formation, serious expressions on their faces. Nearby, people hurried about their business, heads down. No one was strolling along the road, stopping for an idle chat; everyone was in a hurry. Devon Road came into view.

'I understand that your maid is now living with a family on this street,' Mrs Archer said. 'I hope you're able to replace her, should you choose to.'

'I hope the same,' Frances said. 'You're fortunate to still have yours.'

'Actually, we have no servants. Just the boy to help with the animals.'

'Did yours leave as well?'

Mrs Archer laughed. 'We've never had help. Truth be told, my mother was a lady's maid herself, back in Northumberland. Mr Archer's father was a butler, his mother a cook. I was in service myself prior to coming here.'

Pieces of information about Mrs Archer cascaded into place — her competent manner, her independence, the fact she seemed acquainted with the maids of the area. 'Oh, that must be why you always seem so capable,' Frances said. An amusing thought leapt into her head. 'Does Mother know?'

Mrs Archer shook with laughter. 'Not to my knowledge, and I will not be the one to tell her. She would never have extended the hand of friendship to me otherwise.'

'I am ashamed to say you are probably right.'

Frances thought about the well-tended and productive farmland surrounding the Archers' pretty cottage: the garden brimming with vegetables, the healthy sheep and cattle; the fruit grove along the paddock. 'You do it all yourselves?'

'Yes, with our own hands.' Mrs Archer looked quietly proud. 'Of course we've hired farmhands over the years, but not many. Much of the area was a swampy marsh before we drained it, and the rest was scrub. We transformed it ourselves. The family whose house you occupy now did the same, before they moved to Port Chalmers.'

'I hadn't known that.'

'It's so nice to spend time talking to you without your mother present,' Mrs Archer said with startling directness. 'I don't think I've heard you speak so many words in the past year as you've said just now.'

'I suppose you are right. Having made your farm what it is today, you must be worried about losing it if the war doesn't go our way.'

'The thought keeps me awake at night.' Mrs Archer watched some passing soldiers and nodded. They nodded in return. 'We cannot lose the fruits of our labours. I couldn't bear it.'

'I hope we are victorious.' A vision of the Māori women harvesting maize came unbidden into Frances's mind, followed by another of Matāria being led away by soldiers. 'At least, I hope it is over quickly, and there are no lasting effects.'

The general store was now a block in front of them. Mrs Archer drew up to let a cannon pass. It was mounted on the back of a wooden cart pulled by horses.

'At least we have that on our side,' she said, nodding towards the armament. 'I believe it is called a howitzer.'

'Indeed,' Frances said quietly.

'Frances, I must ask you a question. You strike me as being the most sensible person in your household by some margin, so I hope you will take no offence.'

Frances looked away from the howitzer. No one had ever called her sensible before. 'Oh?'

'I have been told your maid left because your brother could not pay her. Is this true?'

'I . . . I don't actually know.' Frances fell silent, turning over thoughts in her mind. Mrs Archer did not interrupt her. Eventually Frances said, 'Do *you* think it is true?'

'Well, your brother does owe my son some money, and he hadn't paid the previous boy either — the one who now works for us. I must be frank and say everybody knows your brother is not a particularly good farmer and won't turn a profit for some time. So I do have concerns that the debt will never be repaid . . .'

Shocked, Frances sat up straight.

Mrs Archer looked away. 'Never mind, dear. I'm sorry. It showed an extreme lack of propriety on my part to raise something as vulgar as money in the first place. I'm sure your mother would blame my breeding. Please forget I said anything. As I said to your mother the other day, we have enough to worry about in these turbulent times. We must rely on one another.'

She pulled the cart to a stop.

CHAPTER THIRTY-TWO

MATĀRIA

The papakāinga was busy. Matāria sat on the chair with dog feet and prepared the kānga pirau. On one side was a large pail full of kānga that had been soaking in water long enough for them to ferment. Mataria's task was to pull the slimy shells off each of their wet bodies, placing the unhusked corn inside a kete. The kānga would then be ready to be prepared by the kuia for eating.

Other women sat outside their huts intent on their various tasks: gutting fish, readying eels for smoking, pulling the stringy fibres from the dried and roasted aruhe fern root so it could be shaped and roasted into cakes. Atarangi and Mere sat in their circle and stripped flax. Still more women arrived from the fields with kānga. Someone had appeared with a barrel of apples, someone else was retrieving kūmara from the storehouses.

Men rushed in to empty their full kete of kai moana for cooking before running back to the sea to catch more. Kuru strode around barking orders at whoever he could see.

'We need more aruhe to take north! He rau ringa e oti ai! And put more aruhe on the fire; we don't have enough for the warriors.'

'Kia tere, wāhine mā. Kia tere! This isn't the old times — we can carry more than we used to take to battle. We have a horse! But you need to work faster.'

'When's that horse coming back? Me hoki ia ināianei!'

'You men — if you catch more fish there will be more to eat. Try to catch a shark — there might be some out past the islands.'

Another group of men walked briskly past, arms full of shiny metal. Rifles from the storehouse. So many guns, but were they enough?

'We're taking too much from the land and sea,' said Hikimapu, a woman who sat in Atarangi's circle. 'We have already pounded all of the fern root into cakes; there's no more unless we venture further into the bush. And all of the gourds are empty — there are no birds left to eat.'

'Then we must collect more aruhe,' Atarangi replied. 'I'll talk to Kuru about sending people to get more, as well as filling their kete with berries and fresh pītau.'

'They're already out there doing that,' someone else said. 'I saw them leave earlier.'

Hikimapu raised her head. 'Ko Tāne mata nui . . .'

Matāria stilled. The woman had issued a rebuke about disrespecting Tāne — the sort of comment usually saved for private conversations or loud arguments. Not kōrero between friends at the harakeke circle.

Atarangi's cheeks reddened. 'Tāne-nui-a-Rangi would understand. He wouldn't have us starve.'

'But rāhui cannot be forgotten,' the woman said. 'Taking more from the land than can be replaced is disrespectful. And foolish.'

'I respect the land more than anyone.' Atarangi's voice was cold.

Hikimapu shook her head. 'We are taking too much from Tangaroa, and I am told that not everyone throws their first catch of the day back into the water. The eel nets were placed yesterday

— too soon since they were last used. We are taking kai from the ground while still plundering from the sea. Soon our lands will be barren until the next harvest, which is not for many months. It will be a long winter with empty fields and hardly any kūmara.'

Atarangi snorted. 'It'll be a long winter regardless.'

'We should go back to Pukeariki and collect the rest of the kūmara from there,' another woman said. 'We were only able to bring half of our stores when we were driven away. If we went back, we could also collect more blankets for all our whanaunga sleeping under the stars.'

'Go back?' said Hikimapu. 'Have your eyes escaped from your head? I saw all those soldiers waving their weapons at us. Did you not notice them yourself?'

Mere sighed. 'We couldn't risk it. Most of us don't have passes and the papakāinga is too close to all those white tents of the British soldiers. It wouldn't be as easy as slipping through the darkness to pull up pegs. I wish we could go back and get more of our belongings, but we can't.'

'I don't want a pass,' said Atarangi. 'It's a betrayal of our—'

'I know. We *all* know what you think, Atarangi,' interrupted Hikimapu. 'But we can't get to those kūmara supplies without them. And we must stop the plunder.'

'We have all these people to feed,' said Mere. Her voice was kind. 'We'll go hungry if we don't borrow a little more from Papatūānuku and Tangaroa. We're sending away most of our kai with the men for when they go into battle. We're not disrespecting the rāhui. There will still be fish to eat.'

'Āe,' someone else added. 'Without food, we can't fight. Without fighting, how can we win?'

'Well, I don't like it,' said Hikimapu.

Mere raised her hand. 'None of us do, Whaea. I don't like having to strip our lands of food when the soldiers simply get theirs sent in on a ship. I don't like that their men get paid to fight, while ours must tend to crops as well. But we cannot change these things. Atarangi is right: it will be a long, hungry winter. This is what we must do.'

Matāria massaged her sore leg and looked at the kānga in the pail. At least she was contributing to the effort, one slimy cob at a time. She might have a bad leg, but she had her uses. She could still demonstrate her worth.

'Māmā.' Betsy slid up to Matāria, Edwin a step behind. 'What are you doing?'

Betsy's face was pink and a bead of sweat ran down her forehead. She must have run here.

'I'm preparing kānga for cooking,' Matāria said. 'See — look at how much I've done already.'

Edwin hovered behind his sister, his face paler than Betsy's, and he had black shadows under his eyes. Neither child had slept well last night. Matāria had heard them stirring each time she woke up herself.

'Have you two packed your favourite taonga like I asked?' If Henry came home with news of a berth aboard a ship, or with some other means of travel, they would need to leave straight away. And if he didn't, they would have to start walking. Either way, their departure was imminent.

'Yes, Māmā,' they said in unison.

'In that case, you may go and play with the other children.'

The twins exchanged a look.

'What's wrong? What is it you're not telling your māmā?'

'Nothing.' Betsy blotted her forehead with her sleeve.

'Nothing.' Edwin's hands trembled.

'You're both as bad at lying as your father. What's going on?'

Betsy and Edwin shrugged, then spoke in unison. 'We don't want you to worry.'

'Please tell me. I'll worry if you don't.'

Betsy's eyes filled with tears. 'They call me fishhhhhh and say that our pāpā is a spy and our māmā is a slave.'

'Oh, do they? Right, well, I'm going to tell them what I think of them speaking like that to you.'

'No!' cried Betsy.

'Please don't!' said Edwin. 'If you do, they won't want to play with us.'

Matāria put down the kānga, wiped her hands on her skirts and spread her arms wide. Edwin and Betsy rushed to her, one on each side. She kissed each of them on the top of the head. Betsy was even warmer to touch than she'd thought.

'I'm sick of playing anyway.' Betsy pulled her frock up over her head, standing in nothing but her shift. 'I'm hot, Māmā. And I want to lie down.'

'Of course, my darling,' Matāria said. 'Go into the hut and rest.'

Matāria's resolve stiffened. These unkind children would not be taunting her twins any longer. They could make new friends, wherever they ended up.

Betsy shuffled into the hut and Matāria turned to Edwin.

'You have done nothing wrong. You have nothing to be ashamed of,' she said. 'Your pāpā and I love you. That's all that matters. Those children are being silly and mean.'

Edwin shook his head. He spoke quietly. 'But that isn't why they don't want to play.'

'No?' Matāria bent close to him so she could hear properly.

'Lots of them are too sick to play.'

'Sick?' The world stilled. 'What's the matter with them?'

Matāria remembered the girl from the other papakāinga she'd

seen lying down the day martial law was declared. The girl had looked deathly tired, but maybe it had been something else.

'Niko's māmā told us he hasn't even woken up yet. And she said some of the other children feel sick and have bad coughs. That's why they don't want to play.'

Matāria felt cold all over. The papakāinga was so crowded, disease would spread swiftly and without mercy. The timing could not be worse. She went to check on Betsy, who lay on her back in the half-light, eyes closed. Her breath came in short pants. Matāria put her hand on her daughter's forehead.

It was on fire.

CHAPTER THIRTY-THREE

FRANCES

Frances and Mrs Archer climbed down from the cart. Over a dozen men stood in small circles in the square, gesticulating and talking loudly. A handful of women were gathered around the bench where Frances had sat with Matāria, and Mrs Archer rushed to join them.

'Good day,' Frances heard her say. 'I thought I might see some of you here. I hope you have left me some oats!'

Snippets of conversation reached Frances's ears as she stood at the edge of the square. Certain words were being repeated over and over: war, fighting, land.

'The natives won't know what hit them,' a man said in a low voice, 'especially once those reinforcements arrive on the *Niger*.'

'I heard talk of more howitzers on board,' said another in moleskin trousers and a blue shirt.

A third interjected. 'I've got a rifle that's ready to be shot for Queen and country.'

Their words gave Frances a headache. Clearly these were not empty threats — what would it mean for George and Mother and herself, for the other farmers, for Matāria and Henry? Everyone she knew had something at stake in this conflict.

She became aware that silence had fallen over the group. The only sound was a lone bird singing from the trees behind the shop: what could have caused everyone to stop talking?

A man walked through the crowd, pretending to ignore everyone's stares. Frances would recognise that gait anywhere. It was Henry, walking towards her. This was the fourth time she'd seen him in New Plymouth, and she was relieved his presence no longer had a dizzying effect. And she was getting used to him being taller, broader and scruffier than she remembered.

Someone muttered audibly at Henry. 'Go back to your Māori wife, traitor.'

'You should be ashamed of yourself, coming here,' someone else said. 'We know you live in that hovel by the beach. That is where you should return.'

'We don't need you spreading our secrets, spy!' a woman yelled from the bench.

Henry ignored them all. From what Frances understood, he had always attracted some disapprobation from his countrymen for his marriage and manners, but he had still retained friends among the settlers. Now, however, no one spoke on his behalf. As he approached, his shoulders were tight and he seemed tired. Very tired. Poor Henry, things must have been so hard for him recently. Him and Matāria both.

He reached Frances and smiled, though his eyes did not crinkle. 'Frances Farrington! We meet again — and here again, of all places. Is your brother with you?'

'No, he and my mother are at the farm.'

Henry exhaled. 'Just you then. Shall we step inside?' He gestured towards the people gathered. 'I don't trust this lot: they have more bravado than sense.'

He opened the shop door and motioned for Frances to enter.

Neither Mr Thorpe nor Dora were in sight. The shelves were largely bare, the wooden boxes usually overflowing with produce contained very little, and the flour bins were similarly depleted. Only three glass jars remained on the counter, all containing a mysterious green salve.

'Oh my goodness,' Frances said. 'Almost everything has been bought.'

'So I see.' Henry's eyes darted around the store. 'I was hoping for more than this.'

'What will you do?'

Henry dabbed his forehead with his sleeve. 'We're leaving very soon. But I've been denied passage on every ship I've approached: all of the berths on departing vessels have already been claimed. We will be walking at this rate.'

Frances laughed nervously.

'I'm not joking,' Henry said.

'Do you mean you would just walk away? As in . . .' Frances searched for the right word. 'Walk?' she said meekly. 'But doesn't Mrs White have a bad leg? I saw her limping that day.'

'She does.'

'Oh. Well, I'm sure you'll find a way.'

Frances wasn't sure of any such thing. The only fact she had a grasp on was that this was the first time she and Henry had been alone in twelve years. This was her chance — perhaps her last chance, if he was leaving. She felt faint, but forced herself to the point. She mustn't squander the opportunity with needless chatter.

'I know this is terribly presumptuous, but there was something I have been wanting to ask you for some time,' she said. 'Every time we meet has been inconvenient, to say the least. We *did* used to talk about all sorts of things, though. Do you remember?'

'Yes.' Henry's voice was hard. 'No. I don't know, I really don't think that much about London. My parents died, as you know, and my siblings have scattered to the four corners of the Earth. And things weren't very good for me in London at the end. I had good reason to forget the place.'

She looked him square in the eye. 'It was the same for me. Only an unmarried woman doesn't have the luxury of leaving a place simply because she wants to.' Frances took in Henry's surprised expression. 'But that is not what I wanted to ask you. I need to talk to you about another matter. My brother, George.'

Henry seemed startled. 'What do you want to know? I . . . I'm not sure where to start. I don't know what you already know.' He looked past Frances towards the door.

'You can assume that I know nothing whatsoever. All I know is that something happened that no one has told me a thing about.'

'I have nothing to say.'

'Nothing to say? All this time, Henry White, I thought you were *dead*. Or gone forever.' Frances spoke quickly, voice low. 'Until that day, right here, I had no idea you were alive and living in New Plymouth. No one told me anything. But now I think my family knew and have lied to me for twelve whole years . . .'

'That is something I can believe all too easily.' Henry picked at his broken fingernails. 'I didn't want to leave you, Frances, but George gave me no choice.'

'What happened, Henry?'

'In short? Your brother fed me a lie, and I was too frightened of his friends to challenge it until it was far too late. Your brother had the power to create trouble for me back then.'

'What do you mean?'

Henry glanced at the closed door and behind the counter. They were still alone.

'I have strong reason to suspect your brother ruined your family's finances, back in London. I went to your home to ask for your hand, on that last day we spent in the park. I remember the conversation as if it were yesterday. Your brother refused. Then he told lies to my employer, and used his contacts to pressure me into leaving England. So I went.'

'What did he say to you?' Frances's voice was hoarse.

'He said we could not marry. And we had a fight.' Henry almost smiled. 'I gave him quite an impressive black eye, from memory. It suited him.'

'Why?' Frances asked. 'On what grounds did he refuse?'

'He said you were already promised to another man and would marry within the month. And, if that wasn't enough, he accused me of courting you for the settlement that marriage to you would have granted me. That chafed my pride, so matters moved quickly from there. And so did my fists.'

'There was no other man.'

Henry gripped his tobacco pouch — a nervous gesture that Frances recognised from all those years ago in London.

'I didn't know that until I saw you here,' Henry said. 'Although I should have tried to find out more at the time . . .'

'I have no settlement to bring to a marriage now,' Frances spoke, almost to herself. 'I learned of our ruin not long after you left — all the money was gone.'

'You did have a settlement back then, though I hadn't known of it until George told me. He said I would never get my "filthy hands" on a penny of your dowry.'

A thought rushed into Frances's head. 'You were sent away so he did not need to pay a settlement.'

George was the reason that Frances was still single. George, with Mother as his accomplice. The room turned upside down. Frances reached out a hand to stabilise herself on the counter, but nothing was there. She felt herself falling.

CHAPTER THIRTY-FOUR

MATĀRIA

Betsy lay on the sleeping mat and Edwin was playing with his timber. As she looked down at her daughter, Matāria's breath quickened.

Before Tai had been cast out from the papakāinga he said illness happened to people with an unclean mauri. This was firmly believed in the old times and some still held on to the the idea. Tai would offer to cleanse a person's mauri, and, in so doing, would restore their good health. Sometimes he would say karakia and sometimes he performed the same actions as the settler doctors: administering an ointment or applying a salve. But it hadn't worked, which was one reason he had been sent away.

Betsy rolled over and groaned. Had Betsy damaged her mauri by telling too many lies, including inventing a new creature that was half-fish and half-bird? If Tai were here, he might have said as much, but, no. *Kāore*. Betsy was just a girl. This wasn't mate atua — an illness from the gods. It was mate tangata. And, in any case, the *why* didn't matter. Betsy was māuiui, and she had to get better. That was all Matāria cared about.

The calming sound of the sea washed over her. She would try not to worry right now. Matāria would husk more kānga and then prepare for their journey. And later, when her daughter was well again, she would talk to Betsy about not telling any more lies. Just in case.

Some fermented corn might be useful for their journey, but she couldn't take it. She didn't want to deprive the people of the papakāinga; those staying would need it more than she did. Henry had money from his work; he could spend it at the store like the other settlers. He'd buy them plenty to take on their travels: maybe some biscuits, potatoes, nuts or cheese, all foods that were easy to carry and prepare.

Kete in her arms, Matāria shuffled towards the women stripping flax, who looked up as she approached. Atarangi's face was expressionless. Matāria held out the bag to Hikimapu, who she'd been told was collecting the kānga — the same whaea who'd objected to them taking so much from the land.

'I have finished these,' Matāria said. 'I can do some more later if that's helpful. Or I could strip flax with you.'

'Thank you,' Hikimapu said, 'but there is no need for you to strip flax. Preparing the kānga pirau is more useful. You were a slave; you are more accustomed to the smell.'

'Yes,' Mere echoed. 'Thank you, Matāria.'

Matāria looked at Atarangi, who said nothing. They could have been like normal sisters, but they weren't, so Matāria needed to stop chasing something not meant to be. But there was something else she wanted to ask the women.

'Edwin said that some of the children are ill. He said Niko hasn't risen from sleep all day — Niko, who is usually full of so much cheeky energy.'

One of the women clasped her head. 'It's true — Niko is so sick he cannot drink or talk. My cousin says he is warmer than hot coals. She has to wash him so often they keep needing to carry more water.'

'Will he recover?' Matāria asked.

Mere's eyes pooled with tears. 'We don't know. We've already lost one child this morning — a young girl from Pukeariki, Niko's cousin. The sickness is sweeping through the children.'

Matāria stood still, taking this in. Niko was always making mischief and yelling fishhhhh at them, but he was just a child.

The women all began speaking at once, interrupting one another with their thoughts.

'There are too many people in the papakāinga.'

'We have nowhere else to go.'

'We need Tai to come back and heal them.'

'Tai took blankets and food from us, and didn't heal the ill in return. He told people they had caught sickness for breaching tapu, when it was mate tangata all along.'

A woman started to sing the old Ngāti Porou mōteatea that had spread from one side of the island to the other, almost as quickly as the initial sickness that gave rise to it — the one the settlers called scarlet fever.

Tiro iho ai au ki ahau
Rinoi rā e te uaua
Te koha kore o te kai ki ahau
Heke rawaho i te kiri ora
Waiho au kia poaha ana
He rimu puka, kei te ahau

Matāria joined in the singing. Once the waiata was finished, they lapsed into silence. Matāria thought about the song's final line: she felt like that same dead weed on the shore.

Atarangi looked at her. 'Are . . . Are The Boy and The Girl well? I saw them sitting beside Niko the day Henare Mā read from the newspaper.'

Matāria faced her sister. 'Betsy's very warm, but I am caring for her. She will get better soon.'

'Do you need me to fetch her some water? I . . . I don't want her to get as ill as Niko. He is very sick — he can hardly move.'

Matāria considered this offer. Atarangi was being nice now, but how long until she said something cutting? It wasn't worth it; Matāria didn't want help from anyone, and certainly not someone who used words as weapons.

'No, thank you.' Matāria crossed her arms across her body. 'Henry and I have done all we can. Betsy will get well soon.'

Atarangi opened her mouth, but Matāria didn't wait to hear what her sister had to say. She turned her back and hobbled to her hut.

If Betsy did have the same illness as Niko, Matāria needed to get water right away. Keeping her daughter cool and clean was important. After she had fetched water she would walk into the nearby bush and collect whatever she could find: kawakawa leaves to boil for a tonic; or bark from the rātā to soak for Betsy to drink. Her leg was worse than ever, but she'd do it.

She had to.

CHAPTER THIRTY-FIVE

FRANCES

When Frances opened her eyes the first thing she saw was Dora Thorpe, hovering over her.

'Frances?' said Dora, concern in her eyes. 'Frances?'

Frances sat up and rubbed the side of her throbbing head. Beyond Dora, Henry jiggled on the spot, holding his hat in his hands.

'Are you alright?'

Henry continued without waiting for a reply. 'I'm sorry, Frances. I shouldn't have told you about your brother's sordid history. Did you not even know about his debts?'

'I did not.'

Dora gasped, looking from Henry to Frances and back again. 'I walk in the room to see Frances fall to the floor, and now this talk of sordid histories? This looks and sounds exactly like the plot of a penny dreadful! You two provide much better entertainment than those tiresome men outside. You need to tell me *everything*.' She tilted her head to one side. 'Although, if it's George Farrington we're speaking of, I may need to fetch Theodore because your brother has not settled his account here for months, and we really do need him to do so.'

Dora put her arm around Frances's waist and helped her stand up. 'Are you quite all right, Frances? Let me fetch you a glass of brandy. My brother has some that is quite good.'

Frances wiggled her arms and legs and swivelled her head from side to side. 'Thank you, I'm not hurt. I just got a shock, I think.'

Henry stopped jiggling. 'Frances, I must go. I need to get back to Minnie and the children.'

'Is there nothing you want to buy?' Dora asked. 'I apologise for our diminished stock. My brother is out the back with one of the shipping workers as we speak.'

'No, I must leave. I bid you both farewell.' Before stepping outside, he turned and faced Frances. 'Be well, my old, dear friend. I'm at the papakāinga near the big rock if you need me. Although I may not be for much longer. But . . . be well.'

Frances felt a lump form in her throat. 'Thank you. And you.' She went to say more, but was too slow. Henry was gone.

Dora dusted the top of a large crate with her apron. 'Here. Sit. I'm going to fetch you that brandy. I don't know what you two were talking about but it sounded important. And you seem to me like a woman who needs some bracing.'

'That's very kind of you, Dora, but I think I need to go. Mrs Archer will be—'

Dora waved her hands, dismissing any objection. 'Mrs Archer seems quite happy outside talking. I saw her right before I came back in here, just in time to see you topple over like a badly made shelf.'

'I'm so sorry, Dora. What a fool I am.'

'Don't be silly. You hardly strike me as the sort of person who would pretend to faint for sport.'

Dora walked briskly into the parlour behind the shop and could be heard rattling glasses and decanters. Frances tried to steady her breathing. So George was in debt all over the place. She had already suspected he wasn't the best manager of money. George must have taken after Father in more than name alone. Frances straightened her old brown dress. She used to wear such fine gowns before Father died. Even her mourning dresses were made from the best velvet.

She sat up straight and gasped. What if the debts had never been Father's and had belonged to George all along?

It couldn't possibly be true. Or, rather, it was too terrible to be true, because of the damage the debts had done to her poor, sweet father's reputation.

And yet it was so obvious — Frances could not believe she hadn't seen it all along. Father had been a careful man who had stayed away from the usual vices. And they hadn't heard anything about debts while Father had still been alive or for over a year after his death. There had been no hint whatsoever of poor management on his part.

Frances felt suddenly overcome with sadness. All these years she'd carried heavy, conflicting feelings about Father. She had welcomed the pain of Henry's disappearance as a distraction from turning over in her mind all the ways her father had failed their family. But it had not been Father. It was George.

The back door swung open and Mr Thorpe stepped through, carrying a glass of brandy. 'Miss Farrington!' He smiled widely. 'Dora said you were here. She poured you this, then was unaccountably called on an errand. I don't know where, but she asked me to deliver it to you in her absence. So here I am.'

'Good afternoon, Mr Thorpe, and thank you.' Frances instantly felt a little better. Mr Thorpe had that effect on her — it was as if he warmed her up, ever so slightly.

Mr Thorpe handed her the glass. 'It is always a treat to see you, Miss Farrington.' He sat on the edge of another crate.

'Please, call me Frances. Your sister does, and it seems absurd to call me Miss Farrington while we're alone in a room, sitting on wooden boxes.'

'In that case, call me Theodore.' He stroked his sideburns. 'Yes, I know. Theodore Thorpe. My parents liked names beginning with "Th". Dora would never tell you this herself, but her name is a shortened version of Theodora. She'd prefer that it was the derivative of Isadora. Much more glamorous, apparently.'

'Both names are more interesting than Frances.'

'I think Frances is a fine name.'

'Thank you, Mr Thorpe.' Frances felt herself blush. 'I mean, Theodore.' To cover her embarrassment, she stood up and extended her hand for him to shake, suppressing the thought that her mother would heartily disapprove her being so familiar with a shopkeeper. 'How do you do, Theodore,' she said with a curtsey.

'I have the honour to be your very obedient servant,' Theodore replied gallantly, taking her hand and bowing.

Frances took a sip of the brandy. The fruity sweetness of the drink brought her back to herself: to the here, the now. It pulled her out of the murky undertow of fear and sadness about the past.

Theodore lowered his voice. 'I wanted to ask you something about our conversation at the public meeting.'

'Oh?'

'You said something about letters from your sister that struck me as odd. So I checked my records to be sure. Just in case I misheard you at the meeting, may I ask again exactly how many letters you have received from your sister since arriving in New Plymouth?'

'Two. Only two,' Frances said. 'If only it were more. How I yearn to hear from her more often.'

'Yes, that's what I'd thought you'd said. Well, according to my records, you have received seven letters from her over the past year. I keep a list, you see. It helps me defend myself against allegations of losing correspondence — you'd be surprised how often I receive *that* particular accusation.'

Frances looked up at him. Her hand was shaking so hard she had to put down the brandy.

'But . . .'

Theodore's face softened. 'I remember I passed two of them to you, as it was you who came to the store directly after the coach arrived from Auckland.'

'And the others?' She knew the answer to her question but felt compelled to ask all the same. 'Who collected the others?'

'Your brother.'

Frances's heart thumped in her chest.

They were interrupted by the store door swinging open. They both looked up to see Mrs Archer framed in the doorway.

'Frances! There you are.'

'I'm so sorry, Mrs Archer. I . . . I got distracted.'

Mrs Archer's eyes were bright. 'Never mind! I only came to find you because we must return home immediately. Everyone outside is buzzing with a new announcement, received not ten minutes ago. It concerns us all.'

'What? What is it?'

'The government has declared that we all must move into the centre of New Plymouth, where we are to reside indefinitely. Boundaries have been drawn, taking in the area around this block as well as a few others between here and Marsland Hill, and all the way down to the sea. That area will be guarded by soldiers to ensure we won't be attacked by roaming bands of natives.'

Theodore looked concerned. 'Where will everyone stay? All the houses in the township are occupied. There are very few spare rooms.'

'That I do not know,' Mrs Archer said. 'All I know is this: we have been instructed to leave our homes. Immediately.'

CHAPTER THIRTY-SIX

MATĀRIA

Matāria carried a heavy pail of water towards the papakāinga. Her māmā always said water had healing properties, which was why, she had explained, water was spoken about with more respect than other food and drink: tōku wai. Not taku wai or tāku wai. The missionary in the north had also said that blessed water was to be revered for it was holy. Holy or healing properties — either way, water was important. It would work together with the plants in Matāria's pockets to heal Betsy, just in time for Henry and Matāria to take their children somewhere safe.

Her leg ached but she couldn't stop. Betsy had been even hotter to the touch, last time she saw her. Matāria wouldn't sit around idly; she would do whatever was needed, and without her sister's help, especially as Atarangi's offer had clearly been hollow. If she had really meant to help, she would be here now.

A clamour sounded from further down the road. Dozens of men were gathering, including some of her cousins and uncles, as well as others from Ōmata, Ōakura and other places in the Ngāmotu area. Some wore traditional battle garments: maro sitting across their loins, war belts of harakeke, mats wrapped around their left arms and hands, war cloaks adorned with feathers and dog skin. Others had donned settler clothes: trousers, shirts and heavy boots. Some had mere made of pounamu, or a wahaika of whalebone either tucked into their belt or looped around their hand with a strip of dog skin. Others carried patu made of stone or wood. Some had old muskets; a handful carried rifles.

All wore serious expressions. Matāria put her pail on the ground and watched the men pass, nodding encouragingly whenever one met her eye. How different they were to the soldiers she'd seen at Marsland Hill. The Māori men seemed much less organised, with their mismatched clothes and obvious lack of marching drill. Matāria smiled. More disorganised, yes, but they were so much angrier and more determined. And they had much more to lose. These men were not yearning for the faraway places Matāria had heard the soldiers talking about while she'd been in gaol. The men in front of her had been trained for war right here, with rods from the mako tree, long before they were old enough to use the weapons they clung to now. They had their tūpuna on their shoulders and desperation in their eyes. They were about to defend their tūrangawaewae. And she'd seen first hand how swiftly those patu could crack a person's ribs.

The men hurried into the distance. Once they were gone, Matāria retrieved the pail, which seemed heavier. She groaned; her arms felt weak. Perhaps she should tip some of it out to make it lighter? *Kāore*. Betsy needed this water, so Matāria would take it to her — every single drop.

She was almost home when she heard hoofbeats approaching.

'Minnie, what in heaven's name are you doing?' Henry leapt from the grey horse. 'Here, let me take that.' He relieved Matāria of the heavy pail, leading his horse with his free hand.

Matāria told him about the sick children and Betsy's fever. 'She's ill, Henry. And at least one other child has died in the past day. I didn't know what else to do.'

'Poor Betsy. We must get her well again.'

'It's mate tangata,' Mataria said. 'Not mate atua. The gods didn't cause this. Even if Betsy did tell lies about fish.'

'Of course, it's not caused by any sort of higher power, Minnie. You've done well. I just wish you'd waited for me to help you.'

'There was no time. I didn't know how long you would be.'

'Where's Edwin?'

'Near the hut. He's not showing signs of illness. Yet.'

Henry looked thoughtful. 'At the store the other day I overheard some people talking about an illness in the town. Some children, as well as a handful of older folk.'

'What about the soldiers? Is there disease on Marsland Hill?' Matāria thought about the stench in the soldiers' camp. 'If the disease has come from their stinking camp, was it me who walked it back from there and gave it to my daughter?'

'Not that I know of — no word of any sick Hickety Pips has reached my ears. Terrible shame, really. Wouldn't it make everything easier if they were all struck down?'

Henry put down the pail to tether the horse. It was only then that Matāria noticed he had no supplies with him.

'Henry,' she said, trying to keep the panic from her voice, 'you didn't buy anything at the store?'

'There was nothing left.' His voice was flat. 'Nothing worth buying, in any case. And, as I was leaving, I heard that the farmers and their families have been instructed to move into a small area in the middle of the town, which will be patrolled by soldiers. I won't be able to go back. They're building another stockade south of the town. And the people I saw today . . . well, let's just say they didn't have much kindness to spare. I don't think I'm welcome there any longer.'

'And the ships?'

'I couldn't find us passage on anything. And they say a warship is due any day now, filled with more soldiers and arms.' Henry looked downcast. 'I asked and asked and asked. Until they sent me away.'

Matāria sank into the grass. Henry sat beside her and put his arm around her shoulders.

'So, we walk,' she said, leaning heavily against him. 'We walk south, as soon as Betsy is well again. We have no choice.'

Henry took a deep breath. 'I saw an old friend of mine in the store: Frances Farrington — I think I mentioned her before. Her brother is that good-for-nothing George Farrington, but she's not like him at all.'

Matāria turned to look at him. Henry didn't meet her eye.

'An old friend?' That was different to what he'd said last time.

Henry shrugged. 'We were courting before I left London, but it was no more than cups of tea and strolls in the park.'

'I met her. She kept apologising for things that were not her fault.'

Henry laughed. 'I'm sure she did. I felt bad for her today, having George for a brother, and her mother is a terrible snob. But my point is that she might help us if we ask.'

Matāria shook her head. 'We don't need her help. That woman needs to help herself first, not other people, especially with that family.'

'You're probably right.'

A man burst out of the papakāinga gates lugging kete of kānga that Matāria may have prepared herself. He tied the bags to the horse Henry had just returned and rode swiftly into the distance.

'Well,' Henry said. 'There goes the horse.'

And there goes the kānga, thought Matāria.

They stayed leaned against each other, heads touching. Matāria closed her eyes and inhaled Henry's musky scent.

A wail interrupted their peace: a small procession of people passed out of the gates of the papakāinga and headed in the opposite direction to the township, towards the urupā. A small body draped in a blanket was being carried by one of the women. Was it the girl she'd seen yesterday, or was it Niko? Or another child entirely? Whoever it was, they were being reunited with the earth a lot faster than usual. The tikanga around tangihanga was complicated in times such as these, especially where disease was involved.

Matāria scanned the crowd. She couldn't see Niko's mother or father, so it must be the cousin. Disease could be so fast — *too* fast. It demanded full attention and sought to punish those who did not pay it enough respect, leaving nothing but tears and pain in its wake.

A tear rolled down Matāria's cheek. It was not rare for children to die, for their bodies are small and not always strong enough to withstand serious illness. Atarangi's own babies had all died before Matāria returned to Ngāmotu. If Kuru had not been so distracted by war, he might have taken another wife by now to ensure his tuakana line would flourish. Sometimes, when Atarangi was absent, her friends in the harakeke circle would whisper that it was only a matter of time before Kuru's gaze fell elsewhere.

Atarangi was not unusual — countless other women had lost children before and since. And then there were the women who sang the waiata of Rangirua, for, like Rangirua, they had caught diseases from the settlers that meant they could never carry babies of their own. Matāria was so lucky her twins had grown to the age they were now. But now her daughter was so sick . . .

'I want to see Betsy.' Henry leapt to his feet and picked up the pail. 'I want to get this water to her now.'

He reached his free hand out to Matāria, and she held it tightly. Together they walked into the papakāinga.

CHAPTER THIRTY-SEVEN

FRANCES

Mrs Archer and Frances drove home from the store empty-handed. The sky was dark blue; the sun would soon set. Birds sang from the trees — a familiar chorus to remind all who listened that night was close. Frances was too tired to engage in chit-chat, so concentrated on saying just enough to not appear impolite. She didn't want Mrs Archer to think ill of her, for Frances respected the woman's honesty and sharp wit, regardless of Mother's view. And Frances had a lot to think about.

'When we saw those carts earlier, I never expected to be instructed to pile my own belongings up like that,' Mrs Archer said. 'Mr Thorpe is right — there is not enough space in that small area for all the souls ordered to relocate.'

'Indeed.'

'Look!' Mrs Archer pointed at three wagons travelling towards New Plymouth, all piled high with household goods.

'Surely we won't be expected to move right away?' Frances said. She thought about all the furniture in their house. There was much less than they'd owned in London, but it was still a lot more than one cart's worth. They would have to leave most of it behind. 'There's not enough time left today to pack and get back into town. I also imagine Mother will need some time to get used to the idea.'

'I am sure she will warm to it if she believes the alternative is being scalped.'

'When will you evacuate, Mrs Archer?'

'I've already decided, Frances. I'm not going.'

Frances gasped. 'You'll stay at the farm? Won't your son be away fighting? And I expect your farmhand will leave — you'll be all by yourself!'

'Mr Archer and I built that house with our own hands,' Mrs Archer said. 'I can see my late husband in every beam and board. He ordered the windows at the front for a wedding anniversary gift, and those at the back were for my birthday. I have spent countless days coaxing my garden into fruition — those peaches I give you come from stones I planted myself. My husband tirelessly turned a barren wasteland into something that provides a good living. This land has given us a life that we never could have dreamed of in England. I'm not leaving.'

Such bravery, Frances thought. 'I can't imagine how it feels to build something from nothing. Perhaps it is the same principle as baking bread, but so much better.'

'It is delightful, Frances. That house and farm are our life's work and I couldn't be more proud.'

'But won't you be afraid?' 'War is coming. You won't have anyone nearby to help if something bad happens. I expect there will be more raids.'

'I've made up my mind. People are falling ill in the township. I'd rather risk being attacked in my own home than die of dysentery in someone else's.'

Mrs Archer looked at Frances, kindness radiating from her. 'I saw you enter the store with Henry White, but please don't worry, I won't tell your mother or brother.'

'Thank you.'

'As I've said many times, we women need to stick together.'

Mrs Archer stopped the cart in front of Frances's home. 'I won't come in, Frances. I hope you don't think me rude, but there are things I must do before night falls.'

'I understand.' Frances climbed down from the cart. 'Good evening, Mrs Archer, and thank you for allowing me to accompany you.'

Mrs Archer nodded. 'Please give my sincerest regards to Mrs Farrington.'

As Frances walked towards the house she noticed George in the front paddock, digging a hole. He was still wearing his volunteer militia uniform, although the big stick was nowhere to be seen. She was relieved. With George distracted, she would be able to avoid talking to him before she had decided what she wanted to say.

She opened the front door. The house was quiet and gloomy inside. Mother would never sit without a candle in this light — she must be elsewhere, or asleep. But when Frances walked past the entrance to the drawing room, a voice came from within.

'Frances?'

'Mother? It's almost dark. Shall I light you a candle? We could light the fire as well. I know it's summer, but it's not very warm, is it?'

'No. I am quite comfortable, thank you.'

Frances paused, waiting for Mother to say more. Had she heard the news that they must evacuate? No, more likely she wanted to say something more about Kitty, or relate some long story about the women from the Floral Society. At the very least, Frances expected her mother to ask about her visit to the store. But she didn't.

'Are you hungry, Mother? Shall I make supper? I think we agreed on boiled potatoes and a poached egg?'

'I am not hungry.'

Frances peered at her mother through the gloom. She was sitting still, eyes fixed downward. 'Is everything all right, Mother?'

'I was tending to my flower garden earlier,' Mother said. Her voice sounded far away. 'The one underneath this very drawing-room window.'

'Oh good. And how is it coming along?' Frances asked. Best to humour Mother when she was out of sorts. Frances would tell her about the order to move into the township later.

'It will grow quite nicely.' Mother's voice was flat. 'But you are right, Frances, something is the matter, and it has nothing to do with the garden. I'm afraid it's something else entirely.'

Frances sat down beside her mother and studied her face. The creases around her eyes were deep and her cheeks were sallow. She was a sad, shadowy version of her usual truculent self. That usual self might fill Frances with exasperation, but she far preferred that to the pain she felt at seeing her mother so defeated. For a moment, Frances wondered whether that infuriating truculence had been her mother's way of helping them all get through the trials they had faced since Father died.

'What's happened?' Frances asked gently.

Mother sighed. 'I was just putting in the last of the pansies and a peach stone hit my hand — it had flown from that broken window.' She pointed to the window with the missing pane. 'And then another was thrown down. And a third!'

Frances looked away. So many overwhelming things had occurred today, and now they were back to the peach conversation. Was Mother going to make her dig more stones out of the garden? She felt a tiredness wash over her.

'Let me light you a candle, Mother,' she said, getting up. 'I'll retire to my bedroom after that.'

'No!' Mother's voice was sharp. Frances sat back down.

'*You* are the one who steals the peaches.' She pointed at Frances. 'We all know this to be true. You squirrel them away in secret, leaving none for anyone else. Not even me. Me! Your mother, who loves peaches so.'

Frances put her head in her hands. 'I don't like peaches,' she said quietly.

'But Frances, you always say this and I don't believe you. Who could not love that sweet, juicy flesh? I was so cross with you — so cross indeed! Until I remembered you were not at home, and we no longer have that uppity maid here either. Only George was here. So, what did I do, Frances? Could you ever guess?'

Frances's head began to ache. Mother was surely setting her a strange new trap. 'I cannot guess.'

'Then I shall tell you. I waited in the garden, as quiet as a mouse. As I waited, twelve more stones came from that window. Twelve! That would have been more than enough to have one each for dessert, some to stew with rice, and perhaps even enough left to make a small peach pudding. That is a dish you could easily learn to prepare. And how delicious would that have been, a peach pudding? It's been so long since we've had the ingredients, and it's such a good use of stale bread. My mouth waters to think about it.'

'Yes,' Frances said. She would not contradict Mother's views on peach pudding. 'Indeed.'

'I spoke to your brother about it just now as he had come inside to fetch a glass of water. He is out in the paddocks now, trying to secure the bullock. His method is to dig some holes to entrap the animal. He should be back soon — it's getting dark. But before he left again I asked him a question. Do you know what I asked, Frances? Do you?'

'No, I do not.' She had no idea where this story was going.

Mother took a deep breath. 'I said, *Why, George, I noticed that the peaches are all gone again*. I told him how disappointed I was, as there had been more than enough for a peach pudding. And do you know what he said in response? Do you know, Frances?'

Frances shook her head.

'Your brother said, *Frances ate the peaches*.'

Frances opened her mouth to reply, but Mother held up her hand to silence her.

'George said he saw you eating the peaches this morning, before you set off with Mrs Archer. He said there was no point asking you about it because you would only lie — as usual.'

'But you said this happened while I was away!'

Mother sank into her chair. 'I know, Frances, I know. You were at the store with Mrs Archer.'

'And I didn't eat the peaches before I went either.'

Mother was grey. 'I also know this to be true. I saw them myself on the kitchen table, right after you'd left. The sight of them brought me great joy. Yet George is the most honest of all of my children, second only to Albert. I also know this to be true.'

Frances inhaled sharply. Her mother's world had been shattered when Father died, the initial grief and shock of losing him being followed by shame and disillusion and even more loss: her house, her standing, and her milieu. Frances understood this caused her mother to cling ever more tightly to what she had left, but she also knew that, knowing now what she had just learned from Henry, she had to shatter Mother's world all over again. '*Is* it true, though, Mother?' Frances spoke softly. 'Are you quite certain George is honest?'

'Yes!' Mother's voice was loud and sharp. 'George has always been honest. Unlike my two daughters, who don't love me half as much as my sons do. Or did, in the case of Albert, God rest his kind soul. Clementine has been envious of George her entire life, ever since she was a little girl. She would always tell lies to make him look bad. And you tell lies also, Frances. You can't deny it. You always have this reason or that reason to be somewhere I am not. Don't think I haven't noticed, because I have. But it is all lies to escape me, your mother! And you didn't tell me you had seen Henry White, either. I had to hear it from George.'

Frances placed her hand on her mother's. 'Mother, listen to me. I did not eat the peaches. I never eat peaches.'

Mother pulled her hand away, tears rolling down her cheeks. 'Then it was Kitty the maid! She ate all the peaches when my back was turned. Wicked, dishonest girl!'

'Kitty has left, remember? We spoke of it not three minutes ago. She's no longer employed here.'

'Oh.' Mother sobbed again. 'Then it was the boy who helps with the horse. George didn't lie. He *didn't*.'

'But what if he did lie, Mother?'

The air chilled. 'What do you mean?'

Frances looked at her dirty fingernails, keeping her voice quiet but firm. 'What if my brother is a liar?'

The accusation hung between them. All Frances could hear was Mother's heavy breathing and, in the distance, the last of the birds singing before nightfall. Eventually, Mother leaned towards her.

'Never.' Her voice was low. '*You* are the liar. You and the stable boy, colluding to steal the peaches.'

Frances bowed her head. Mother would never take her side. Ever.

CHAPTER THIRTY-EIGHT

MATĀRIA

Henry returned with yet another pail of water and flopped onto the chair.

'Are you feeling all right?' Matāria asked her husband.

'I'm just tired.'

'I don't want you to get ill as well.'

'I won't.' Henry lay down on the mat not far from his daughter and curled into a ball. 'I'll just close my eyes for a little bit. Then I'll be fine.'

Matāria looked at Henry and Betsy on their mats. She turned to her son. 'Come, Edwin, let's go over by the kūmara storehouses and look down at the sea. We might see some more waka.'

They walked towards the side of the hill, Matāria's leg slowing her down. Edwin followed her, head bowed, feet dragging. She observed him out of the corner of her eye. His colour was normal, and he did not need to rush to the stick over the swamp to do his business. Edwin wasn't ill. Yet.

Atarangi pushed out in front of them.

'Matāria?' Atarangi pinched her lips. 'The girl is māuiui. The Boy came and told me so.' She patted Edwin on the head. He smiled up at his aunt.

'Betsy is doing well,' Matāria said.

'I will help you. I can take The Boy. You're limping like a broken horse, the sort they put in a paddock to die before its meat is fed to the dogs.'

'I am not a broken horse. I am a tired horse. There's a difference.'

Atarangi grimaced. 'That came out wrong. I've just bid Kuru farewell; I'm not thinking properly. Regardless, I can see you limping, and I know The Girl is sick. Let me help your children, if not you.'

'The children you said don't belong, you mean? The children whose names you won't even use?'

'Stop being stubborn!' Atarangi's eyes flashed. 'Stubborn like a limp old horse.'

The two sisters faced each other. Between them stood Edwin, looking from his mother to his aunt and back again.

'Māmā? Whaea?' His eyes filled with tears. 'Māmā?'

Matāria put one hand on his shoulder. This conversation needed to stop. 'We are doing well enough, Atarangi, but thank you for your concern.'

She turned to walk away but Atarangi blocked her.

'They lost Niko — the boy that played with your children. He went to walk with his tūpuna this morning.'

Edwin gasped. 'Fishhhh.'

Matāria stood still, shocked at the news. That boy had been alive and teasing her children only a day or two ago, and now he was gone. *Haere rā, haere atu rā ki ō tūpuna*, she thought. He had gone to his ancestors, as Atarangi said.

'I . . . I hadn't realised. Please tell his māmā I'm sorry.'

'Tell her yourself.'

Matāria glared at Atarangi. 'As soon as Betsy is better, we're leaving. We're going somewhere safe — we would have left by now if she wasn't ill. So I won't dishonour our parents anymore by bothering you. I know you think I should have stayed in Waikato as a slave forever.'

'I never said that.'

'You said enough for me to know exactly what you meant.'

'I have been thinking about it after what Mere said—'

'I don't care what Mere said.' Mere had supported Matāria with soft words that had landed on Atarangi like heavy stones. Matāria was grateful but it was too late. 'Don't you see? You're not my sister anymore. You're just someone I knew as a child. Much like every other adult in this place.'

'What's got into you, Matāria? You weren't like this before.'

Matāria's voice broke. 'That's because I thought — I hoped — that one day you'd accept me, but now I know that will never happen. I might as well wish for our parents to come back to life. I have been hoping for things that can never be.'

'Matāria, your daughter is ill. *Very* ill. Her playmate has died. The Boy might be next. Please let me help you.'

'I don't need your help. I don't need anyone's help. I can solve my problems myself. This broken kōtuku doesn't need you.'

'So I'm just someone you knew as a child?'

Matāria raised her chin. 'Nothing more. Nothing less.'

Atarangi made a guttural sound. She turned and walked quickly away.

Matāria watched her sister leave. Had she had been too harsh? No, it was the other way around. Atarangi had been hard on Matāria ever since the day Matāria arrived back at the papakāinga from the Waikato. Even recently, after Matāria had spent time in that horrible prison, Atarangi had greeted her with nothing but unkind words.

She heard a whimper and looked to see Edwin staring up at her. She'd completely forgotten he was there. His lower lip quivered;

tears pooled in his eyes. Matāria patted his head, but he pulled away.

'I like it when she calls me The Boy. Tama. Tama is a Māori name, at least, not like Edwin. And why aren't you more like the other women here? Why doesn't your hair hang down like theirs? You don't look like the other women at all.'

Edwin ran off in the direction of the hut.

'Edwin!' she called. But he was gone.

The hairs on Matāria's arms stood up. Edwin had never been cross with her before — it was Betsy who had all the feistiness. She should have told her children she wore her hair rolled and bound for good reason: when it fell around her shoulders, she was reminded of how long and dishevelled it had become when she was a slave; unkempt like a hairy animal in the wild. And Edwin was a good name — the name of the kind missionary who lived in the north with his wife Betsy. They'd taken Matāria and Henry in when the twins were born, paid Henry to look after the cattle, and helped Matāria learn English. English names had made sense when the twins had been born. She had one herself by then: Minnie. Henry hadn't spent any time in the papakāinga so didn't know Māori. Neither child had complained about their names before. But she and Henry should have told them. They were old enough now.

Matāria walked back to the hut but Edwin wasn't there. She sat on the dog-foot chair and looked at her daughter. Betsy was neither better nor worse. Her hair was stuck to her forehead, her skin pink.

'Māmā,' Betsy suddenly cried out. 'Māmā! I saw a rainbow fish!' Then she rolled over and closed her eyes again.

Henry still lay behind their daughter, hugging his knees. His face was also sweaty, his hair was plastered to his face.

Matāria leaned over him. 'Henry?'

Henry opened his eyes halfway. 'I'm cold.'

'You look hot.'

'I'm not hot.' Henry began to shiver. 'I'm cold. And my middle hurts. Badly.' He groaned and covered his eyes with his forearm. 'Ohhhh, I am so cold, Minnie.'

Outside the hut came a yell. Matāria looked up to see Mere and some other women rush past, kete in hand.

'Quick, the waka are leaving,' someone said. 'We need to give them this fruit.'

'If they run out of bullets, they can use the stones instead.'

'Kia tere, then. Hurry up.'

But Matāria hardly heard them. Henry had caught the disease that was killing children. Now she had to deal with this alone.

CHAPTER THIRTY-NINE

FRANCES

In the two weeks since they had moved into town, Frances had been busier than ever. The area in the centre of New Plymouth that had been allocated to farmers was scarcely three blocks wide and five deep, flanked by the sea in the west and Marsland Hill in the east. It was far too small to accommodate them all.

The move had been fraught. George and Frances had stacked the cart with some basic furniture, bedding and other supplies, but Mother was adamant there was room for more.

'I wish to take my card table,' she had said. 'I cannot bear to be without it, nor my favourite chair.'

'Mother, they will not fit,' George had said. 'We're taking your rosewood work table. Surely one table is enough?'

'Of course I need to take my rosewood work table: I was lucky to keep it when so many of our other possessions were sold. But the card table is *equally* special.'

'But we need to fit in the bags of oats and flour,' Frances had said. 'And as much other food as we can carry. We also need to take some more pots.'

'Nonsense,' Mother had replied. 'We can buy such things in the township, when it is only a matter of time before we have a maid again to use them. We must fill our cart with valuables of the sentimental variety, such as the tables. And my napkins and cloths and shawls and hats. I have already packed the daguerreotypes of Albert and your father of course. They shall have pride of place in our new lodgings.'

'I would also like to add my snuff boxes and collection of cravats, as well as *my* favourite chair,' George had said, 'but I cannot. This is all we shall take. I insist.'

Eventually it was time to leave. Frances sat on a pile of blankets and clothing, hugging to her chest the only personal possessions she had allowed herself: the tin box of letters and cards, the cushion she had made of chicken feathers, and her half-finished embroidery. Everything else had to remain behind. Waiting for George to start the cart, she gazed at the homestead: the small house, Mother's fledgling flowerbed, her own feeble vegetable garden, the fowl house to the side of the kitchen.

'Perhaps we should take some chickens,' Frances had suggested. 'They will be useful and there is still some space if we stack things differently.'

This time George had been listening. 'True. And if we take our pig and chickens we will have more to eat.'

'But my card table . . .' Mother had wailed though her tears. 'It came all the way from London. I cannot abandon it now.'

It had been no good telling her that the table was likely to be waiting for them on their eventual return. Mother demurred eventually after exhausting herself with her histrionics, and her table remained. She cried the entire way into New Plymouth, and became completely inconsolable when, upon their arrival at the edge of the town, the pig and three of the hens escaped into the scrub.

Helping Mother settle into their new quarters and adjust to a different lifestyle had swallowed up the next two weeks, until their attention was diverted by some alarming news: the first shots of battle were to be fired the following day.

Frances had heard it from George, so decided to walk to the store to see what Theodore and Dora had to say on the matter. It was as good an excuse as any to get out of their cramped lodgings. In other circumstances, she might have said the short stroll was a chance for some fresh air, but that was now a scarce commodity in New Plymouth. The population had doubled in the past fortnight, and the stench from overburdened privies and rubbish pits was so foul in places it was impossible to pass without reaching for a kerchief.

There were even more animals than humans. Valuable livestock had been brought from the surrounding countryside, and Frances's family were not the only ones who had lost pigs and chickens, which now roamed freely. More animals meant more manure. And more waste and filth meant more mice and rats, darting around Frances's feet as she made her way through town. It would have been enough to make her vomit if she had anything in her stomach. The dull ache of hunger was now her constant companion. She really ought to have pressed her point about packing more food.

Outside the store, she stopped to read the notices. There were dozens posted to the board, each half-obscuring others. She read those on top.

WANTED: Lodging for a tidy couple and six children.

WANTED to rent or purchase — a cottage containing two or three rooms, which, if outside the entrenchments, would bear removal.

WANTED: Female servant, apply to Mrs Newell.

WANTED: Boy to milk a cow and make himself generally useful in a small family.

WANTED: Two rooms to let.

Frances hurried into the store, where the Thorpes greeted her with their usual warmth. They had little to offer in the way of goods, but were happy to share what they knew.

'The soldiers plan to march at first light,' Theodore said. 'I have had it from at least three of them. It's all anyone is talking about.'

Dora snorted. 'When they're not complaining about their inadequate lodgings or berating us for running out of supplies, you mean. There's talk of confiscating all the Māori crops to feed the people of New Plymouth, but that hasn't happened yet. Not that we would see the benefit anyway — it would all go directly to the 65th.'

Theodore winked at Frances. 'Is that what you're here for, Frances? To tell us that our store is deficient?'

Frances laughed. 'You read my mind.'

She and Theodore looked at each other and smiled. He was wearing a colourful necktie that she'd not seen before. For a moment, Frances almost forgot her troubles. Almost.

'I don't know what we can do to prepare for this battle,' she said. 'And those complaining about their living conditions aren't wrong. George, Mother and I have only one room to share, as George has not been invited to sleep in the barracks. It's cramped, to say the least.'

Not to mention smelly and disgusting, she mentally added. The worst part for her was her constant close proximity to George. Whenever her brother was nearby, Frances felt skittish and tense. But she didn't need to share that with Theodore and Dora. Given how kind they had been to her, she suspected they already knew how unhappy she was.

'Our home is cramped also,' Dora said. 'We have another family staying with us, and you could hardly swing a cat without hitting someone. But what we can do? We can't leave the town anymore, so all we can do is wait.'

Theodore stroked his moustache. 'There simply isn't enough

space in this town for over two thousand people here and all of the soldiers on Marsland Hill. I intend to raise it at today's meeting of the volunteer militia.' He opened his pocket watch to check the time.

Frances studied Theodore. His face was worn, like so many others hereabouts, but with none of the smarmy arrogance of George's acquaintances. She could picture Theodore chopping down trees and clearing farmland, but not engaging in battle. 'I hadn't realised you were in the volunteer militia.'

'I'm not, but I've been invited due to my commercial interests.'

'I suppose George will be attending as well,' she said. Her brother hadn't mentioned it, but that was hardly surprising. Over the past few days he had barely been home, and when he was, he spoke in little more than grunts.

Theodore nodded. 'I imagine so.'

This meant Frances could go back to their room knowing George would not be there. *What a relief.*

'Oh, and Frances?' Theodore rummaged under the counter. 'There is something Dora and I wanted you to have.' He held out his hand, which contained three fresh carrots. Frances blushed — what a treat, given the circumstances. She hadn't eaten fresh vegetables for over a week.

'Thank you very much indeed.'

She took her leave of the Thorpes and set out for her lodgings on foot, carrots in hand. The streets were busy with foot traffic today, people walking in pairs and threes, talking loudly in anxious voices. A sharp odour pierced the air — on top of the smell of sewage. She wrinkled her nose. It was the miasma of illness, wafting from a small cottage. Frances recognised it as the way Father's bed chamber had smelt the day he'd died. She covered her face with her hand.

Around the corner was a road of wooden cottages and behind them sat three single-storey dormitories around an unpaved courtyard. They had originally been built as sleeping quarters for single men, and were the only accommodation the Farringtons could find. Some of their neighbours idled in the courtyard alongside a pig that lay in the sun. Frances made her way inside, ignoring the stares of the men. The air in their room was heavy and stale. There was only one small window, allowing for very little natural light unless they kept the door to the courtyard open. Inside was a narrow bed for George, mats for Frances and Mother, and space against the wall for their trunks. There was no room for Mother's rosewood work table, which sat outside their door, covered in a piece of scrim. Frances didn't dare tell Mother she'd spied the resident pig rubbing against it the previous evening.

She stopped in the open doorway. George was sitting on his bed. How disappointing. Shouldn't he be on his way to the volunteer militia meeting?

Mother was perched on one of the metal trunks. 'It isn't right, living here,' she wailed. 'I am not a servant and will *not* be treated as such. Your Father might have left us destitute, but this is just too much.'

'I agree, Mother.' George looked around the room. 'I *will* find something better. Just give me time.'

'I'd wager even our former maid Kitty has nicer quarters,' Mother went on. 'I saw her yesterday with that young man she is stepping out with. Unchaperoned, I might add. I was going to cut her but the rude girl interrupted my reverie to demand I pay her some wages. Would you believe it? *So* ill-bred of her.'

'I'm sorry that happened, Mother,' George said, 'but I wouldn't worry about her. We'll have another maid soon enough, when all this inconvenience is over. We'll have more land, too — that hill behind the house for all the sheep I shall buy. And, as I said, I am seeking out better lodgings. In the meantime, you are welcome to join Mrs Archer if this room is not to your liking. During a raid, you can fight off the natives together.'

Frances stepped inside while Mother continued, oblivious to George's sarcasm. 'I cannot! We would both be scalped! Mrs Archer is a fool sitting up there alone. I know what you are thinking, Frances — you are about to tell me that Mrs Archer said the Māori people don't scalp people. Well, she'll regret those words when it happens to her. I'll only be sorry she won't be alive for me to tell her *I told you so*. Though living here is almost as bad, if I take scalping out of the equation.'

George waved his hand dismissively but Mother was undeterred. 'I don't understand why we couldn't let rooms at the new public house. Two of the women from the Floral Society are staying there. They say that all the available rooms face south, but it is pleasant enough nonetheless. There are stables there, as well. If we had stables nearby, our horse and cart would not need to be kept two whole blocks away. That is much too far to walk in the rain, especially considering all the filth on the roads.'

'For pity's sake, Mother. You know those rooms are too expensive.'

'We can surely afford them with the profit you have turned on the farm. Why, were you not telling me just last week how well everything was going?'

George's eyes flashed. 'The publican raised his prices when I asked. He has it against me. I could offer him thrice what those others pay and still he would reject me. I blame Henry White for speaking ill of me around the town. I had no problems here before him.'

'Oh, that odious man.' Mother glared pointedly at Frances. 'And isn't he also the one who turned the butcher against you, making him close our account? Not to mention why no one will sell you glass for our drawing-room window.'

'The one and the same.'

Frances bit her tongue. In all the business of packing up and moving, she had not yet had a chance to confront George, much less tell Mother what she had heard. She would have to choose her time carefully — and not while they were confined to living in a single room.

'Your Father wouldn't recognise us, staying in servants' quarters.' Mother closed her eyes and hugged her body.

George clenched and unclenched his fists. 'He would not, particularly now I am to fight in a war. He would be surprised — but happily so.' He jutted his chin. 'I am going now to receive my instructions for battle. I will take my rifle tomorrow at first light and I shall fight. We'll show those Maoris a thing or two.'

Mother smiled, her litany of woes seemingly forgotten. 'I'm sorry, George. You are right: your Father would be so proud of you.'

'He might even remark on how Albert never would have done such a thing,' George said. 'My older brother didn't have the constitution — he was far too sickly. Unlike me. I wouldn't have died after being scratched by a stick.'

Mother looked over at the miniature of Albert she had placed beside her mat and said nothing.

Frances cleared her throat. 'Are you attending the volunteer militia meeting today?'

George turned towards her. 'What are you talking about?'

'I was at the store just now.' Frances set the carrots down on a chest. 'Theodore —Mr Thorpe — mentioned he was going to a meeting of the volunteer militia today. He was about to leave when we spoke.'

'A meeting? Right now?'

'That's what he said.'

'Why wasn't I told?' George frowned. 'What does that merchant know that I don't? You must have made a mistake.'

'Yes,' Mother said, 'or perhaps the organisers didn't know to find you in this hovel. Word might have been sent to the farm instead.'

'But I saw the other men at the public house last night. I'll go and find out what's going on.' He faced Frances. 'You're blocking my exit. Move.'

Frances scuttled out of her brother's way.

Leaving Mother napping on the bed, Frances walked through the courtyard — past the pig, past the cottage that reeked of illness and down the muddy road towards Mt Eliot, the area near the sea. There were some large buildings in this area: a warehouse, the home of former governor George Grey, a courthouse with empty stocks in front. She continued towards the sea. How refreshing to smell the crisp air. The house on the farm had felt barren and lonely but now she thought of it fondly. How she would love to be in her small bedroom, looking out on the hill bathed in evening light. Perhaps Mrs Archer had made the right decision after all.

The sea stretched out in front of her, rocky islands in the distance. She stopped near the shore, beside a seemingly abandoned Māori village on a hill. A brown fence surrounded small, low houses dug into the earth. Some of the homes were long and thin, some on stilts. None were big enough to hold much furniture, and there was not a glass window to be seen. Frances noticed evidence of the village having been lived in recently: some blankets lay discarded on the ground, and the small garden inside the fence had been carefully tended. But Frances was alone with the wind — there wasn't a single person in sight. They must have left to fight, or escape.

Looking more closely, Frances could see that the village was cleaner and more orderly than the slums of East London — or what little she'd seen of them, anyway. Pleasanter, in fact, than the room her family currently shared. At least here the wind from the sea would carry away any hint of disease-carrying miasma. There was a pride evident here that was endearingly familiar to the way she had felt on their farm, even as she struggled to keep up with the chores.

Henry must live in such a place now. She couldn't imagine the Henry she'd known in London thriving in this sort of village, but the man she'd met here — she could see that it suited him. The more she thought about Henry of New Plymouth, the more her memories of London slid around until she could see the new Henry lying dormant within the old Henry. He had always been less concerned about societal etiquette and had a keen sense of adventure. Frances had just forgotten.

A yell came from the sea. In the distance were a cluster of Māori canoes, their prows standing tall against the sky. They were made of dark wood and covered in what looked like carvings, although it was difficult to tell from this distance. There were many of them — half a dozen, if not more: they cut through the water too swiftly for Frances to count — heading north, where everyone said the first shots would be fired in the morning.

Inside the canoes, men paddled with all their might. Frances shivered. She'd heard about Māori warriors but never seen any with her own eyes. They chanted in unison: a loud, fierce song. She didn't understand the words but their intent was clear.

These men intended to win.

CHAPTER FORTY

MATĀRIA

Matāria stood tall in the salty air and watched the waka being launched from the beach. Pride swelled in her chest as the men paddled into the distance, Tāwhirimātea carrying their chants on the wind. She recognised so many of these warriors: Kuru, her other cousins, boys she'd played with as children. They were joined by men from Taranaki iwi and other iwi in the south, who had put aside their old grievances and travelled here to help Te Ātiawa. So many men, fighting for the same thing, determined to die like sharks, not octopuses.

Beside her, Henry whistled. 'I wouldn't want to take those men on. Those settlers in the volunteer militia won't know what's hit them.'

'You mean men like George Farrington?'

'Exactly. From what I hear from his neighbour, Farrington can't even keep his bullock contained in a field.' Henry's eyes followed the waka. 'But unfortunately it's not just the volunteers they'll be facing. The British Army are out in force, and they've had plenty of practice suppressing rebellion in India and elsewhere.'

'It's not a rebellion to try to keep what is already yours.'

Henry laughed. 'True. But rebel is a name given to anyone whose cause you don't agree with, when you have power and they do not.'

They watched the waka until the chants could be heard no longer. Henry stooped to the stream and filled his pail with water. He was not showing many signs of illness at that moment but Betsy was getting worse; they needed to keep her clean and cool. Henry's face was flushed with the exercise.

'I can do it,' Matāria said. 'You look hot.'

'No, Minnie. I can tell your leg is as bad as it's ever been.'

They walked back to the hut.

'I hope this finally breaks Betsy's fever,' Matāria said as they approached their hut and stood outside the open door. 'And I've soaked some more rātā bark, and boiled more kawakawa leaves.'

'Is there anything else that might help?'

'Nothing I know of.' She wondered what Tai would have recommended. Another balm, perhaps, or some other rongoā that Matāria did not know. Or maybe he would have insisted the illness was Betsy's own doing, which would not have been helpful. But Tai was long gone.

Henry ran his hands through his dusty blond hair. 'I ought to have bought something at the store,' he said. 'There was a green ointment. I couldn't tell you what it was, but it might have helped. My mother used to give me Sweet Spirit of Nitre, along with some water mixed with brandy. But I don't think they had any of that at the store.'

'What can we do?'

'I don't know, Minnie. I bloody well hope those rats are staying away. If any come sniffing around my sick daughter they'll get what's coming to them.'

'I haven't seen any — all the noise in the papakāinga must have driven them away.'

'Māmā. Pāpā.' Betsy's cry interrupted their conversation. 'I'm hot.' Her eyes were closed as she spoke and her arms and legs were a mottled pink. 'Make me colder. I don't like being so hot.'

'Betsy's sick, Māmā,' said Edwin.

Matāria looked at Betsy, her eyes filling with tears. 'I know, my darlings. I know.'

Betsy sat up and vomited all over herself. Then she lay straight back down and closed her eyes, covered in the meagre contents of her stomach. Matāria stripped off her clothing and used the water in the pail to clean her. She placed Betsy's frock and blanket in a kete to take to the beach to wash. She looked up at Paritutu through the doorway. They were supposed to be leaving this place — it was too dangerous to remain — but Betsy couldn't travel in her state. Betsy could not end up in the urupā. Matāria would *not* let that happen. Not that she had any way to ensure her daughter would get well again. There wasn't any light; there were no guiding stars.

CHAPTER FORTY-ONE

FRANCES

The soldiers marched as soon as light broke through the darkness; they would soon see the men pass by in formation. Dew was still on the ground and the air was cool. Frances stood on the side of the street, a knitted woollen shawl around her shoulders. Mother and George were on either side of her, Mother guarding against the cold by wearing her paisley shawl over her mourning shawl, and George in his volunteer militia uniform. The Thorpes stood at the end of the row of bystanders. Theodore gave Frances a friendly nod and Frances smiled back. Around them stood residents from other houses on the block, all waiting in respectful silence: the regiment had requested that the people of New Plymouth not yell or cheer.

A bugle interrupted the stillness. Its crisp sound carried from the direction of Marsland Hill, followed by the rhythm of beating drums.

'They're coming!' Mother sounded excited, her breath visible in the cold air. 'I understand there are hundreds of soldiers — brave men, every last one. I can hear their footsteps, marching in unison. Marching to victory!'

'Of course,' George said.

'Are you sure the volunteer militia has not been called up for duty?' Mother asked.

'Yes, I'm sure.' George shrugged. 'I thought the order would have come by now, but not yet.'

'One of the women from the Floral Society told me—'

'Stop.' George held up his hand. 'It is nothing to me what those blathering women think. The volunteers will be called up shortly. I am sure of it.'

'But she said—'

'Mother, are you calling me a liar?'

'Of course not!' Mother pulled her shawl even more tightly around her hunched shoulders. 'I know you do not lie. You cannot be a liar. You simply cannot.'

'Of course I am not,' George said.

'Yet you ate the peaches.' Mother's voice was soft.

George turned his head sharply towards her. 'I beg your pardon?'

'Oh, nothing.' Mother waved her hand. 'I had so little sleep last night in that horrid room. Ignore me.'

George clenched his fists. 'I shall not ignore you. I heard you clearly. You said that I ate the peaches.'

Mother looked overcome with sadness. 'You were the only one home that day.'

George's face was reddening; there was a familiar tightening in his jaw. Frances knew that expression: her brother was about to lose his temper. She stepped back involuntarily.

The soldiers' footsteps grew closer, the sound of drums echoing around the otherwise silent town.

'The soldiers are about to march past,' George snarled. 'I'll be fighting a war shortly. Who cares who ate the blasted peaches? Whether it was me or someone else — what of it?'

Mother stared straight ahead, the colour draining from her face. She seemed suddenly very old. Frances herself felt a strange tingling in her body. How dare he?

The first row of the 65th Regiment came into view around the corner, followed by another row and another: a blaze of blue jackets, white trousers and long rifles. Some of these men might have been Frances's age, but most were younger. Very young in some cases — they were barely more than boys. Older men sitting tall on horses trotted alongside them.

A woman cried out, breaking the silence. 'Good luck to you!'

Mother shook herself back to life and waved a large lace-trimmed handkerchief. She was joined by others around them, the women silently waving handkerchiefs or their gloved hands, the men lifting their hats.

There were more soldiers than Frances could count, now passing by them in quiet ranks. She waved her own handkerchief, a stirring of pride in her chest at the brave Englishmen, but the feeling was swiftly dampened by her vivid recollection of the empty Māori village she'd seen the previous day and the warriors in the canoes. Her hand dropped to her side. She turned to where Theodore and Dora stood, but they had both gone.

'This is a mistake,' a deep voice near her said. 'This is a grave mistake.' It was the German missionary, Schmidt. He must have relocated into the town also.

George spun to face him. 'Hush, traitor. Go back to your Māori friends. You're not welcome here.'

Schmidt shook his head and looked at George with a forlorn expression. 'The Māori say I betrayed them by trying to broker peace. All I did was recommend that they give away some of their land. Not to enable the purchase of the whole block, but to avoid war and death.' He sighed deeply. 'They will not talk to me anymore.'

'Any man worth anything will be fighting for our cause today,' George said. 'That's why I'll be fighting with the volunteer militia.'

'But the Taranaki Rifle Volunteers have already mobilised,' said

Schmidt. 'They're assembling at the barracks as we speak. I'm told they're being armed to the hilt with rifles, carbines and even swords.'

'How can that be?' Mother said to George. 'How can they gather without letting you know? Although, I did try to tell you that the ladies from the Floral Society—'

George interrupted her. 'I intend to get to the bottom of this right away.'

'They must have the wrong address,' Mother said. 'As I said yesterday.'

Schmidt shook his head. 'With due respect, ma'am, everyone knows you are staying in the servants' quarters near the miners' cottages.'

George paled. 'You offend me, sir. What are you implying?'

'It's none of my business.' Schmidt said. 'I must be going, I do not wish to stand here any longer in the cold, watching these men march towards an avoidable conflict that will most certainly result in some of them meeting their maker far too soon.'

'No.' George's voice was sharp. 'You owe me the courtesy of an explanation. If the militia knew how to contact me, why would they not? I'm strong and clever. I can fight as well as anyone.'

'There is talk . . .'

'Talk of what?'

'It's not my place.'

George reached out and pushed Schmidt's shoulder. Frances watched in horror, heart pounding. How could George lay his hand on a man of the cloth?

'Oi, there!' someone else yelled.

'Talk of what?' George glowered at the missionary.

'Talk of unpaid debts and a love of cards. I'm not party to the details.'

'Henry White!' Spittle flew as George spoke. 'Henry White is behind this. He's deliberately ruining everything I have worked so hard to achieve.'

Frances felt a pulse through her body. Anger, like she'd never felt before. It was like a bullet from one of those rifles the soldiers carried — and she would deploy it with cold accuracy.

'No!' she shouted at her brother.

George glared at her. 'What do you mean, *no*?'

'I've heard about your debts and I know about your lies,' Frances said. 'I know what you did. You can't blame it on Henry this time. This is your own doing!'

George's face drained of colour. 'How dare you speak to me like this, sister? I keep you because no man will have you, and this is how you repay me? By believing Henry White's lies?'

'He didn't lie. You did.' Frances's voice wobbled but she was determined to finish what she had to say. 'All those years ago you let me believe Henry had left me, but he hadn't. You made him go because you had gambled away my dowry and could not admit it. They were your debts all along — not Father's. *You* caused our family's ruin.'

Several other pieces of the puzzle slotted into Frances's mind. 'Clementine found out, didn't she? That's why you have been stopping me from reading her letters. Is she trying to claim her dowry too, what rightfully belongs to her husband?'

The soldiers had disappeared into the gloom of the morning and most of the townsfolk had retreated to their homes. Schmidt shot Frances a sympathetic glance and slunk away. There was no one left on the street except Frances and George and their mother.

Don't look away, Frances told herself. *Don't let him stare you down. Be like Matāria.*

Mother looked stricken. 'George? What is Frances talking about, George?'

George broke eye contact with his sister. 'She's lying, Mother. Frances always lies. You know that.'

'My late husband's debts, God rest his soul,' Mother said quietly. 'Were they . . . were they your debts, George?'

George spoke through gritted teeth. 'Frances. Is. Lying.'

Mother was still. 'George, did you eat the peaches?'

'Good God, Mother. Peaches again? What is it with you and those godforsaken peaches?'

'*Answer me.*' Mother squinted at George, a note of steely coldness in her voice. 'Did you, or did you not, eat the peaches?'

'I refuse to answer your ridiculous questions. Maybe. Maybe not. I don't keep a detailed log of all the food I consume, Mother. Why do you care so much?'

'I wanted to have a peach pudding!' Her voice softened. 'I could have taken it to a Floral Society meeting. If the women had liked my peach pudding, they might have stopped laughing at me behind my back. They think I don't know, but I do. A delicious pudding and my fine garden might have made it all better.'

'Why does it matter whether you made a pudding of peaches or apples or even slop? Who cares?'

'I care,' Mother said. 'Because if you lied about that—'

'Mother, you've lost me.'

'Albert never told lies.' Mother folded her handkerchief with trembling hands. 'Albert was a good boy.'

'Albert is dead! And he wasn't a good boy when he was alive — he wasn't. I remember what he used to do to me, not that anyone ever believed me. And Father is dead too, leaving behind him a trail of debt.'

Mother's face crumpled. She turned to Frances, sobbing loudly, and Frances took her mother in her arms.

George and Frances glowered at each other.

George broke the silence. 'Apologise, Frances. This is all your fault.'

'It is not, and I will not.'

'You caused this with your hysteria. You're no better than Clementine.' He shook his head. 'No, I take that back: you're worse. At least Clementine found a husband so she didn't leech off me. You're nothing but an old maid who sucks the joy from a room with your melancholy.'

Frances blinked back hot, angry tears.

'There was a man who wanted to marry me, but you sent him away!' she shouted. 'And I will *not* apologise to you. You are such a liar, you have lost all sense of what truth is!'

Mother sobbed louder against Frances's shoulder.

George's voice was a low growl. 'Henry White did this,' he said. 'Everything was going well for me in New Plymouth until I saw him again. He has ruined everything for me because he is envious that I am a gentleman while he lives in filth in a native slum. But I will fix him. Then I can clear my name and take my rightful place as a respected citizen of this town.'

CHAPTER FORTY-TWO

MATĀRIA

Matāria sat outside her hut on the chair with dog feet, watching the sun rise. A new day —what would it bring? A runner had arrived earlier that morning with two pieces of news: the men from their papakāinga had arrived safely in Waitara to join Wiremu Kīngi, and the British soldiers were marching towards them. In Pekapeka they would fight.

Very few men were left behind — only the elderly or injured. Even the sentries were boys not much older than Edwin, being overseen by a kaumātua. There was nothing more to be done. With Betsy still sick and Henry not much better, Matāria couldn't leave. All she could do was wait for updates while preparing further supplies for the warriors. It was all any of the women and children could do. They stripped flax, they prepared kānga and other kai, but mostly they sat, fidgeted, and asked the same questions over and over. Was anyone else ill? Had anyone else succumbed to the disease and begun their long journey to Hawaiki? Had anyone heard any news?

Atarangi rushed back and forth telling everyone what to do, but her instructions made no sense — her head was in disarray. She was clearly worried about Kuru. Matāria wondered whether she should try to comfort her sister but thought better of it.

Betsy was still flat on her back but hadn't vomited all day. Henry, on the other hand, was becoming more febrile and unable to keep liquid in his body. Allowing him back up to help collect water had been a mistake. He now spoke very little, and when he did, he appeared delirious.

'Minnie!' he'd cried. 'I want to jump in the Serpentine.'

'My pipe is on fire!'

'I saw Betsy's rainbow fish!'

Matāria hoped he would get better soon. He was a healthy man, not a child or a sickly elder. She *needed* him to get better soon. She was only just managing to fetch enough water for two sick people. Beside his father lay Edwin, staring at the wall. He had barely spoken to Matāria since their argument; his silence was like an angry scream that only she could hear. And of course the illness had finally reached her son — something as inevitable as the moon replacing the sun at the end of each day.

Edwin was not very ill: his forehead wasn't as hot to the touch as Betsy's had been, and he hadn't covered himself in waste. But he wasn't well, and who knew what path the disease would take? Henry claimed that miasma spread it, so Matāria had recited karakia, she had washed away unpleasant smells, perfumed the air with ambergris she'd found floating on the sea, and sprinkled fresh water over their sleeping mats. There was no miasma here. She sat back in the chair and closed her eyes. If she ignored the women talking and Henry moaning, she could hear the waves breaking against the shore. It calmed her.

A sound cut through her thoughts and her eyes flew open. What was that? The women nearby had all leapt to their feet, fear etched on their faces. Matāria realised the pahu was being struck by the sentries at the gate: an echo bounced off the walls of the papakāinga each time the wooden stick hit the instrument's matai body. The sentries usually hit the gong once or twice, but today it was being beaten continuously. Matāria heard a loud voice at the gate: angry shouts that thundered over the pahu. An English voice.

She had thought the battle would be fought north of New Plymouth, not here, in an unarmed, undefended papakāinga full of women, old men and children. They were all so vulnerable here. More vulnerable than Matāria should ever have allowed herself to be.

CHAPTER FORTY-THREE

FRANCES

Frances looked down at Mother, now sitting on a tree stump, watching George hurry towards the stables.

'Are you all right?'

Mother didn't respond. She was a quivering mess. Frances knew George was on his way to attack Henry — what should she do? She needed to ask someone for help. She looked one way up the road and then the other but saw no one. What about Father Schmidt? He was obviously staying nearby, and he understood her predicament, but she had no idea where he was lodging. Nor could she bother her other neighbours, whom she barely knew. What would she tell them? This story was too painful and complicated to put in words. She'd sound every bit as hysterical as George kept accusing her of being. What a pity Frances didn't have any friends. *Real* friends.

But she did have the Thorpes. They would not think her hysterical, and they obviously knew a bit about her brother. *Yes*. She would ask Dora and Theodore to help her.

Mother's looked up at her. Her eyes were red, her face stained with tears. 'Oh, Frances. I'm sorry.'

'We don't need to talk any more now, Mother. But I need to go to Mr White. I think George means him harm, and being associated with me has already ruined his life once. I can't let it happen again.'

'He wasn't good enough for you, Frances. I didn't want you to marry him, not when George said he was a wastrel, just courting you for your settlement. He was not a gentleman, and you are a lady—'

Frances pulled off her gloves and held her hands out in front of her mother. 'Are these the hands of a lady? I don't think so. These are the hands of someone who can bake bread and light fires and tend to animals. I may be the daughter of a gentleman, but I have not had the luxury of being a lady since George lost my inheritance playing cards.'

Mother sobbed. 'I have been so angry with your father for all these years. Was it really all George's fault? Your poor father, having his reputation sullied in this manner. Clementine said as much and I dismissed her. You have to understand, Frances, George was my only remaining son. I have never understood money matters and I relied on him. I trusted him. Who will keep me in my old age now?'

'I don't know who will keep either of us, Mother. Let's worry about that later. Here, let me help you up.'

Mother gripped Frances's hand and allowed herself to be pulled to her feet. 'I had forgotten something important, you know,' she said. 'When George was a boy, he told lies about Albert. Beastly lies. Of course they weren't true — that's what your father and I decided. Albert always was the better of my sons; what George said about him could *not* have been true. I saw George's lies as the jealous moaning of a young boy — nothing more, nothing less. Now I see it for what it was: a pattern. George has always been a liar.'

'I don't remember Albert being anything other than kind and good,' Frances said. 'And I'm going to leave you now. Go back to our lodging and lie down.'

'No! I don't want to be all alone in those dark servants' quarters.

If you go, who will fetch me tea and poach me an egg? Please don't leave me. George will be back shortly, and all will be well.' Mother sobbed again. 'All will be well.'

'I have to go, Mother. I am not asking permission. I am going now.'

She set off swiftly towards the Thorpes' store. Mother's sobbing grew louder with each step she took, but Frances didn't stop. She had something more important to do: warn Henry that George was coming for him.

CHAPTER FORTY-FOUR

MATĀRIA

A woman ran up the hill — one of Matāria's cousins, who often sat with Atarangi in the harakeke circle.

'What's happening?' one of the other women yelled.

'There's a crazy man coming — a settler. He's not a soldier, but he has violence in his eyes. He's already pushed Mere over, and hit the sentry boy with the pahu stick.'

'Where is he now? Should we hide?'

'Hide where?'

Matāria watched as the women gathered crying children and led them away. Some ran down the other side of the hill, several rushed into the kūmara storehouses. Others climbed over a low fence at the back of the papakāinga. Matāria stood rooted to the spot in her doorway. She couldn't leave her family lying sick in their hut. If this angry man made it this far, he'd have to get past her.

She thought about finding a weapon, just in case. There were some large sticks beside the fire. She wouldn't be able to save her family with her bare hands.

But she couldn't fight. What was she thinking? Her leg was still weak after the walk back from Marsland Hill. If only she'd accepted the Thorpes' offer of a ride, or Atarangi's offer to collect water. Matāria always made things worse for herself with her stubbornness. She hoped the strange angry man wouldn't see her in the shadows. She hoped he would go away. *Hope*. That useless emotion again, but it was all she had. And hope was far more comforting than the empty void of nothing. Perhaps it had some value after all.

From the darkness of the doorway, Matāria saw the man. He wore a uniform she didn't recognise and his hair was dishevelled. He was waving the pahu stick. Matāria gripped the doorframe; her heart raced. It was George Farrington. There could only be one person he was here for: Henry.

Before Matāria could react, Farrington saw her. His upper lip curled, displaying a row of yellow teeth. 'I remember you being led away to gaol like an animal.'

Matāria was as still as a tuatara. She looked him directly in the eye.

'Why are you here?' Her voice was hoarse. 'The war is somewhere else. Are you lost?'

'I am not at war because your scoundrel husband spread lies about me!' George shouted. 'He has ruined my reputation. And now he has turned my own mother against me.'

'How could he have done such a thing? Henry has no such power. He lives a simple life, here with me and our children.' *Keep him talking*, Matāria thought. Distract him long enough for help to arrive. She knew she couldn't solve this problem on her own.

'Henry has not done those things,' she said to George. 'He would not.'

George spat on the ground. 'You're wrong. He did. And now I can't fight in the war. I *wanted* to fight, as it would have made my mother proud. She would have seen that I was better than Albert. Albert wouldn't have fought — he was the sort of person who punched where the bruises didn't show. He would slap my body and make me swim in the lake in the middle of winter. He threw rocks at my pet dog and laughed when she ran away, never to return.'

Matāria had no idea what he was talking about. Who was Albert? Was Farrington delirious? Did he have the illness too? She didn't care. All that mattered was that this dangerous man leave them in peace. Matāria planted her feet on the ground, holding her space like a tōtara in the forest of Tāne-nui-a-Rangi.

'Perhaps your mother is ashamed of you because you act like a wild animal,' Matāria said.

George shook his head. 'It's not true!' he yelled. 'You don't know what you're talking about.' He growled loudly and ran at her.

Matāria came towards him, spinning off and landing on the ground with a thud. George pinned her chest to the ground and punched her. Matāria inhaled sharply, struggling to breathe. He hit her again and again, landing blows all over her body. She rolled over and tried to crawl away, but George leapt at her, putting his full weight on her bad leg. Pain exploded through her body. He flipped her onto her back and kept punching.

'Stop!' she tried to say. 'Stop—'

But he didn't.

Matāria's vision blurred. She might have seen Henry, standing at the doorway of the hut, leaning against the doorframe to steady himself. 'Minnie?' she might have heard him say. 'Oh my God, Minnie!'

Then she could see no longer.

She tried to focus on the sound of the waves breaking on the shore in the distance: the same sea she'd heard since she was a child. But the only noise filling her ears was the dull thudding of George Farrington's fists on her body.

CHAPTER FORTY-FIVE

FRANCES

Frances rode with Theodore and Dora in their cart. They travelled south of the township, towards the giant rock, as fast as they could. On the way they passed a cart in a ditch. Furniture was strewn in the grass and broken crockery lay on the road. A dog sat beside an overturned wooden dresser, looking forlorn.

Around the corner was a farm with part of the front fence ripped apart. Cows stood on the path, refusing to move until Theodore yelled at them. In the distance was a farmhouse that had been burnt to the ground, its ruins charred and black. Nearby was a timber barn — or, rather, what had once been a barn: only two of the four walls remained. Alongside, Frances saw as they came closer, lay three bloated dead sheep.

So this is what war looks like, she thought. It sickened her.

Theodore took a circular route, avoiding the blockhouses. 'If anyone stops me, I shall say I am collecting supplies.'

'You didn't have to come,' Frances said to Dora. 'I wouldn't want to put you in any danger.'

'Don't be a goose,' Dora said. 'I wouldn't miss this excitement for the world. And I don't trust Theodore to find the village without me.'

'I returned his cart when he was arrested, remember?' Theodore said. 'I know where to go: it's right under Paritutu. It is easy to find.'

'Thank you, both of you,' Frances said. 'Thank you so much.'

Theodore gave Dora a pointed look. 'Tell her,' he said. 'We need to tell her.'

Frances stiffened. 'Tell me what?'

Dora sighed. 'If you insist. It wasn't Henry who told people about George's past.'

'Who was it, Dora?' Theodore's voice was light.

'Very well,' Dora said. 'Please don't be cross. It's my fault people know George's business, not Henry's. I was worried about you, you see. I overheard what Henry said to you in the store, right before you fainted. Of course I was already aware of your brother's reputation in the town when it came to his finances. And many of us women have also experienced his unwelcome attentions, and his fantasies of grandeur. I only mentioned the matter of your own inheritance to one or two others — and only because I was worried about you as my friend. I should have known how quickly word would get around our small town.'

Dora looked down at her hands. 'I'm sorry, Frances.'

Frances turned over the information in her mind. Two words stood out: My friend. She smiled. 'Please, don't berate yourself,' she said, taking Dora's hand. 'It was the truth. It needed to be said.'

They pulled up outside a Māori village near the base of the giant rock. Frances had never been here but the wooden fence was similar to that surrounding the village she'd seen the day before. This settlement was larger, and built on a bigger hill, and, unlike the other village, this one was occupied.

At the gates sat a young boy, groaning, with his head in his hands. An older man had an arm around the boy's shoulder. Two children watched on, weeping. Nearby, women ran this way and that, yelling words that Frances did not understand. Yet she understood their intent.

Something had frightened them.

CHAPTER FORTY-SIX

MATĀRIA

Matāria opened her eyes. Her face was in the dirt; dust filled her mouth. She rolled over and tried to open her eyes. *Ow*. Her head pounded; sharp pain darted up her arms and legs. Her face throbbed and a warm liquid trickled down her cheek.

Henry was leaning over her. 'Oh, Minnie. I'm so sorry I didn't help. I was too sick and confused — it's over now and the children are still asleep. Please tell me you're all right.'

Matāria looked past her husband to where George Farrington lay on the ground with his eyes closed. His arms stretched out in front of him, one of them bent at an unnatural angle. His chest was moving up and down so he wasn't dead, but he wouldn't be getting up again easily.

Matāria sat up with Henry's help. Someone was standing above George's twisted body, holding the chair with dog feet so tightly that their knuckles had turned white. A chair that was covered in smatterings of blood.

Atarangi.

'You may say *I'm* just someone you knew when you were young,' Atarangi said, 'but *you* are still my sister.'

Atarangi threw the chair down; it landed with a crack. She rushed towards Matāria and wrapped her arms around her shoulders. Other women ran towards them both; chaos erupted around the hut.

Matāria clung to her sister and wept.

CHAPTER FORTY-SEVEN

FRANCES

Frances stood with Dora and Theodore beside the cart. Henry was with them, his face pale.

'They were about to send us away,' Theodore said. 'The women over there threatened to hit us with pots. Luckily I thought to ask for you.'

Henry shook Theodore's hand and bowed at Frances and Dora. He told them what had happened, then said, 'I must get back. I'm not that well, you see, and waking to find that brute pummelling my wife didn't help. She's badly hurt.'

'I'm so sorry,' Frances said.

'It's hardly your fault. Anyway, George will be here in a moment. Please take him somewhere far from here, where I never need to see his rodent moustache again.'

Henry waved goodbye and left. Frances watched him walk back towards the village. A feeling of shame crept over her body. What a terrible thing her brother had done, both to Henry's wife and to the young boy sitting beside the gate. Apparently he had knocked down another Māori woman as well. These poor people, who had done nothing to deserve it.

She had an idea. 'Henry!' Frances called. He turned and she

rushed over to him. 'You could stay at our farm. There are hens and a cow still there — we couldn't take them with us. You will find a little food in the kitchen, and probably plenty of eggs in the fowl house. There is also a bullock. Please go there, for we cannot, not at the moment. Use some of what you collect to feed these poor souls my brother has hurt. You have my permission.'

Henry smiled. 'Thank you. We would appreciate that very much.'

'No, thank *you*,' Frances said. 'We are old, dear friends after all.'

'We are indeed. Despite your brother, which makes it all the more pleasant, don't you think?'

Two women carried an unconscious George towards the village gates. They walked slowly, struggling under the weight. Theodore rushed forward and relieved them of their burden. He rolled George into the back of the cart, right into a damp patch near the back. Frances studied her brother. His face was bruised and bloody, but he was alive.

One of the women leaned over the edge of the cart and spat on George. 'He beat my cousin Matāria,' she said in English. 'No one comes to our place, the place of our ancestors, and hurts one of us.'

The other woman glared at George's battered body but didn't say a word. They both nodded at Frances and walked back through the gates to their village on the hill. The women both had loose hair and tattoos on their chins — this was a place Frances couldn't have described to Clementine even if she'd tried. But one thing she knew: these women did not feel like enemies on the other side of a war.

Theodore looked at George. 'We'll need to get him seen to. He won't be going anywhere interesting for some time, not with that bump on the side of his head and the way his arm is positioned.'

'That man deserves everything he got,' Dora said.

According to Henry, Matāria's sister had laid George out — with a chair. Those two women must be cut from the same cloth: fierce and strong. Women Frances would love to emulate. She still had a way to go, but she would keep working at it.

'Fortunately, George's sister is nothing like him,' Theodore said quietly. 'What she has got lately is not so good . . . she deserves better.'

Frances smiled widely at Theodore, her crooked teeth visible, but it didn't seem to matter anymore.

George groaned and rolled onto his side, the woman's spittle dripping across his forehead and into his eyes. 'My head hurts,' he mumbled.

'Oh, stop being so hysterical, George,' Frances said.

The giant rock caught her eye. In the distance was the mountain, outlined against the crisp blue sky. Between here and there were rolling hills covered in thick bush, which Frances now considered quite beautiful — in its own way.

CHAPTER FORTY-EIGHT

MATĀRIA

The months passed. Matāria sat on the hill, where Tāwhirimātea blew a cool breeze on her face. *Keep blowing*, she thought. Blow away the soldiers. We have won some battles already, so let us win some more. Let us keep our lands — at least the parts that haven't yet been sold, like this hill.

Henry had come here to the farm numerous times to collect food and supplies, but Matāria hadn't been ready to join him until today. So many years had passed since she was last here, back when she was small. Now she was Matāria, she was Minnie, she was Māmā. She was Te Ātiawa, the woman who could prepare kānga better than anyone else in the papakāinga. She was a sister.

She was once the child who was captured, right in front of those trees. She was the daughter who howled as she watched her own māmā being killed. She was the little girl who had looked out at the rocky islands off the coast and thought: *I should have gone in the waka with Atarangi*. She was still all of those versions of Matāria. The important thing, she now knew, was not to linger on the bad things she had endured, but draw on the things she had learned, and put that knowledge to use at every opportunity.

She stood up and looked around. The vegetable garden had

nothing worth taking but there was a very pretty flower garden underneath the front window — what a pity flowers were no use to anyone. The house was large: at least four rooms. From where Matāria stood, she could see a bedroom at the back of the house, with a small table and narrow bed. That would be the best room in the house, the one that got all the evening sun.

Beside the house, the kitchen still had its door, unlike other farms in the area. Nor was this farm littered with dead animals and broken furniture — items the raiding parties deemed too troublesome to carry away for food or firewood. Kuru had kept his word to Henry: the cousins had stayed away.

It was kind of Frances to allow Henry and Matāria to use this house. Frances now lived in the town with her new husband. Henry said she lived behind the store, with Mrs Farrington.

Henry had returned recently from a visit to New Plymouth to find out what he could about the progress of the war, and had returned agitated and upset.

'The area in front of the store is a makeshift hospital,' he'd said. 'There are so many injured men. Frances helps them, she told me. And the smell of the town! There are too many people stuck inside that barricade. Folk are sleeping in churches and in the saloons of public houses. They all complain of being hungry. Rats are everywhere, and people die of sickness every day.'

'You know we have our own injured and dead,' Matāria had replied. 'We, too, are hungry. These people invoked Tūmatauenga. Now they feel his wrath.'

'Most of the settlers think they are winning the war, illness and discomfort notwithstanding.'

Matāria had shook her head. 'No one is winning. We are just losing in different ways.'

'I am pleased to have seen Frances, though. I want to help her where I can,' Henry had said. 'Although, I hardly recognised her mother — she barely uttered a word. Frances said all her mother speaks of is her late husband, and how she'd never imagined she would one day live in a shop. The poor old lady seems terribly confused: upset at living with the merchant class, while also being grateful to live in more comfort than in the servants' quarters.'

Henry also had news of George. George had made it to the front eventually; the regiment's losses made them less picky about the calibre of their volunteers. But Atarangi had injured George's arm so badly that he would never hold a rifle, so his only option was to go as a barracks servant. He had died of illness within a fortnight.

The sickness that swept through the town and papakāinga had spread everywhere else that Taranaki could see: to the pā where men fought; to the few farms still occupied by settlers; to the soldiers' camps. When Matāria heard that George Farrington had caught the illness she had heard the voices of the old people, whispering of a mauri that was unclean. Yet no mother should lose a child, including Mrs Farrington. Matāria hugged her twins tight every day and felt thankful that they had both healed after their own brushes with the afterlife. And she felt so grateful for Henry.

Henry also said Frances had asked him to call on the woman living alone on the neighbouring farm. 'We need to pass on Frances's regards to Mrs Archer and ask if she needs anything,' he said. 'Although, if I remember Mrs Archer correctly, she will be perfectly fine. She and her husband were very kind to me when I first arrived in New Plymouth, if you recall. And she's hardier than you and I combined.'

The woman was also benefiting from Kuru's protection, although she knew nothing of that. Kuru had also indicated that Henry was now out of favours and Henry agreed not to ask for any more.

Would Matāria live in this house until the war was over? Frances had said they could. Maybe. Maybe not. It actually didn't matter — the land of her tūpuna stretched from here to the papakāinga, and even further still. Either way, she was on her lands. She couldn't make Tūmatauenga go away. Hundreds of people, Māori and Europeans alike, would die before Rongomatāne returned and sowed his peaceful seeds.

But at least now she had options of where to keep the children, depending on what happened. She wouldn't leave Ngāmotu again, not now. She'd walked too far to get home. She owed it to her people to fight alongside them, in this space, until the very end of the war — whenever that might be.

When that time came, she would come here with Atarangi. They could sit in this very spot on the hill together, remember their parents, and watch as the children played — embracing the puna that connects the tūpuna of the past with the mokopūna who are yet to come.

Haere whakamua, hoki whakamuri. They could look back, but move forward.

Together.

HISTORICAL NOTE

Like so many Te Ātiawa, I grew up in the shadow of a loss that occurred many generations before I was born. Many of my childhood memories swirled around this feeling of trying to regain what we no longer had: watching an old woman cry as she told our story at Parihaka; hearing my grandfather talk about where his own parents gathered seafood when they were children; my father pointing out this housing block or that playground and saying, *That used to be a pā.*

Another memory I have is of being a young girl attending hui — *so* many hui — and hearing my grandad and my uncles and aunts and my parents talking loudly about the Māori Land Court and all sorts of other things to do with 'the claim'. Attempts to seek acknowledgement of, and redress for, raupatu (confiscation) was a defining feature of my family for longer than I have been alive.

One of the proudest moments of my life was joining my aunt, Wikitoria Keenan, for the June 2014 initialling of the Te Ātiawa Deed of Settlement in Parliament, where I was able to sign the document myself. Wiki was one of the Te Ātiawa negotiators who worked tirelessly on the historical Te Ātiawa settlement. Sadly, she died shortly after it was finally signed, so never saw the legislation pass in Parliament.

She was not alone. Between the passing of the New Zealand Settlement Act 1863 (which triggered the land confiscations) and the Te Ātiawa Claims Settlement Act 2016, countless Te Ātiawa agitated for recognition. Most did not live long enough to read the words now enshrined in legislation: 'The Crown unreservedly apologises for its actions during the Taranaki Wars which resulted in the destruction of Te Atiawa property, hardship, and the loss of life of your people.'[1]

I tell this story to illustrate that sometimes the past permeates the present, and, as a result, it can be difficult to separate out the stories I have heard from the historical sources I have since read. Nonetheless, I am a historian by training, so will endeavour to faithfully capture my method in a note.

Much of my initial research for this book occurred while trawling through oral submissions made by people of Te Ātiawa to the Waitangi Tribunal between 1991 and 1995 as evidence for WAI 143, the Taranaki claim. At the time, I didn't have fiction writing in mind: it was for my Master of Arts thesis on oral evidence, historical methodology, Te Ātiawa history and the Waitangi Tribunal. But the stories stayed with me. As I studied, I spent many hours determinedly ignoring academic analysis, instead reading and re-reading the oral submissions — people recounting stories they themselves had been told — all the while thinking: *what did it feel like to live through that?* I have since supplemented that with a number of other historical works and compilations of primary sources, which I have listed in the bibliography at the back of this book. I could write an essay about New Plymouth in early 1860, but it was such a complex time in our nation's history I wouldn't want to do it a disservice by offering less than a full exploration. If you're interested, I recommend the sources in the bibliography, as they tell a fascinating story in a variety of ways and from a range of perspectives.

In this novel I have tried to capture the essence of my reading as faithfully as possible, and all major political events that I write about took place in early 1860. This includes the requirement for Māori to carry passes, the forcible removal of the inhabitants of Pukeariki

---

1 www.legislation.govt.nz/act/public/2016/0094/25.0/DLM6460017.html

Pā, the arrival of the ships, the order for all the settlers to move into the township, and the rampant march of disease. Both Frances's witnessing of the waka paddling north the day before the battle and the soldiers marching at dawn the following day are based on eyewitness accounts.

With the exception of Native Secretary and Land Purchase Commissioner Donald McLean, all the speaking characters in the book are fictitious. Some contemporary people are referenced, however: Mr Black did indeed own a bakery in New Plymouth at that time; Mary Bishop caused great scandal by proposing to a Māori man; and of course Wiremu Kīngi and Te Teira were central to the dispute over the Pekapeka Block near Waitara that led to war. Some characters are also inspired by real people. According to records, there was a former slave called Mitai who was driven away by a German missionary, Riemenschneider, after Mitai purported to be a healer. Johann Riemenschneider was himself a fascinating figure in New Plymouth history: he was close to the Māori, and is even said to have taught a young Te Whiti o Rongomai. But he fell out of favour with Te Ātiawa after his unsuccessful attempts to broker peace in the lead-up to the Taranaki War, and left the district soon after.

Another thing to note is some changes in geography between 1860 and today. When the New Plymouth port was constructed, part of Paritutu was removed, turning it into a far narrower rock than it would have been in Matāria's time. Mikotahi — one of the islands to which Te Ātiawa fled during the Waikato invasion of the 1830s — is also no longer an offshore island, on account of reclaimed land in what is now the New Plymouth Port area.

Like all writers of historical fiction, I had to make a series of decisions about what I included and what I altered. Of note, I've opted to call Devon Street what it was known as then — Devon

Road. I've also deliberately not referred to my hapū, Ngāti Te Whiti, as Māori living there in 1860 would not have conceived of the same hapū boundaries that we in Te Ātiawa use today. The greatest historical differences relate to language for readability. I've added the macrons to Māori words throughout the novel, as well as opting to use more contractions in speech. I have also deliberately used less formality — for example, my characters become on first-name terms far earlier than they would have ever been at the time, and much of their sentence structure is less turgid.

Similarly, I've taken the decision not to use certain words or phrases that might have been in common use then but are offensive or outdated today, most notably turning the word Māori into a plural by adding an 's'. Not because I am shying away from the past — far from it. It is because I don't want to distract from what is otherwise, I think, a fascinating period of our history.

ACKNOWLEDGEMENTS

Writing *The Space Between* was like hurtling a snowball down a slope — it gained mass and momentum with every passing second. This story started as a vague idea scribbled in a notebook in Kailua, Hawai'i, where we were living at the time. It ended in the depths of the Wellington winter less than twelve months later, after we decided to move home to reconnect with our whenua. And what an exciting time it has been.

But long before this book were the people whose lives were severely impacted by the events I have written about: my tūpuna. I also want to recognise all the claimants who gave evidence during the Waitangi Tribunal's Taranaki claim hearings in the early 1990s, as well as other members of my whānau who have allowed me to share our stories. Thank you.

I acknowledge the many women settlers who wrote to friends and family about their experiences in the colonies, as recorded in the excellent book edited by Frances Porter and Charlotte Macdonald, *My Hand Will Write What My Heart Dictates*. I only wish we historians had more such important records to draw from as we seek to understand the past. I harbour dreams of one day discovering such documents written by my own ancestors, Māori *and* Pākehā.

Back to the present. My husband, Tāne, and our kids, Amotai and Lily-Raema, not only enabled me to write this book, but were constantly on hand to offer advice and suggestions. Their support and encouragement made all the difference in the world — I could not have done it without them. I must also acknowledge the feline members of our family, Pali and Akumu, who only ever strolled over the keyboard on two occasions, typing a few lines of asdsaijfihioasdfoiuasdf before being strongly encouraged to relocate themselves elsewhere.

Special thanks go to my historical consultant and friend Stephen Deed, whose eye for detail and extensive knowledge of Victorian New Zealand assisted me greatly. So much of what I know about the period has come from visiting historical homesteads and museums with Stephen over twenty or so years. I am only sorry I could not find a place in the book to showcase his personal collection of hideous blue Victorian vases. (Perhaps one day I will feature them in a gothic horror novel.)

I would also like to acknowledge my dad, Dr Danny Keenan. His ongoing support has gone so much further than closely reading my text and sharing his deep expertise in Taranaki Māori history (not to mention letting me peruse his book collection). It's my delight to have been able to incorporate the title of his PhD — 'Haere Whakamua, Hoki Whakamuri' (We go forward, but we look back) in the novel in a way that grounds both fact and fiction in the area where we are ahi kaa.

My mum, Raema Merchant, listened to me talk ad nauseam about my ideas, offering sage advice where appropriate. Then there are my sisters — Philippa Thomas, Dr Erin Keenan and Dr Ngaire Keenan. It never fails to delight me that all four of us are committed to the same kaupapa as adults, even if it is expressed differently via our diverse professions.

Other people to acknowledge are Gaylene for bouncing ideas around with me (including the title), Dr Raymondo, Charlotte and Sarah-Jane for the 'Shut Up and Write' sessions, and my lovely friends and colleagues in both Hawai'i and later in Wellington for indulging me as I talked at length about my writing. You know who you are.

Lastly, the team at Penguin Random House, especially publisher

Harriet Allan, from whom I have learnt an immense amount, as well as editor Rachel Scott. I have never before been so excited about a project — an excitement that has continued unabated, even during that point of editing where it felt like (in Isaac Asimov's words) chewing gum once the flavour has gone. Thank you for your time and wisdom.

SELECT BIBLIOGRAPHY

In addition to the books cited below, I made extensive use of Submissions D1–D18 to the Waitangi Tribunal's Wai 143 (The Taranaki Claim), as well as the National Library's *Papers Past* website.

Barker, Lady, *Station Life in New Zealand*, Viking, Auckland, 1973.

Belich, James, *The New Zealand Wars and the Victorian Interpretation of Racial Conflict*, Penguin Books, Auckland, 1986.

Caughey, Angela, *The Interpreter: The biography of Richard 'Dicky' Barrett*, David Bateman, Auckland, 1998.

Cowan, James, *The New Zealand Wars and the Pioneering Period*, vol.1, Government Printer, Wellington, 1922.

Deed, Stephen, *Unearthly Landscapes: New Zealand's early cemeteries, churchyards and urupā*, Otago University Press, Dunedin, 2015.

Dieffenbach, Ernst, *Travels in New Zealand (facsimile edition)*, Capper Press, Christchurch, 1974. (Originally published: John Murray, London, 1843.)

Greenwood, William, *Riemenschneider of Warea*, AH & AW Reed, Wellington, 1967.

Hood, A, *Dickey Barrett: With his ancient mariners and much more ancient cannon! At the siege of Moturoa. . .*, Southern Reprints, 1890.

Hunt, Leigh, *Confessions of A Leigh Hunt*, AH & AW Reed, Wellington, 1951.

Keenan, Danny, *Te Whiti o Rongomai and the Resistance of Parihaka*, Huia, Wellington, 2015.

Keenan, Danny, *Wars Without End*, Penguin Random House, Auckland, 2021.

Ogle, Nigel, *Traders and Whalers: Taranaki*, Tawhiti Museum, Hāwera, 2010.

Paterson, Lachy and Angela Wanhalla, *He Reo Wāhine: Māori Women's Voices from the Nineteenth Century*, Auckland University Press, Auckland, 2017.

Polack, J. S., *New Zealand: Being a narrative of travels and adventures . . . (facsimile edition)*, vol. 2, Capper Press, London, 1974. (Originally published: Richard Bentley, London, 1838.)

Porter, Frances and Charlotte Macdonald (eds), *My Hand Will Write What My Heart Dictates*, Auckland University Press, Auckland, 1996.

Smith, Ian, *Pākehā Settlements in a Māori World: New Zealand archaeology, 1769–1860*, Bridget Williams Books, Wellington, 2019.

Smith, S Percy, *History and Traditions of the Maoris of the West Coast North Island of New Zealand Prior to 1840*, Thomas Avery, New Plymouth, 1910.

Vayda, A. P., *Maori Warfare*, AH & AW Reed, Wellington, 1960.

Werry, Philippa, *The New Zealand Wars*, Upstart Press, Auckland, 2023.

Lauren Keenan (Te Ātiawa ki Taranaki) is a writer of creative non-fiction, novels, short stories and popular psychology. Lauren was a winner at the 2017 Pikihuia Awards for Māori writers and a finalist in the 2019 awards. She was also a participant in Te Papa Tupu mentoring programme. Her short stories have appeared in *Huia Short Stories* collections in 2015, 2017 and 2019. In 2020 her book *The 52 Week Project: How I Fixed My Life by Trying a New Thing Every Week for a Year* was published, followed by a children's novel, *Amorangi and Millie's Trip Through Time* in 2022, which was a finalist in the 2022 NZ Book Awards for Children and Young Adults and longlisted in the ARA Historical Novel Prize. It also won the 2023 Booklovers Award. Lauren has a Master of Arts in Māori History.

ALSO FROM PENGUIN RANDOM HOUSE . . .

PUBLISHED: 30 JANUARY 2024

ISBN: 978-1-77695-054-6

Fly Bird, fly Child, in every direction.
Know what there is to know of everything terrestrial,
Of all that has been laid out by Tāne-nui-a-Rangi.
Fly high. Fly high.
Know all that is celestial.
Attain the uncountable stars.

Mythology and contemporary Māori life are woven together seamlessly in this spectacular collection by Aotearoa's foremost short story writer.

The titular story 'Bird Child' plunges you deep into Te Kore, an ancient time before time. In another, the formidable goddess Mahuika, Keeper of Fire, becomes a doting mother and friend. Later, Grace's own childhood vividly shapes the world of the young character Mereana; and a widower's hilariously human struggle to parent his seven daughters is told with trademark wit and crackling dialogue.

Moving artfully across decades, landscapes, time and space, with tenderness and charm, *Bird Child and Other Stories* shows an author as adept and stimulating as ever.

"*Grace's stories make a shining and enduring place formed of the brilliant weave of Māori oral storytelling.*" - Joy Harjo

ALSO FROM PENGUIN RANDOM HOUSE . . .

PUBLISHED: 30 MAY 2023

ISBN: 978-1-77695-048-5

First released 50 years ago, *Tangi* was Witi Ihimaera's debut novel and the first to be published by a Māori author. A landmark literary event, it went on to win the James Wattie Book of the Year Award. He was just 29 years old at the time.

At the centre of the novel is the story of a father and son set within a three-day tangihanga. Those who love *Pounamu Pounamu* will immediately recognise that already present are the hallmarks of classic Ihimaera storytelling.

Revisiting the text for this special anniversary edition, Witi has added richer details and developed the nascent themes that have continued to preoccupy him over a lifetime of writing. Return with him to where it all began.